PRAISE FO

The Matchmaker's List

"Sonya Lalli offers up a tale of familial pressures, cultural traditions, and self-discovery that is equal turns heartbreaking and hilarious. . . . Lalli tears down stereotypes with humor and warmth."
—*Entertainment Weekly*

"An engaging love story that delivers on the promise of true love forever. . . . *The Matchmaker's List* comes through in spades (and hearts)."
—NPR

"A funny and moving exploration of modern love."
—Balli Kaur Jaswal, bestselling author of *Erotic Stories for Punjabi Widows* (Reese's Book Club Pick)

"A warm and refreshing look at cultural identity, unexpected romance, and unbreakable family bonds."
—*Kirkus Reviews*

"Bright and vivid, and fresh and funny—I was utterly charmed by this insight into Raina's struggle to be the perfect Indian daughter."
—Veronica Henry, author of *How to Find Love in a Bookshop*

"A riotous odyssey into the pressures of cross-cultural modern dating that will chime with every twentysomething singleton."
—*Elle* (UK)

"Lalli's debut is a delightful, multicultural romantic comedy full of humorous banter and loads of life lessons about family, happiness, love, honesty, and acceptance."
—*Booklist* (starred review)

"Lalli's sharp-eyed tale of cross-cultural dating, family heart-break, the strictures of culture, and the exuberance of love is both universal and timeless."   —*Publishers Weekly* (starred review)

"Absolutely charming."   —*Woman's Day*

"A knockout romantic comedy debut."
                              —Washington Independent Review of Books

ALSO BY SONYA LALLI

The Matchmaker's List

Grown-Up Pose

SONYA LALLI

BERKLEY
NEW YORK

BERKLEY
An imprint of Penguin Random House LLC
penguinrandomhouse.com

Library of Congress Cataloging-in-Publication Data

Names: Lalli, Sonya, author.
Title: Grown-up pose / Sonya Lalli.
Description: First Edition. | New York: Berkley, 2020.
Identifiers: LCCN 2019033239 (print) | LCCN 2019033240 (ebook) |
ISBN 9780451490964 (paperback) | ISBN 9780451490971 (ebook)
Subjects: LCSH: Self-realization in women—Fiction. |
Psychological fiction.
Classification: LCC PR6112.A483 G76 2020 (print) |
LCC PR6112.A483 (ebook) | DDC 823/.92—dc23
LC record available at https://lccn.loc.gov/2019033239
LC ebook record available at https://lccn.loc.gov/2019033240

First Edition: March 2020

Printed in the United States of America
1   3   5   7   9   10   8   6   4   2

Cover art and design by Vikki Chu
Book design by Kristin del Rosario

For Mom and Dad

chapter one

Anu Desai tied her hair back with the elastic around her wrist and broke into a jog as she turned into the back alley. She hadn't taken this path in more than ten years, yet it looked exactly the same. A near-rotting wood fence still ran the length of the alley, vines draped over the planks intermittently. The gravel crunched conspicuously beneath her sneakers, and she slowed her pace as she made a right onto another backstreet. After the third garbage bin, she traced her hand along the wood, three large paces past the fire hydrant, and found the latch. Opening the gate just a sliver, she slipped through and closed it noiselessly. She glanced up at Mrs. Jenkins' bedroom window next door—if it was Mrs. Jenkins who still lived there. The lights were out, and so Anu tiptoed toward the shed.

She stuck her back foot on the fence to push herself up the wall and was surprised by how easy the familiar motions felt. She stepped fully onto the fence and then leaned against the outer wall of the house. From there, it was just one step onto the rain gutter—she tested it first, to make sure it was still sturdy—and then another onto the windowsill.

As always, the window was open just a hair. It was one of the best parts about living in Vancouver. Even if it was chilly outside, like today, nothing beat that fresh Pacific northwest air. Anu pressed her face close in toward the window as she found her footing, and her stomach growled when the smell of deep-fried *pakoras* hit her. While Anu's own mother had experimented with non-Indian food, going so far as to serve the family pasta and pad thai on occasion, her soon-to-be ex-mother-in-law, Priya Desai, had stuck to her roots. The only stains on her kitchen counter were from turmeric, and if the spice or vegetable wasn't available at her local Punjabi grocery store—well, Priya had probably never tried it.

Anu settled her butt down and then gently tapped her fingers against the glass until it opened. Back first, she pushed through—but where there used to be a bench, there was nothing but air, and she toppled over into a large crash onto the floor.

A light switched on while she was sprawled on the ground, and Anu tried to sit up in a blur, ignoring the pulsing sensation in her left ankle.

"Anush?"

"Mother *Fiona* that hurt."

She felt hands on either side of her pulling her up, then spotted two dark brown feet sticking out from beneath the legs of khaki trousers.

"Why didn't you use the front door?"

The room stopped spinning. Anu moved to massage her ankle and winced at the pain.

"Here, let me take a look—"

"Ow!"

"That doesn't look good." Neil Desai rolled up the hem of her jeans and inspected her ankle, squatting down in front of her. This was the most physical contact they'd had in months, nearly a year, and she wondered if he was thinking the same thing.

"Do you know what you're doing?" she said quickly to break the silence. "Are there any doctors downstairs?"

He snorted. "Don't need one. I took a first aid class, remember?"

"In two thousand seven."

"But that's basically the same thing as medical school."

"Oh, really?"

He grinned again, and she winced. But this time it wasn't from the pain.

She pulled her leg away from him and stepped gingerly onto the floor. After testing her weight, she stood up straight with Neil's help.

Neil's bedroom used to have baby blue walls and ugly wicker furniture—not that Priya had ever allowed Anu to go upstairs to his room when they were dating. Now it was their daughter's, Kanika, room, with every Disney figurine, plush toy, or poster imaginable living within its blush pink walls. Her Moana backpack and matching suitcase were open on the floor, clothes and books spilling out. Neil crouched down and started tucking everything neatly away.

"Do you want any help?" Anu asked.

He shook his head, and so she walked toward the far window, pressed her head against the glass.

Anu should have waited to come over until the party had concluded or offered for Kanika to sleep there an extra night. The front lawn was crowded with the aunties and uncles of her community, dressed up in a rainbow of red, saffron, and gold in tribute to Diwali. Some had firecrackers, candles, or sparklers—others watched the festivities from the sidelines. Anu didn't have the energy to face them today, although she knew she would have to on the way out. She couldn't climb out of Neil's bedroom window with a five-year-old in tow.

She spotted Priya climbing up the porch stairs, slowly, leaning her weight onto the handrail, and then Kanika darting past her in the opposite direction, waving two long sparklers. Anu inhaled sharply. Someone had dressed her in a neon pink *lengha* so long she could trip over it. And why hadn't anyone put a coat on her? Couldn't they feel the biting October wind?

"I know she's not wearing a coat," Neil said behind her. "She refused. She's getting more stubborn every day."

"Just like you."

"I was going to say, just like you."

Anu smiled out the window, watching her daughter prance around the lawn, basking in the attention of being the only child at the party. "Why aren't you down there?"

"There was a minor fire-related emergency."

She spun around to face him. Tucking Kanika's favorite plush walrus into the backpack, he gestured to his right forearm, at a bald patch the size of a baseball.

"Prabha Uncle brought firecrackers, and I got caught in the cross fire when he tried to light one in the kitchen sink."

"He tried to light it inside the house?" Anu laughed. "They make these things childproof. Who knew it needed to be uncle proof."

She went to reach for the bald patch but caught herself just in time. Instead, she planted her hands firmly on her hips.

"It's just hair," he said quietly. "It'll grow back."

She nodded, even though she didn't agree. Not everything came back.

Anu sat down at the foot of the bed, and she wondered if it was the same twin bed Neil had slept in until they got married. She leaned her head back against the wall and closed her eyes. For the first time since he had moved out, they were back on good terms. They were civil, and sometimes on Saturdays during the pickups and drop-offs—on nights like these—they even laughed together.

But she knew Neil, and now everything was about to change.

She opened her eyes. He was examining her more closely as he closed up the backpack with its palm tree zipper.

"Everything OK, Anush?"

She pressed her lips together, cringing at the sound of his nickname for her; the way the tone dropped off at the elongated *oo* sound. Once upon a time it had been romantic.

And now?

"Ryan and I. . . ." She caught his eye, and there was no need to say more.

He dropped the backpack to the floor, rubbed his hands through his hair.

She sat forward on the bed. "Are you OK?"

He didn't reply. She could hear him breathing over the sounds of voices downstairs, chattering filling up the house.

"I haven't told Kanika. She hasn't even met him yet—"

"You . . . you *climb* in here like nothing has changed . . . and just spring this on me." Neil was pacing now, and his voice was on the rise. He was on the cusp of snapping. That temper of his, the one that reared its petty, unruly self so rarely, was on its way up and out. "She hasn't met him *yet*? Is it serious?"

"Neil, lower your voice." She stood up from the bed, keeping the weight on her right foot. "It's only been a few months, I swear. I didn't want you to find out from anyone else."

"So everyone knows you're with *him* now? Is that it?"

"Neil, please calm dow—"

"Don't you—"

"*Beta.*" A sharp voice from the doorway. "*Hush.*" Her mother-in-law, Priya, was standing at the entrance of the room, her sari a sheath of orange tie-dye. "We have *guests.*" She gave them both a stern look. "What is this nonsense?" She paused, breathing hard. "I thought fighting time was over."

Anu relaxed her hands, only then realizing they were clenched. "Neil and I were discussing—"

"How Anu's got herself a new boyfriend."

Anu's stomach dropped. He was telling on her to his mother?

"Already? Is it that *white* man?"

"So what if he's white, Auntie?"

Priya's cheeks flushed, and immediately Anu felt regret. She was not usually so vocal with her opinions. As Neil's girlfriend, she'd tried to ignore Priya's constant demands, her placations and opinions, the way she made and unmade everything they did, like a bed, like a chore. When they got married, she couldn't ignore them; rather, she obeyed them. Now she didn't have to, but she still wasn't used to the idea that she was *allowed* to do and say as she pleased. In their culture, you couldn't be honest with elders without disrespecting them.

"I'm sorry, Auntie," she said finally, sincerely. She met Priya's gaze. "I didn't mean to snap at you."

"You mean every word, dear. Except the promises you made to my son."

Anu took a deep breath as she tried to remain calm. She was used to the guilt; it was the pain she was still coming to grips with. She chanced a look at Neil. His arms crossed, he was staring out the back window that she'd first climbed through twelve years earlier.

Why couldn't she reach out to him, press her hand against his chest, and make him understand that this was for the best?

He turned around and caught her eye. Staring at her like a stranger, he opened his mouth as if to say something, and then he closed it.

Maybe because, deep down, he knew there was nothing left to say. Not a scrap left to tussle over or work through. *This* was all that was left. And now wouldn't it be easier to play the cold estranged wife? The one who only eight months into their separation was starting to fall for another man; who would be ready for a divorce when the one-year separation mark rolled around and she was legally entitled to ask for it.

The one who didn't look back.

Swallowing hard, Anu walked out the door and down the stairs, ignoring the throbbing sensation in her ankle. The kitchen and the living room were full of people, and she smiled and nodded at everyone as they greeted her. There was a thundering on the stairs behind her.

"Anu, you forgot her bags," she heard Neil say.

"Thanks," Anu mumbled.

"Mommy!"

Kanika ran halfway up the stairs to greet her, squeezing her around the middle. Anu fought the urge to cry and widened her eyes so the tears didn't spill. She bent down to kiss Kanika and, following her down the stairs, nodded intently at what her beautiful daughter was saying.

But Anu couldn't hear the words. She could only watch Kanika's tiny, full lips move. *Neil's lips.*

The way her eyes widened and contracted in animation, the same way Neil's did when he was excited or joyful—a look Anu would probably never witness for herself again.

Coming and going. Going and coming. These were the routines of Anu's life now, except it still didn't feel like her own.

"Here."

Anu turned toward the voice. Without meeting her eye, Priya handed her a heavy plastic bag.

"It's OK, Auntie. I already ate."

Priya didn't reply as she disappeared into the kitchen.

"Thank you," Anu called after her, but she didn't think Priya could hear her over Kanika's whines and pleas to the entire room as Neil tried to dress her in a coat. She didn't want to leave the party yet, she cried. Why didn't Mommy want to stay? Why didn't Mommy ever want to have fun?

Anu tried not to wonder this herself, but when you married the first man you ever kissed, these weren't the questions you were used to asking yourself. Lately, she was realizing she never stopped to ask herself anything, let alone find the answer. Why had she lived her life like it wasn't her own? Why had she followed the wind without wondering where it was blowing, or why?

Anu took a deep breath—counted in for two, counted out for two—just like her mother had taught her. Clutching the bags in one hand, she gave Kanika her most serious look. "Please, baby. It's time to go."

Kanika pouted—that way she did often, the way she knew worked on everyone. "Can Daddy come, too?"

Every time, it ripped. Just a little bit more.

"Daddy will walk us to the car."

chapter two

One year ago

Have you given more thought to renovating kitchen?"

"Um." Anu wiped her hands on a tea towel and turned around to face her mother. "Not really."

"Why not?" Lakshmi stirred the dal that was simmering on the back burner, setting her other hand on her hip. "Is it money? We can lend."

"No . . ." She trailed off as her mother-in-law appeared in the doorway. Priya's face was flushed from the November cold, and she handed Anu the bag of groceries she'd left in her car. As Anu turned to set it on the counter, she accidentally bumped Lakshmi's arm, sending a spatula flying from her hand.

"Sorry!"

"See?" Lakshmi smiled as she picked up the spatula and tossed it into the sink. "Priya-*ji*, don't you think this room is too small?"

"*Hah*, why have there been no renovations?"

"Anu, you need to take down this wall." Lakshmi rapped on the far kitchen wall with her knuckle. To Priya, she said, "It will open up the whole space, *nah*?"

Anu nodded, grabbing a bunch of coriander from the bag. "Good idea." She had already explained to both of them that the wall Lakshmi was hell-bent on knocking down was load-bearing, and the kitchen was too crowded only when all three of them were in there, but she didn't bother repeating herself.

Instead, she washed the coriander and pinched off brown leaves, zoning out of the conversation as Priya and Lakshmi discussed what color Anu should paint the kitchen, then in what crockery to serve the *aloo gobi.*

If Anu had cooked herself, she would have been done an hour ago. Rather than chop it all by hand, she would have used the food processor to chop all the chilis, garlic, onions, and ginger required in the four-course Punjabi feast Lakshmi had envisioned for the evening. She wouldn't have soaked the rice and lentils in cold water for thirty minutes, but only five, because it really didn't make a difference, no matter how much they insisted it did. There would be a dozen fewer dishes to wash and fewer surfaces to scrub, and she would have managed to squeeze in a forty-five-minute yoga session in the rec room downstairs before dinnertime.

But Priya and Lakshmi liked to stretch chores out in leisure, taking breaks from chopping, frying, and stirring to set their hands on their waists and gossip about the latest drama at their temple, exclaim at the state of Anu's Tupperware cupboard, rearrange the jars of cumin or cinnamon in Anu's spice rack.

"That is very brown, *nah*?" she heard Lakshmi say.

"Sure is, Mom." Anu nodded, continuing to pick at the coriander. "I'm working on it."

Lakshmi switched to Punjabi and said something to Priya about hardwood flooring, and Anu fought the urge to scream.

Anu's Tupperware cupboard.

Anu's spice rack.

Was this really her destiny, to be stuck here between the two of them, practically invisible?

She pressed the back of her hand hard against her mouth, and after a minute, the feeling passed. She should have been grateful. She was lucky to have a wonderful family, a mother and a mother-in-law who had become as close as sisters.

This was everything she could have ever wanted.

"I hear her!" Priya exclaimed, just as Anu noticed Kanika's laughter ringing through the front hallway. "They are back!"

Anu dried the coriander in a paper towel as Priya and Lakshmi rushed to the front hall. Her dad, Kunal, and Neil had taken Kanika to skate at the rink a few blocks away, the one where Anu had spent countless afternoons that month teaching their daughter how to skate.

"Since when did Kanika become the next Tessa Virtue?" she heard Neil say.

No one had the answer, and from the other room, Anu didn't volunteer it.

"Nanaji skated, too!" Kanika told the others. "He fell on his butt."

"Uh-ho!" Lakshmi's voice. "Kunal, do you need an ice pack for your *butt*?"

"Oh, yes, *please*," he replied. "Maybe my sweet wife can give me a massage, too?"

Everyone in the hallway laughed. Anu did not.

She heard the pattering of footsteps as the family moved into the sitting room, and the conversation switched to the upcoming play at Kanika's day care.

Was it possible to be *jealous* of a four-year-old? Anu pondered the question as she chopped the coriander, eavesdropped on her family as they obsessed over the lion costume Kanika was planning to wear—the one Anu was in the middle of sewing.

Anu couldn't remember if she'd told her family that she was the one to write the play, after the day care coordinator told her she had "just too much on her plate." So Anu had read a few Wikipedia articles on playwriting and bashed out a child-friendly script about safari animals and inclusivity one Saturday night after Kanika had gone to bed, and she had been directing the thing ever since. For the past month, she'd shuffled and reshuffled her schedule at the medical clinic where she worked as a nurse to make sure she could be there for every rehearsal. She'd e-mailed the newsletter to all the parents explaining which costume each child would be required to wear. Several times, she'd bailed on lunches or after-work drinks with her best friends, Jenny and Monica, to finish the set backdrop or props or pick out paper stock for the programs.

She didn't mind. It was important work, being a mother. She wasn't allowed to mind.

The *subjis*, curries, and rice were cooked, heated through. After ladling them into crockery and putting it all to warm in the oven, she started on the dishes. Scrubbed each pot, plate, and pan as slowly as possible, as the others chatted away in the sitting room.

"I am thinking about going back to university," she heard Lakshmi say through the wall. "I have always thought I would. Perhaps, it is the time. I have started an application."

Anu resisted the urge to roll her eyes. How many times had she heard her mother say that? She'd believe it when she saw it.

"My lovely lady, a student—me a professor," Kunal said softly, as Kanika banged at the piano in the background. "It would be a Bollywood love affair, no?"

"I would watch that," Priya said in earnest. "It really *should* be movie."

"Uh-ho. Kunal, you think I would be so sleazy as to have affair with my professor?" Lakshmi asked. "*Nah*, if I am to have an affair, it would be with *fireman*. I have always liked fireman."

"Like Chuck Norris?" Priya asked. "He was *so* handsome."

"Chuck Norris was the Texas Ranger, *nah*?"

"Would you like me to leave the room while you pick your suitor?" Kunal harumphed for effect. It reverberated through the whole house just as Lakshmi squealed in delight.

"Look at him Priya-*ji*, so jealous!"

Anu was startled by a noise behind her. She glanced back, moving her neck only in the slightest, and with her peripheral vision caught sight of Neil chugging orange juice from the carton, one hand leaning against the open refrigerator door.

She squeezed her eyes shut as the tears started to form, unable to remember the last time he had greeted her when arriving home—with a kiss, a smile, even a hello. The last time he had held her because he wanted to and not just because Kanika had jumped into their bed and there wasn't enough room for the three of them.

She heard the refrigerator door close, a cupboard door open.

Would he come to her? Would he slink toward her and set his hands on her hips? Whisper something into her ear—something silly, maybe romantic? Or maybe he'd simply walk over without saying anything at all, pluck the tea towel from her right shoulder, and wipe down the dishes drying on the rack.

That would be enough. Right now, wouldn't that be enough?

She heard the rustling of a chip bag and then the cupboard door close.

Where had he gone? Where was *it*? The olive branch. A sign

that their marriage was more than their daughter. A home. A union of nice Indian families.

That she was more than just his lackluster Indian wife.

She held her breath, her heart pounding in her chest as she waited for him. And she kept waiting until she heard Neil's voice in the other room.

There was a glass bowl in her hands caked in turmeric, salt, and flour. It fell to the floor, and nobody else heard it shatter.

chapter three

❦

SARA: Hi, Anusha, this is Ms. Finch from school—but call me Sara. Hope it's OK that I've texted instead of e-mailing! Anyway, thanks for signing up to build the set for the Christmas (I mean holiday!) concert. I've ordered the supplies, but it looks like you're the only kindergarten parent that's signed up to help. . . . Is that OK? I will try and rally more volunteers but no guarantees.

ANUSHA: Hi, Sara—texting is easier for me, too. I only work part-time, so no worries. I've got time to build the set. ☺

SARA: You are such a lifesaver. Thanks!

He kissed my *thumb*."

"He kissed your *what*?" Anu exclaimed.

"My thumb." Jenny repeated, sticking her left thumb up like a hitchhiker. "He leaned over across the couch, and so I closed my eyes—" Jenny closed her eyes, replaying the whole scene for them like the total drama queen she was. "And I waited, because I thought he was going to kiss me. . . . And then I feel this wet thing on my hand."

"It was a *wet* kiss?" Monica asked.

"On your *thumb*?" Anu added.

Jenny reached for her wineglass, nodding. She took a long sip, clearly enjoying making her friends wait for the rest of the story. "He *Frenched* my hand, you guys. My thumb, in particular."

Anu made a face at them both. "So what'd you do?"

"Well, to be honest, I was curious. He seemed to think this seduction technique worked. I was quite impressed by his confidence, actually."

"What did he go for next?" Monica said. "Your baby toe?"

"He sort of . . . worked his way up my hand." Jenny traced a line up her thumb and then flipped over her wrist. "It took about ten minutes to get to my inner forearm. I know this, because I was *literally* watching his microwave clock."

Monica laughed and let her head fall down onto the bar table. "This would only happen to you, Jen."

"Did he ever get to your lips?" Anu asked.

Jenny shook her head in disgust. "It felt like a wet centipede crawling on me. And by the time he got to my elbow, I was bored out of my mind and ordered a taxi." She winked at them both. "You know, with my other thumb."

"What a weirdo."

"The weird thing is," Jenny said, glancing at her phone, "if he'd just kissed me on my mouth, I probably would have slept with him."

Anu sipped her wine as she listened to Jenny go into more detail about her "wet date" with Ronny the personal trainer. Anu and Monica had been best friends since childhood; even though Anu's family was Hindu and Monica's was Sikh, they were both Punjabi and had grown up in a similar community. Jenny hadn't joined their group until years later, after she and Anu became friends in nursing school. Monica, who had already started work as a real estate agent by then, had been jealous of Anu's new friendship— until she, too, met Jenny, and the rest was history.

Nearly ten years later, all three of them had solidified their places in one another's lives. They were inseparable, and by any definition, Anu was the "Charlotte" of their group. The first one to get married, the *good* girl, although even Charlotte had dated around before she settled down. Monica was a self-proclaimed "Carrie," while Jenny—wild, cynical—was equal parts "Samantha" and "Miranda."

And now that Monica had gotten engaged to Tom, it was only Jenny who had the dating stories worthy of their namesakes from *Sex and the City*. But as with the many other dates Jenny had told them about before, Anu didn't understand why Jenny was so quick to dismiss Ronny. She had been looking forward to going out with him for weeks, and until his admittedly odd way of kissing, it had sounded like the date had gone just fine.

"What's with your face?" Jenny said, midstory, turning to look at Anu. She pushed the bowl of wasabi peas across the table, and Anu scooped up a handful.

"Nothing's wrong with my face."

Jenny rolled her eyes.

"OK, fine." Anu sighed. "I'm just wondering why you're writing this guy off so quickly. I thought you liked him, and now you're saying you need to switch gyms to avoid him."

"Did she not hear my story?" Jenny asked Monica.

"I heard your story, but—"

"*But*, Anu, dating is hard, and you have to trust your gut. You'd know that if you'd ever actually *dated*."

"I've dated," she said quietly, anticipating Jenny's raised eyebrows.

They'd gone over this time and time again: Anu and Jenny had very different definitions of the word "dated." To Anu, it was the handful of coffee, study, or lunch dates she had gone on with Neil twelve years earlier before he had worked up the courage to hold her hand and change his relationship status on Facebook. It was the six weeks of wining and dining her boyfriend, Ryan Fraser, subjected her to before she asked him if she was his girlfriend and he said yes, and so she finally agreed to sleep with him.

"*You* have not dated," Jenny said predictably. "*You* married the first man you ever kissed."

Anu had spent the entire day swimming with her daughter at the wave pool and then snuck in thirty minutes of yoga after dropping her off at Neil's, so she was too tired to argue. "You're right. I haven't."

"Don't be condescending."

"I'm not!"

"You are, too."

"And you're trying to pick a fight."

Jenny stuck her tongue out.

"You're such a child, Jen."

Their plate of nachos arrived, and Anu could feel Jenny glaring at her as the waiter took his time setting out small plates, cutlery, and napkins, then refilled their water glasses.

"The only child at this table," Jenny said after the waiter left, "is the one who can't drink more than two glasses of wine without going cross-eyed."

Anu's jaw dropped as Monica giggled.

"The only *child* at this table," Jenny repeated, "is the woman who thought people had *organisms* during sex until her *eleventh*-grade biology midterm."

Anu gasped, hitting Monica on the shoulder. "You told her?"

"The only child at this table," Jenny said, slowly this time, "is the *thirty*-year-old hiding her new boyfriend from her parents."

Anu knew Jenny was only trying to be funny, and she didn't want to make a scene, but the last one still hurt. Still, her ears were burning.

"Jen," Monica said, "that's enough. You know she's not ready."

"I wanted to tell Neil first," Anu said defensively.

"You told him a week ago."

Anu couldn't think of what to say in her own defense, so she ripped into the nachos instead.

"He's not taking it well," she said finally, wiping salsa off her lips. "He sent Priya Auntie to pick Kanika up today. He hates me."

"And you're worried your parents will, too?" Monica said helpfully for Jenny's benefit.

Anu nodded, even though "hate" wasn't the right word.

It was "disappoint."

She had been twenty-nine years old the first time she let them down, the first time she ever saw their faces fall, their unpracticed looks of dismay.

"Neil is moving out."

The concept was so foreign, it was like she was speaking to them in French. Why would she ask her hardworking, loyal husband to move out? Why did she need *space*? Their house was two thousand square feet!

How could Anu be so selfish as to do something for herself?

Still, more than eight months later, her parents remained convinced it was temporary. That their separation was a "blip," as Lakshmi liked to call it to her friends. And so Anu still hadn't made it clear to her parents that her marriage was really over—so *over*, in fact, that she'd become serious about another man.

"I don't understand why you're so scared of them," Jenny said. "What are they going to do, ground you? And don't say this is because you're Indian—Mon's Indian. She stood up to her parents."

"I'll tell them eventually, Jen. But right now . . . it's easier just to let it be." Anu smirked. "Like the Beatles."

"That song is about how much Paul McCartney loved his mother, not how much he *lied* to her."

"I'm not lying," Anu said, reaching to dip a chip in the salsa verde. *"Technically."*

The previous summer, her parents had moved to London for the year so Lakshmi could "finally" pursue a master's degree in socio-something-or-other, and Kunal had taken a sabbatical from the university and gone with her. And so they weren't around to notice that when Neil had their daughter, Anu had spent her nights at Ryan's house and started to keep a canvas shopping bag full of spare blouses and underwear in the trunk of her car.

"Why are your panties *lace*, Anu?" she imagined Lakshmi saying if she were to discover them during one of her daily snoops through her daughter's life. "Do the holes not make you feel *cold*?"

Anu knew they wouldn't approve of Ryan, and right now she couldn't even fathom their reactions to the fact that he was an important part of her new life. The situation lacked precedence; Anu had never dared to do anything that required her to lie and then muster up the courage to come clean.

"You only have two weeks, Anu," Monica said as they made their way through the plate of nachos. "You need to tell them before my wedding. People will talk when they see you and Ryan together, and word will get back to your parents—I don't care how many time zones away they are."

"Wait. Why are you even bringing Ryan?" Jenny asked.

"I might as well. Neil's not going to be there." Jenny's jaw dropped, and so Anu continued. "He's been invited to speak at a prestigious conference in San Francisco the same weekend. He can't miss it."

"And we understand," Monica said, squeezing Anu's hand. Neil, one of Tom's oldest friends from Calgary, had introduced him to

Monica in the first place. "It's a really big opportunity for Neil. Tom would *kill* him if he missed it."

"No, I mean why bring Ryan? Just because Neil won't be around doesn't mean you need to bring some other guy."

"Ryan's not 'some guy'—"

"Right, he's a new boyfriend. You introduce your friends to a new boyfriend. You tell your *parents* that he exists, but bring him to your best friend's wedding? That's . . . *serious*."

"We are serious."

Jenny snorted. Anu reached for her drink and, finding it empty, twisted the glass hard in her hand. Having sex and spending almost every night together (that she wasn't with Kanika, of course) didn't count as *serious* to her best friends?

"You don't like Ryan," Anu said, refusing to meet Jenny's eye, "do you?"

"Ask Monica if she likes him."

"I like him just fine"—Monica slapped Jenny on the arm—"and I think what Ms. Diplomatic is trying to say is—"

"What I'm *trying* to say is that Anu claims she left Neil to find herself, yet here she is jumping into a so-called 'serious' relationship."

"I was with the wrong guy before. Ryan is different. He's—"

"This isn't about Ryan!" Jenny cried. "You need to get to know yourself, let yourself make some mistakes along the way. Anu, if you've never been single for more than five seconds, how exactly are you supposed to know what kind of guy you even want? Or what you want out of life—"

"I—"

"How are you ever supposed to grow up?"

"Are you kidding me? I was the first of us to grow up," Anu fumed. "I'm raising a daughter. I have a good job, a house, a boyfriend, a mortgage—"

"Except that's stuff you have, not stuff you *are*."

Anu threw a pleading look at Monica, but she was picking at the nachos. "Fine." Anu sat up straighter in her chair. "I *am* financially responsible and live within my means. I put my family first. I'm a role model to my daughter. I chose a suitable life partner—"

"You mean *Ryan*?"

"Of course Ryan! And so what if I can't handle my liquor well? I can control my urges. I do things in moderation. I'm responsible."

"Responsible or. . . . scared?"

Anu looked up, meeting Jenny's gaze. They were fighting and not fighting simultaneously. They were honest and brutal, but this was the way they always were.

Anu exhaled slowly. She could sense there was something else Jenny wanted to say, to push them even further, truly test the notion that they loved and fought as hard as sisters, but luckily Monica stepped in. She yanked them both by the ear.

"Ow!"

"Monica, that *hurts*!"

"Are you fools done yet?" Monica said. She sounded annoyed. "The nachos are getting cold."

"I'm done," Jenny said.

Anu smiled at the table, victorious. "I'm done, too."

They returned to the food and their conversation about Ronny the personal trainer. Anu didn't need to prove herself, to convince Jenny of something she was simply incapable of understanding.

Anu *was* a grown-up. After all, she had everything a woman was supposed to want in life. *Could* ever want in life.

Even if for the first time in her life, things weren't going according to what she'd always planned.

chapter four

�֎

LAKSHMI: I am trying to call. There is no answer. Have you dropped your phone into the toilet again?

(two hours later)

LAKSHMI: YOO-hooo! ALL OK?? Your father cooked tonight. It is a British dish called a sheep herder's pie. I will e-mail you the photo.

ANUSHA: Busy, Mom. Talk later. Enjoy the pie!

Ryan hadn't texted in more than an hour, and so Anu decided to go for a walk. She tried not to feel disappointed. Sure, he was MIA half the time, but he was an environmental lawyer, so at least the work that kept him so busy was legitimate. And besides, he was working late so he didn't have to go into the office that weekend. Monica's wedding was tomorrow. It had been stress overload for the both of them all week—all year, really. Anu had helped Monica plan the whole thing. Because Anu worked part-time, the weeks Kanika was with Neil, she'd found herself with whole days during which she was free to sample entrées and wedding cakes, drive from Indian store to Indian store to pick out the perfect bridal shoes, or brainstorm fusion-inspired centerpieces that represented both Monica's Indian heritage and Tom's Anglo roots.

Now, the night before, there was absolutely nothing left to do. All Anu had to do was show up.

The November wind was cold around her neck, and Anu tucked her collar up around her throat. She kept walking, taking random turns, and eventually found herself next to the shops on West Broadway. Although she'd spent a lot of time at Ryan's house, she had never fully realized he lived so close to this neighborhood. They always seemed to order in or cooked at home—and when Ryan did take her out, it was always somewhere splashy, a bit too lavish, downtown by the waterfront.

She trudged west, along a cute villagelike block, staring into shop windows as she passed them. A sushi restaurant. Coffeehouse. Bookstore. Marijuana dispensary. Vegetarian restaurant. She used to ride down this road every single day to and from the university—usually on the express bus. She had been jealous of the students who got to live around here and then, later, her friends who could afford to buy property in the area. She and Neil had considered a town house not too far from here in Kitsilano, their dream neighborhood being close to downtown, the university parklands, the beach. But as her parents pointed out, the properties around here didn't have many bedrooms (for children), and they could get a much larger house for the same price in the suburbs near them, near Priya. Staying close to their parents was the financially responsible decision. What a grown-up did, and so that was what they did.

Anu slowed down as she passed a yoga studio and stole a look inside. There was a girl with a mop of fiery red hair who looked a bit younger than Anu. The sign reading "Mags' Yoga Studio" had paint chipping off, so it read "Ma s' Y g S u io." As Anu moved to walk on, she caught sight of the girl waving. Anu pointed at her chest, and when the girl nodded, Anu hesitantly pushed through the front door, stamping her boots off on the mat.

"Are you here for the six p.m. class?"

"Who, me?"

"Is there anyone else in here?"

Anu laughed nervously, glancing around the room. The foyer looked a lot like the sign outside: cute, bright, but rather worn down.

"I was just walking by."

"If it's your first class, I can give you a discount," the girl said, standing up from her chair behind the front desk. She was wearing a hot pink top and black shorts, and her red hair was messily parted into French braids. "Usually it's twenty bucks for a drop-in fee, but I can give you the first one for ten."

"I don't know," Anu said, smiling. "I don't have anything with me."

"We provide the mats. And you're dressed just fine."

Anu glanced down and realized that she was indeed wearing yoga pants—one of the many pairs she wore grocery shopping or to the swimming pool and didn't actually use for yoga.

"Have you practiced before?"

"Yeah," Anu said, nodding. "I've been practicing for years, actually."

"What studio? I bet it's not as good as Mags'."

"Oh, I used to go to . . ." She trailed off, blanking on the name. "It closed a few years ago. Anyway, since my daughter was born, I only practice at home. YouTube videos in the basement. That sort of thing."

The girl nodded. "Well, I think you should give us a go. You've got nothing to lose, except an hour."

"I'm not sure. . . ."

"Come on. You're the only one who has shown up, so I can give you a one-on-one lesson. That's worth *way* more than ten dollars."

"Is it usually this dead?"

"No," the girl said, sounding rather offended. "So are you in? Come on. Please? Otherwise I won't get paid."

One last time, Anu checked her phone. Ryan still hadn't texted, and feeling rather pathetic, she put away her phone. Offering the girl a smile, she said, "Sure. Let's do it."

She followed the girl—Imogen—into the studio, which was bare, clean, and simple, just like the studio Anu had gone to in high school and university, before she got too busy to take formal classes. The tasteful birch panels on the wall were whitewashed and reminded Anu of the beach house she and Neil had once rented while she was pregnant with Kanika. Instantly, she felt at ease, unlike some of the studios she'd tried for one-off classes over the past few years. Yoga had become so on trend, so over-the-top, sometimes she didn't even recognize it. Anu didn't need an Ayurvedic juice bar or an in-house naturopath or for the Hindu Om to be spray-painted on the bathroom wall like some appropriated decoration and not the scared mantra that it was.

All Anu needed was a yoga mat and a quiet room. Something like *this*.

Anu's doubts about Imogen's young age (twenty-one, she said) vanished by their first downward dog, and the more Anu kept up, the swifter Imogen moved her from pose to pose—*talasana* to *vriksasana* to *sirsasana*.

But Anu wasn't used to practicing for so long or holding her poses—as Imogen insisted—in perfect alignment, and so she was puffing and sweating hard by the time she collapsed out of the revolved triangle. Squinting, she looked up at Imogen and watched her lift up and into a crow pose, shins on elbows, her pointed toes hovering effortlessly into the air.

"I still can't do crow pose," Anu said, panting. "And I've been trying for years."

"Give me a few weeks, and you'll be able to," Imogen said. She ejected her legs out and landed in plank, then pulled down and out with a graceful *chaturanga*.

"Damn. You're good."

"Yoga isn't about being *good*."

Anu blushed. "I know that."

"Do you?" Imogen leaned back into downward dog, and Anu followed.

Stretching deeper into the pose, Anu lifted her left leg high and straight behind her until it was in perfect alignment with her back.

"It's not about showing off, either."

Anu set her left leg down, lifted her right. "I'm not showing off."

"You are, too. You're sucking in your stomach too much. I can tell."

"Don't be a smart-ass." Anu smiled, and then cringed. That was something she would have said to Jenny, sometimes to Monica, not to a total stranger. She caught Imogen's eye, tried to gauge if she was offended.

Deadpan, Imogen said, "At least I'm not an *old* ass."

It was a great workout, although they kept saying things that cracked each other up—or like what happened in wind-relieving pose, when Anu let out a fart. Anu was surprised by how good, how *light* she felt by the time Imogen told her the class was over. She couldn't remember the last time she had felt this way.

Back in the studio foyer, a gray-haired woman was hovering in the doorway, fighting against the wind to push the door closed. Imogen rushed over to help.

"Thank you, dear," the woman said after they shut it. She touched Imogen's arm and then glanced in Anu's direction.

"That's Anusha. A new customer."

"*Anusha*." The woman smiled and offered her a warm hug. She looked to be about her mother's age. "So lovely to meet you."

"This is Mags. She runs the place."

"It's lovely to meet you, too."

Mags surveyed the room, as if momentarily fixated on the texture of the walls, the worn-down grains of the hardwood. "Are we all done for the day, love?"

Imogen nodded, zipping up her hoodie.

"Right, then. Who needs a cuppa?"

Upstairs, Anu drifted in and out of the conversation that Imogen and Mags were having about the new hot-yoga studio down the road. The mug of tea was warm in her hands, and she'd given up thinking that Ryan would finally text and tell her he was on his way home, so she'd left her phone in her bag by the door. Mags' apartment above the studio was crammed full of odds and ends, but for whatever reason, the space didn't feel crowded or suffocating. Her limbs heavy in the chair, for the first time in several years, Anu felt calm.

"This building has a *positive*, affirming energy to it—don't you reckon?" asked Mags, startling Anu. At that very moment, she'd been thinking the very same thing.

"It does, Mags. Thanks so much for having me over. I feel so relaxed right now."

"You aren't the first one to say that." She patted Anu's hand. "Relax away. Just *be*."

Anu smiled in return, resisting the urge to say something snarky—her usual reply whenever her own mother told her to *be*, or chant *om*, or something that could sound like a line from a *Star*

Wars movie about becoming one with the universe. Instead, she changed the subject.

"So is that a British accent I detect, Mags? How did you end up in Vancouver?"

"It's a great story," Imogen said.

"I followed my partner here more than thirty years ago. Then she went ahead and died, but such is life." She gestured to her tea set on the table between them. "Sugar?"

"Mags, that's not the story." Imogen leaned forward, spooned sugar into her cup. "Mags' wife was in the Canadian foreign service. She was stationed in England and just happened to be passing through her town of Hambridge—"

"Henstridge—"

"Henstridge," Imogen repeated. "And they fell in love that very day."

"It took at least a week, dear. And *passing* through?" She laughed, the corners of her mouth tightening into crisp folds. "More like she was the only girl on the drink in my father's pub."

"What was the pub called again?"

"The Dog and Du—"

"The Dog and *Duck,"* Imogen finished, laughing. "You English people, you have such weird names."

Imogen pointed across the room. There was an urn on the fireplace mantle, a small bronze Ganesha—just like one Lakshmi had in her bedroom—and right next to it was a framed black-and-white photo of a thirtysomething-year-old woman in a denim jacket. Red hair and kind eyes. *Eyes*, Anu thought, *like Neil's*.

"Anyhow, Anusha, I followed her to London, and then to New Delhi when she was stationed in India. That's when I fell in love with yoga." Mags laughed, as if this was a private joke just for her. "It was quite the experience. We had a one-bedroom flat, and everyone *still* believed we were cousins." Mags glanced back at the photo. "When we settled here, I opened up the studio."

"It was a great class," Anu said, nodding toward Imogen. "I'll be sure to try one of yours, too."

"I haven't taught since Tara passed away—it's been months now." Mags shook her head, brushed a stray hair out of her eye. "Actually, I've been trying to find someone to take over for me. My sister lost her husband last year, and well, I thought I'd move back home so we can be alone together. Thought we'd start some sort of *club*."

"If only I had a bit of money," Imogen said, "I would, Mags."

"I have three years left on the lease, and these hipsters keep offering on it. They say it's prime real estate for another coffee bar."

Anu laughed.

"I'm really trying to find someone who will keep the studio alive. Our regulars are few and far between, but they are as loyal as *anything*."

"The teachers, too." Imogen snapped a biscuit in half, setting the bigger chunk back on the tray. "We're loyal, too."

"What about you, Anusha? Are you in the market?"

"For a yoga studio?"

"Sure. Why not? It's surprising the sense of purpose building something like this can give you."

The words startled Anu, but they didn't seem ridiculous. At least, ten years ago they wouldn't have.

Anu had started yoga when she was fifteen years old, and she had been hooked within months. She had spent each day leading up to her high school graduation saving every penny from her part-time jobs serving pizza or washing cars to pay for the pricy monthly membership. Secretly, she had also been saving up toward yoga teacher training. There were courses in Vancouver, but she wanted to enroll in one far away—Costa Rica, Los Angeles, maybe even Europe. That had been the plan, the dream, the *journey*. She'd graduate high school one day, and the next she'd be on an international flight toward an adventure.

But then she'd told her parents.

"So what do you say?" Mags said. "Shall I draw up the paperwork?"

"Sorry," Anu said, snapping back to reality. "I don't know the first thing about running a yoga studio."

"But I do. I've been working for Mags for a while. . . . Anusha, I could be your manager!" Imogen said.

Anu laughed, but stopped when she caught Mags' eye. There was something about her that made the idea seem not so ridiculous. Like she could see through Anu's thin veneer and see point-blank that Anu was searching—for what, she didn't know. A university education, a career, marriage, and motherhood were supposed to have given her sufficient direction—yet here Anu was, and living with *purpose* was something she couldn't claim to have felt.

Was it possible to be grateful and feel fullness from each aspect of your life and still feel like you were missing something?

Anu stood up and stared out the window. It was darker now, and the clouds were so thick, she yearned to reach out and touch them. Mold them with her fingers, her palms, and transform them into something else.

chapter five

❧

KUNAL: Your mother is trying to call again. Is there problem? Beti, she is growing upset and you are putting me in bad position.

(forty-five minutes later)

KUNAL: Anu, I know what it means to be left "on read."

"Come here. Give me a kiss."

Anu glanced out the car window. She had instructed Ryan to park as far away from the entrance as possible, and the coast being clear, she gave him a quick kiss on the lips.

"Remember. Don't kiss me in front of any Indian people."

He grinned as he stretched his right arm into the backseat, fetching his umbrella.

"I'm serious," she said. "Some of my parents' friends will be here. If anybody asks, you're *Tom's* friend, not my date."

"Tom's friend, check. Which one's Tom again?"

"Um, the groom."

"Right. Sorry."

"And you're sure you don't mind pretending we're not together tonight?"

"Why would I mind?"

She hesitated, digging her fingers into her cuticles. If Ryan had been the one hiding their relationship, wouldn't she mind?

"I get it, babe. We haven't been dating that long. You don't want"—he waved his hand like he was swatting away a fly buzzing around his face—"all the old 'aunties' to know. By the way, have I mentioned how *hot* you look in Indian clothes?"

Anu rolled her eyes and opened her purse. She pulled out a stick of black eyeliner and flicked down the visor. Glancing into its small mirror, she carefully smeared a spot of black in her hairline just above her ear. Turning to Ryan, she did the same to him.

"What was that?"

She laughed, looking at him. "I guess it doesn't camouflage as well beneath blond hair."

He looked at himself in the rearview mirror, pulling it down toward him. "Is this some kind of brown voodoo?"

"Uh, no. It's called *nazzar*. . . . It's this thing my mom does whenever one of us is dressed up or something fortunate happens." Anu watched his face, but she couldn't read it. "She's very superstitious and thinks a black mark gives you an imperfection . . . and wards off the evil eye."

Ryan snorted. "The evil eye?"

"I know, I know . . . ," Anu said. "It sounds stupid, but it's just eyeliner."

"If it's just eyeliner, why do you do it?" He stroked her forearm with the tips of his fingers. "You're not superstitious, are you?"

Anu tucked the eyeliner back in her bag, snapped the gold clasp shut. Was she? Until that moment, she'd never really thought about it.

"I don't know. I guess . . . not." She turned back to Ryan. "Sorry, sweetie. Do you want me to take it off?"

Ryan took another look at his reflection and then gave himself a big wink. "*Nah*, I reckon I look pretty good in eyeliner."

. . .

nside the hall, Anu left Ryan with Jenny, who was setting up a vase of blush pink peonies on the guest book table. It could be a disaster, the two of them together; on the other hand, maybe their spending time together was all Anu needed to get Jenny on her side. It was still two hours until the guests were due to arrive, and Anu found Monica upstairs behind a door marked "power room."

There had been twenty women—only half of whom Anu actually knew—helping Anu get ready the day of her own wedding, but she found Monica all by herself, half dressed in her bridal *lengha*. A suitcase was open in the middle of the floor, and there were a chair and a mirror set up where she assumed Monica would have gotten her hair and makeup done.

"Your sisters aren't here?" Anu asked hesitantly. "Mon, we could have been here hours ago. You said it was going to be just the three of you this morning."

"I didn't realize," Monica said flatly, "that my sisters think it's more important to get *themselves* ready."

Anu reached for Monica's hand, but she flicked it away.

"Can you tell me what this thing does? Jenny had no clue. You remember, right?" Monica thrust a garment at her—sparkly, thick silk—and then grabbed for another one hanging behind the door. "What did the woman say? You wrap it *where*?"

Anu fumbled with it, racking her brain from the bridal appointment a few weeks before.

"And do you know the difference between a lacto-ovo vegetarian and a pescatarian?"

"I think—"

"And it's started raining?" Monica gestured a vulgarity at the window. "What the hell!"

Anu wrapped the silk around Monica's waist, fumbling with hooks to see if it fit, but then Monica pushed her hands away.

"Anu, am I making a mistake? Should I have just married an Indian guy?"

"Mon . . ." Anu turned to face her. Monica had asked her and Jenny variations of this same question time and time again. Unfortunately, it had never mattered to Monica's family that Tom treated her with respect or had bent over backward to understand their cultural and religious traditions; the only thing that mattered was that he was white.

Anu's heart was breaking for her best friend. Monica's sisters lived in their own world, and her parents had made it clear that they might or might not even show up for her big day.

Taking a deep breath, she grabbed Monica by the hands. "You'll look gorgeous, even if we put this thing on wrong. If the vegetarians are being picky, they can eat rice. Rain on your wedding is a good omen for marriage, or so my mother tells me, and"—Anu caught her breath—"you and Tom are perfect for each other. So no, you should not have 'just married an Indian guy.'"

Monica shrugged, crossing her arms in front of her. She looked beautiful and bridal, and Anu wished she could do or say the right thing to cheer her up.

On an impulse, she grabbed her phone and loaded her favorite Spotify playlist. She raised an eyebrow at Monica just as "Wannabe" came on.

"What are you doing?"

"What?" Anu started dancing, gyrating, mouthing along to the lyrics. Like every other girl their age, she and Monica had been obsessed, dreamed of being one of the Spice Girls.

Except she and Monica were going to be the Spicy Girls.

Singing along, for the first time, Monica cracked a smile, and just then they see a text on her phone. Monica's parents had arrived.

A nu had meant to avoid Ryan during the cocktail hour for the sake of appearances, but she couldn't even find him in the first place. The wedding ceremony now over, she grabbed a flute of prosecco and started mingling with Monica's and Tom's families, the aunties and uncles she recognized, and then her friends and acquaintances from high school and college.

She couldn't remember the last time she had seen most of them, yet because of Facebook, she knew exactly what was going on in their lives. Who had gotten engaged at the summit of Mount Haleakala on vacation in Maui, who had painted their master bedroom eggshell white, who had popped a balloon full of baby pink confetti at their gender-reveal party.

Once upon a time, Anu had had dozens of friends—and her schedule had been full of coffee or movie dates, party invites or casual brunches organized on a whim. Now if Jenny and Monica were busy, Anu stayed home and baked gluten-free cookies for Kanika's class, watching Netflix or *The Late Show with Stephen Colbert*.

She couldn't remember why she had lost touch with so many of them, and feeling bad, Anu quickly found herself making up an excuse to move on. She circled the room and joined Jenny, silent and sulking by herself at the bar. A few moments passed, and Jenny still hadn't said anything. Was she mad at Anu for bringing Ryan?

Determined to dispel the awkwardness, Anu turned to her. "A twenty-one-year-old kicked my ass in yoga yesterday. I haven't felt this good in years."

"Oh, yeah?"

"I'm thinking about joining a studio on West Broadway, actually. Why don't you come with me sometime? We could go after work."

"Don't we spend enough time together already?" Jenny raised her eyebrows at Anu. It was true. They did spend a lot of time together; they worked in the same clinic.

"Come on. I know you think it's airy-fairy, but honestly, at minimum it's great exercise."

"It's not exercise. And why would I pay twenty-five dollars to roll around on the floor and *stretch* with a bunch of—"

"Watch it . . ."

"Lululemon-sporting, plant-based-cappuccino-drinking soccer moms who spend thousands of dollars a week getting lip fillers and balayage treatments?"

Anu suppressed a smile. "You get balayage treatments, Jen."

"That's not the point!"

Anu turned to face her more fully. What had started out as a peace offering had somehow turned into one of their battles. "Try it, Jen. One class. For me?"

"Will I get to say 'nuh-*maas*-tay' with a horribly offensive accent?"

"If you want."

"Will you go running with me after?"

"Joke all you want, yoga can be challenging. You're going to be too tired to run after."

"Maybe . . ." Jenny shrugged. "OK, sure. Why not? And who knows? I might meet a guy."

Anu grimaced, shaking her head. "No, you won't."

"How are you so sure?"

"There are only three types of guys who go to yoga, and none of them is your type."

"Oh, yeah?"

Anu gave her a look. "Type one: beardy white guys who can do the splits standing up and like to spend their holidays at ashrams in India."

"Pass."

Anu giggled. "Thought so. Type two: middle-aged men who recently suffered some sort of health scare and are now determined to be flexible." Anu bent her arms into a stiff-eagle pose, and Jenny burst out laughing.

"*Hard* pass. And the third type?"

"Are married," Anu said flatly. "They're dragged there by their wives."

A few moments passed. Jenny turned quiet again, and Anu hoped she wasn't thinking of a certain married man named Blair.

"I wonder if he ever told her about me," Jenny said after a while, resting her forearms on the bar. Anu winced, feeling bad she had inadvertently brought up the man who a few years earlier had bashed Jenny's hearts to bit.

"It's not your fault," Anu said, even though Jenny never believed her. "You didn't know."

Jenny shrugged and then turned to face toward the crowded hall. "Shit," she said suddenly, bolting upright. "He's here."

The way Jenny said "he," Anu knew before she even looked. The hair on the back of her neck prickled as she turned around and saw Neil walk confidently into the crowd, a small carry-on suitcase in tow behind him.

He was wearing the same suit he had worn to their own wedding reception, but with a lighter shirt, a different tie. Was Priya back to doing his shopping?

"He made it back," Anu heard Jenny say, following him with her eyes as he crossed the room toward the coat check. She looked ahead and for the first time in hours saw Ryan. He was standing right in Neil's path, with a group of Monica's friends.

Neil and Ryan hadn't ever met. They probably didn't even know what the other one looked like, yet here they were together. Her two worlds—one past, one future—colliding.

Priya and Lakshmi had planned everything about her weeklong wedding celebration. Neil had been hard at work as Google's newest junior developer, and Anu—nose deep into her clinical practicums—had been too stressed to care whether they served naan or poori at the *sangeet*, if her bridesmaids' saris were melon or apricot orange.

But Monica looked so happy up there standing next to Tom, their eyes and hands locked together. That was how Anu and Neil used to look. Their marriage hadn't always been so bad.

With Ryan, could she do it all over again?

After dinner, Anu found herself painfully sober on the dance floor, doing her very best to keep a smile on her face. Most of the aunties and uncles had left, and almost everyone under the age of forty-five got completely smashed; Monica always knew how to throw a party.

Ryan was at the bar again, and she tried not to feel annoyed that he had assumed Anu would be the one to drive them home. She set down her half-drunk prosecco glass and slipped away, maneuvering around the tables toward him. It was dark, and it was too late to turn around by the time she spotted Neil in her path, slouching at a table by himself. His legs were spread wide, a bottle of beer dangling between his pinkie and ring finger.

She had to walk right by him, and she slowed her steps. Smiling, she stopped short just in front of him. "Hi."

"Hello."

She wanted to ask him about how his presentation had gone in

San Francisco, the one he'd been preparing for six months and how he'd managed to get away early. Did she have the right? Would he even tell her if she asked?

"It's nice to see you," she said finally. He looked up at her as if he couldn't quite believe her. But wasn't she telling the truth? That, despite everything, she was genuinely happy to see him.

She gestured to the chair next to him, and when he didn't say no, she sat down.

"How was the ceremony?"

"Beautiful." She nodded. "Monica cried. Tom cried. Everyone cried. It was really nice."

Was he also thinking about their own wedding day? Remembering what it had been like for them?

Sipping from the beer bottle, Neil looked over his left shoulder. "So you brought him."

"I'm sorry. I would have warned you if I knew you were coming."

He shrugged.

"Are you OK?"

"Why do you ask questions you don't want the answer to, Anush?"

She winced. Why did he still have to call her that? Why did his nickname for her still hurt so much?

"Do you want me to go?" she whispered.

"Sure, I'm used to you leaving."

She stood up, cupping her right hand over her mouth. "Look . . . I know you're hurt. . . ."

He stared at her, and it was so cold, it was as if he wasn't looking at her at all.

What was she supposed to say? She didn't want to feel responsible for his feelings anymore . . . but it was still not easy to see him hurting.

"I . . . I'm sorry."

"For what?"

Why *was* she sorry? Their marriage was broken, and now it was over. What did she have to feel sorry about?

He stood up, too, set down the beer bottle with a thud. She'd forgotten how tall he was, how small she felt standing next to him.

"You should stay," he said, brushing past her. "I'll go."

chapter six

✿

Eleven years ago

Hello, Uncle. Hello, Auntie."

"Hello, Neil," she heard her parents say in unison.

"How are you this evening?"

Anu crept down the carpeted stairs a few steps as Lakshmi prattled away about the *mattar paneer* simmering on the stove, the latest plot twist in her favorite Hindi soap.

"Your mother likes watching the show, too, *nah*?" Lakshmi asked. "You must tell her. If she is lonely on your nights out with Anu, she must come over. We can watch together."

"That's very nice. I'll tell her, Auntie. Thank you."

Anu chanced another step and then sat down on the staircase. She lowered her head just a bit and peered through the banister. Neil was wearing dark jeans, a collared shirt, and the brown leather jacket he rarely wore. Lakshmi, more than a foot shorter than Neil, was standing just in front of him; even though her mother hadn't left the house all day, Anu smiled, noticing her mother had put on lipstick.

"You can stay and eat with us, no?" Kunal asked. He was standing a few feet back from Lakshmi, his arms crossed tight.

"Uncle, I made a reservation. . . ."

"Surely, there is no punishment for canceling."

"Kunal," Lakshmi tutted, "let the children go eat."

"Yes, they are children, and they should eat with their *parents*."

"Do not listen to my husband. He is very grumpy he is stuck with me this evening."

"Uncle," Neil said, "that's nothing to be grumpy about. Auntie looks so pretty."

"All right, then I will go with Anu to the restaurant. And you can stay here with my *pretty* wife."

Neil laughed, and just then he locked eyes with Anu. She sat back startled, and when he didn't reveal her presence, she leaned back in.

"Before I forget," Neil said to Lakshmi, "I brought you these." He held out a box of chocolates, the brand they sold at the fancy department store right by campus. Lakshmi beamed as she took it.

"Neil, are you here to see Anu or her mother? Be careful how you answer. I can be a very jealous husband."

"Well, I figured I first need to win over Auntie if I want to see Anu."

"And what about me?" Kunal's face was flat, but his eyes were sparkling. "You are not trying to win me over?"

Neil winked at Lakshmi and, laughing, said, "Oh, Uncle, I already know *you* love me."

Anu was grinning as she snuck back up the steps toward her room. She pulled on her black pea coat and a scarf she'd nicked from Monica's closet the week before, and then she grabbed a tube of lip gloss from the bathroom.

It was their six-month anniversary and, officially, only their tenth date. The tenth time Neil had picked her up, made overtures to her parents—who had warmed to him considerably over the past six months, especially her father—and then taken her out to dinner.

But in reality, she saw Neil every day on campus—even on the weekends. They studied together and with friends in the library and at coffee shops constantly. Sometimes, he came along to her favorite yoga class in the strip mall a twenty-minute bike ride from her parents' house, although with the demanding university classes she needed to take to qualify for nursing school, she didn't have much time to go anymore. Among the many rules her parents had laid out for her was that if her grades slipped, she and Neil were over.

Anu padded down the stairs and caught the three of them in conversation about Neil's latest midterm. They all looked up at the same time, and she had a sudden sensation of lightheartedness.

"Hi, Anush."

"Hey . . ." She blushed as she stepped into her boots and hoped her parents wouldn't notice the way he was looking at her.

"Doesn't Anu get chocolates?" she heard Kunal ask.

"*Dad*, he's taking me to dinner."

"But your mother got chocolates!"

"Kunal, *really*—"

"A man who doesn't bring his date chocolate?" He winked at Anu. "I cannot allow you to leave with this monster."

As Lakshmi hugged her goodbye, she whispered, "Be home by ten," into Anu's ear. Annoyed, Anu nodded and then followed Neil out to his car. Only when they were several blocks away did he pull the car over and kiss her.

They were by far the youngest customers in the restaurant, and Anu's eyes bulged at the prices on the menu.

"Thirty dollars for *chicken*?" she asked Neil. He rubbed her shin with his leg beneath the table and told her not to worry about it; he had saved up from his internship the summer before, and he wanted to treat her.

They ordered dinner and, after each was carded by the waiter, a small carafe of wine to share. Neil made Anu drink most of it, because he was driving, and her head felt light and airy by the time he paid the bill and they left the restaurant.

After, it was only eight thirty p.m., and they were not sure what to do next. They could go back to Anu's and watch a Hindi movie with her parents, but they wouldn't even be allowed to sit on the same couch. So they drove around aimlessly, past a movie theater, bars, and restaurants, and then they did another loop around the neighborhood.

Resting her chin in her hands, Anu sulked in the passenger seat, thinking about how if she had just lied about whom she was going out with that night, she wouldn't have had a curfew. If she had told her parents she was with Monica or another *female* friend, she could have stayed out with him the whole night.

"We might as well just go home," she said after a while, staring out the window.

"Is that what you want?"

She shrugged and then grabbed his hand on the stick shift. "Not really."

Neil cleared his throat and then hung the next right into a parking lot behind a big-box store. It was mostly empty, and Neil pulled into a spot on the far end.

Without saying anything to each other, they both got out of

the car and into the backseat. Scooting into the middle, she leaned into his chest as he wrapped his arm around her.

Here, in his mother's car, was the only time they ever got to be alone. The only time their legs could touch and their fingers intertwine and they could sit together like they were in love, do *something* more than just say it.

"Do you want to listen to music?" he whispered.

"Your weird punky-funk music?"

"Hey, my music isn't weird."

"I hesitate to call it music to begin with." She leaned forward between the front seats, and he swatted her butt just as she switched on the radio. "Hey!"

"Get back here," he said, pulling at her jacket.

She laughed, switching between stations. Billy Idol. The twenty-four-hour Punjabi station. The Mandarin channel. Shania Twain. She clicked SEEK one last time, and Rihanna came on. She beamed at him as she shifted backward, leaving no space between them on the seat.

"This isn't music, either," he warned her. He sounded hungry.

Emboldened, she went in for the kiss, and their mouths collided, perhaps too hard, but it was funny and so they laughed. His hands were cold on her cheeks, her neck, but they were warm by the time they slipped beneath her shirt. He kissed her harder now, and she slid closer, then pulled herself onto his lap.

She felt him pressing against her hips, and instinctively, she moved against him. As his hands moved from her hips to her stomach, and then higher, she pulled one leg over to straddle him.

This was always where he stopped her, where in a moment, maybe two, he'd stop her again. He sat up straighter, and she slid in closer, a soft moan escaping her lips. She wanted to be closer to him, push herself harder against him. She knew he wanted that, too, as he fumbled with her bra, helped her move her body up and down against him.

She was taller than him sitting like this, and pulling away, she leaned down and kissed his neck.

She loved him so much. She wanted him *so* much.

She could feel him shiver, and she kissed him in that spot again. He was squirming beneath her now, and she slid her mouth up to his ear, let her tongue dart in and then out.

"*Anush.*" He pulled at her waist, her jeans, like he wanted them off, but he'd never actually tried. Would she let him if he did? She kissed him, and everything became more hazy, more abstract, as he ground against her, and then suddenly he stopped.

He always stopped. Right now she wished he wouldn't.

Her vision blurred as she crawled off him and then into the front seat. Neil was red in the face as he started the car. The clock came to life. It was nine forty-three p.m.

"Time to go," he said, his voice catching.

They both knew where they were going—and that they'd be there together forever. But they were only nineteen, and it wasn't coming fast enough.

chapter seven

KUNAL: Hello, sir or madam, this is Kunal Kapoor, the father of Anusha Desai. If you are reading this, it is because you have kidnapped my daughter and are holding her hostage. I respectfully decline to pay the ransom. However, if you allow Anusha to call back her mother, who has left her 8 messages and will speak to me about nothing else, I will reconsider.

Should I watch *Miss Congeniality* or *Hitch*?" Anu pressed her lips together furiously. "Yes, I realize I've seen them both before." She paused. "Fine, *more* than once before."

Anu reached for the bag of chips sitting on Ryan's end table and suddenly noticed it was empty. She'd eaten the whole thing the evening before, sitting here, watching a different romantic comedy she'd seen a dozen times before, waiting for him to come home from work.

"I'm talking to myself, aren't I?"

A Buddha statute that Ryan said he'd gotten at Urban Barn, staring at Anu from a high bookshelf, didn't respond.

Anu stood up and, feeling incredibly pathetic, grabbed a pair of yoga pants from her overnight bag. There were too many hours to fill in a day ever since the separation, when she and Neil had agreed on joint custody. She couldn't even remember what she used to spend her time on before Kanika was born when all of a sudden, Anu's whole life evaporated into her daughter's health and appetite, amusement and emotions.

She had liked reading and going for hikes with her dad or Neil. She had hung out with her friends, although the only two she seemed to have these days were often busy, like tonight. Monica had just left with Tom for her honeymoon, and Jenny was at her sister's book club.

She sighed as she pulled on her workout pants, stretched the elastic material up her calves and thighs. Anu used to be interesting and fun and passionate. She used to have yoga.

Fifteen minutes later, she found herself outside of Mags' Studio. The lights were out, and disappointed, she blocked her eyes with her hands and peered through the glass.

"Anusha?"

Anu whipped around toward the voice and spotted Imogen's signature hair. Instead of yoga clothes, she was wrapped up in a faux-fur coat, and her hair was parted down the center, buns above her ears like Princess Leia. Her boots, matte black leather, stretched high up her thighs.

"Hey . . ."

"Were you here to make Mags an offer?"

"Pardon?"

"On the studio." Imogen smiled. "Mags says she has a good feeling about you. She's convinced you'll be the one to take it over."

Anu rolled her eyes, pulling her scarf tighter around her neck. "As if I can run a studio." She shook her head. "No. I couldn't find your schedule online, but I thought I'd try my luck."

"There are no classes on a Friday night. The last class of the day finished up hours ago. I was upstairs getting ready at Mags'."

Anu took notice of the bright pink lipstick on Imogen's lips, her smoky eyes, her contoured cheekbones—a cross between Pippi Longstocking and Kim Kardashian. How did women manage to put on makeup like that? It was art. It was pure, magical art.

"The next class isn't until eight a.m. tomorrow. . . ."

"Damn," Anu said. "Oh, well. I'll come tomorrow. Have a nice evening."

"You, too . . ." Imogen trailed off, and then shoved Anu lightly on the shoulder. "Actually, you wanna come with?"

"With who?"

"Me?" Imogen laughed. "*Out*. I'm seeing this guy. It's his friend's birthday." As if noticing the hesitation on Anu's face, Imogen shook her head. "You won't be the oldie, I swear. I think the guy is turning like twenty-seven or something."

"But I won't know anyone," Anu said, even though what she was really thinking was that she barely knew Imogen. She *didn't* know Imogen.

"I won't know anyone, either. It's casual. Some bar downtown. He said anyone's welcome."

"I don't know. . . ." Anu stuffed her hands into her pockets. She couldn't go out to a bar with perfect strangers, could she? At her age? She hadn't been capable of summoning that sort of spontaneity even at *Imogen's* age.

"Oh, live a little, Anusha. Come drink with me."

Live a little. It was something Jenny would have said to her—likely *had* said to her in the past.

Kicking at a loose rock on the pavement, Anu racked her brain for a reason not to go, but the truth was, she didn't have one. There was no reason why she shouldn't. No family, boyfriend, or friends to stay home for. She checked her phone. Ryan hadn't replied to one of her text messages in hours, since he had said he was going into an urgent closed-door meeting for one of his cases.

"Come on," Imogen said. "Did you have anything better planned?"

"Not really. My boyfriend's working tonight. I suppose I'll just watch Netflix and chill. Why are you laughing?"

Imogen keeled over in a fit and then threw her head back, hair falling everywhere. "You're going to Netflix and chill, *alone*?"

"What?"

"Do you know what that *means*?"

Anu shook her head, mildly irritated. "I have no idea what we're talking about right now."

"Netflix. And. Chill." Imogen stared at her, and still Anu didn't get it. "It's code. It's, like, *slang* for sex."

"No, it's not! I Netflix and chill by myself all the time. Hey, stop laughing at me!"

"Sorry. Sorry," Imogen said, composing herself. "But you really need to stop saying that. I swear people will make *assumptions*."

Her cheeks burning, Anu shrugged. "Noted."

"*Anyway.*" Imogen linked arms with Anu and started leading her in the direction from which Anu had come. "Where do you live? You need to change."

Anu gestured at the next corner, and so they turned. "My boyfriend's house is just down the block."

"Perfect," Imogen said. "And to be clear, *we* are not going to Netflix and chill. I'm not hitting on you."

"That didn't even cross my mind."

"Really? That's the *first* thing that would have crossed my mind."

"Is it a millennial thing?"

Imogen eyed her playfully. "I think it's a redhead thing."

Two hours later, Anu was in a crowded bar she had never noticed or seen before, but was only two blocks away from the office building where both she and Ryan worked. She thought about texting him to see if he'd like to join her after he was done, but she didn't want to seem needy, so she decided against it.

The bar was dark and dingy, and there was a handful of pool tables by the jukebox and a line of picnic tables stretched along the far wall. Anu didn't have much clothing at Ryan's house, but somehow Imogen had convinced her to wear her red lipstick and faux fur. She had felt like an impostor walking out the door, utterly ridiculous, but here suddenly she seemed to fit right in.

"It's Haruto," Imogen said, gesturing to her phone as they made their way to the bar. "They're in the back. But let's get a shot first."

"So Haruto is your boyfriend?"

"He's *not* my boyfriend. We're sleeping together. But we also sleep with other people, you know?"

Anu nodded as if she understood, even though she had no idea how dating worked these days—or had ever worked, really.

"I met him at Mags' a few months ago. He took my class."

"Aw, that's cute."

"Cute? Sure." Imogen shook her head, laughing as she tried to get the bartender's attention.

As they waited for their shots, Anu tried to remember herself at Imogen's age. Sure, she'd *gone* to bars like this; a few times, she'd drunk one too many vodka 7 Ups with her friends and Neil, but she'd never been stupid about it. Neil would sit with her in a booth, bring her water, and protectively drive her home when a party got too wild. Anything that had even come close to "stupid," she had shared with Neil.

Their shots arrived, and just as Anu went to pay, a man's arm pushed in front of her and handed the bartender a twenty.

"Keep the change, toots," said the voice, and Anu and Imogen both turned to look. He was very ordinary looking, except for the blond porn-star mustache crawling down his face.

"I'm Bob," he said gruffly. "What are your names?"

Anu glanced at Imogen, and she could tell the young woman, too, was trying her best to suppress a smile. She coughed, covering the giggle.

"Thank you for the drinks, *Bob*," Imogen said. "You didn't have to."

"I know I didn't. But I'm in town on business and thought I'd spoil a few good-looking gals."

"Is that so?"

He grinned, and the porn-star mustache morphed into a butterfly spreading its wings. "What's your name, sweetie? And what do ya do for a living? Bet you're a model, aren't ya?"

Eyes gone wide, Imogen answered, "My name is Fern. And I'm . . . a parade float designer. For the Macy's Thanksgiving Day Parade."

"Really?"

She nodded, and Anu did her best to hold in her laughter as she caught Imogen's eye.

"That's very interesting, doll." He turned to Anu. "And you?"

"My name is Mango."

"Mango?"

"It's Indian. Indians eat a lot of mangoes. And I'm an . . . heiress." Anu swallowed, smiling. "I'm very rich. I don't need to have a job."

The man gasped. "Are you one of those Indians in the Patel family?" he continued, oblivious to the unimpressed look on Anu's face. "The Patels that own half the logging industry in this town?"

"No. The Patels are basically paupers when it comes to my family. You see . . . my *grandmother* invented . . . yoga."

"*Did* she now? I've heard of yoga, you know. But I thought it was invented by Gwyneth Paltrow."

Anu pursed her lips like she was evaluating a fine wine. "Common misconception, Bob. Common misconception."

They fled the scene close to tears, and after meeting up with Haruto and his friends, Imogen disappeared with him outside to smoke a joint. Anu, who had never tried marijuana even after it became legal, stayed behind at the table. Suddenly, the rush of energy she'd felt dwindled when she saw a text from Ryan saying that he wouldn't be home for a few more hours.

"Do you want a beer?"

Anu looked up to find the guy next to her pushing a plastic glass toward her, reaching for a half-full pitcher of beer with his other hand. He was young, handsome in a nondescript kind of way—brown hair, green eyes. With his denim jacket, he looked a bit like one of Kanika's Ken dolls.

"Sure. Thanks."

He poured the beer, and when she reached for her purse, he shook his head. "Don't worry about it."

"I'll buy the next pitcher, then," she said, and the guy smiled at her. Was it because she'd offered to buy a round, or was it a different sort of smile? Jenny would have known. Leaning away from him, Anu reached for the glass. "So whose birthday is it?"

"My brother's. Tim." He pointed to a guy at the far end of the table, one with the same green eyes and dark hair. "And I'm Jake."

"Nice to meet you, Jake."

Their conversation started and stalled, and Anu wondered if Jake was acting awkward or she was. Where the hell was Imogen? Anu tried asking Jake questions about where he worked, what area of Vancouver he lived in, but he kept switching the conversation away from himself. And so, beer after beer, they mostly talked about her. How she'd come out with Imogen only on a lark after learning her boyfriend had to work late. By the time Imogen and Haruto came back in, the bar was even more crowded, and inadvertently, Anu was drunk.

Quite drunk.

Imogen pulled her up to the dance floor, and Anu obliged, her limbs loosening with each R&B song. Haruto, Jake, and the others joined them, and when a Tupac song came on, nobody but Anu knew the words. They formed a circle around her as she rapped the lyrics, jerking her torso up and down with the beat.

Everyone was egging her on, and pretty soon the whole dance floor was cheering, and Anu felt completely exhilarated by the time she bowed and the DJ transitioned to a different track.

"Girl, you've got some *moves*!" Imogen squeezed her shoulder, pulling her toward the edge of the dance floor. "And here I thought you were a square."

"I'm not a square!" Anu laughed, fanning herself with her hand. "Are you hot? I'm *hot*."

"You *are* hot, Anusha. You just don't act like it."

"I am not."

"Don't fish!" Imogen's eyes were wide. "You are hot, and you don't need to pretend like you don't know that"—she paused, rushing and stumbling over her words—"or *fish* for compliments."

"I wasn't fishing." She threw Imogen Tupac's signature "west side" hand sign. "I was rapping."

Suddenly, the room spun as she tried to remember how many beers she had drunk. She could feel a breeze on her face, and she positioned her body toward it. The entrance door was open, with people pushing their way in and out. She blinked at the blur of them coming into focus.

Her chest tightened.

She wasn't seeing straight, was she? She *was* drunk.

She blinked again, and her arms went limp as she caught sight of the familiar face in the doorway.

"What is it?" Imogen turned on her heels, followed her eyes to the door. "Who are they?"

"I don't know about 'they.'" Anu swallowed hard. "But *he* is my boyfriend."

Her mind raced, and there was barely time to process any of it as she spotted Ryan's hand slip around a woman's waist. It was like Anu's feet were glued to the floor, her eyes glued to *him* as he moved his hand from her waist to her shoulder.

"Maybe it's . . ." Imogen trailed off as Ryan bent down and kissed the woman's neck. "Oh, sweet Jesus."

Anu couldn't breathe; she couldn't move, even as Ryan and the woman started walking in her direction. A deer caught in headlights, she couldn't do anything but stare at them, the floor spinning beneath her.

"Are you going to say something?" Imogen grabbed her by the elbow, squeezed her until she felt more alert. "Anusha, *do* something."

Do something. But what exactly?

Anu nodded and, shaking her arm free, stepped forward just as Ryan and the other woman were about to pass.

She wanted to scream. She wanted to *slap* him, but when their eyes met, she couldn't do a thing.

"Anu?" His face went beet red as he stepped toward her, recoiled away from the other woman. "I—I was just . . . finishing up, and the team wanted a quick drink. . . ." He paused as if waiting for her to intervene, but she didn't. What was there even to say?

"Tammy"—he gestured to the woman—"is one of my associates. The rest are coming in a minute. Aren't they, Tammy?"

The woman smiled nervously and then looked down at the floor.

Do something. Anu's ears rang as she tried to muster the courage, but her lips wouldn't stop trembling, and her hands stayed limp.

"His *associate*," Imogen muttered. "What a fucking cliché."

"I should have texted you I wasn't coming straight home," Ryan said, his eyes briefly leaving Anu for Imogen. "Anu, I'm so sorr—"

"You can stuff your sorrys up *Tammy's* asshole."

"Imogen!" Anu waved her off, just as Ryan's face drained of color. The way he was staring at her reminded her of Monica's rescue dog when he had been only a puppy and he would have accidents all over the floor.

What would she say, if she allowed herself to scream?

"Anu, it's not what it looks like."

But what did it all look like, really?

. The man she had taken a chance on, the one who held the promise of a new start and a new kind of life, was a *jerk*.

A goddamn cheater.

Like Imogen had said, the whole thing was a fucking cliché.

Without tears, without words, she walked out the door. A beat later, she felt a coat on her shoulders, Imogen's hands helping her arms into the holes.

They walked in silence onto a less crowded street. The air was soggy and suffocating, and her chest hurt and her head pounded, and she wondered if anything on earth that she'd touched or felt had ever been real.

Her face felt wet. She licked her lips and tasted the salt.

chapter eight

Eleven months earlier

She'd seen him around for months, maybe even years. He stood out from among the bluish gray rainbow of suits that rode up and down her building's elevator, all of them conventionally handsome—but not *too* handsome. He easily could have blended in with the rest of them, but for that charisma of his, that way he held open the door for women or always remembered to bring his eco-friendly coffee mug with him to the lobby Starbucks.

It was early summer, her birthday, and in the elevator she caught him glancing at her legs. The day before Thanksgiving he winked, while carrying a stack of steaming pumpkin pies through the lobby. Was it for her? (The wink, not the pies.) She didn't know. Then the first day it was cold enough to wear her favorite parka—heavy wool, navy blue—he smiled at her, but this time just a bit too long. She felt guilty. Exhilarated. A passing crush on a stranger, one she was certain would depart as quickly as it came.

The chill set in; the mountains clouded over. One night in early winter, she went out for happy hour with Jenny at the bar and grill around the corner. Jenny was tipsy, and Anu, sober, made an excuse again for why she couldn't attend their girls' trip to Seattle. She felt a hand on her shoulder, and there *he* was, just inches away.

"It's you."

"It's *you*."

"And you are?" she heard Jenny say.

"I figured it's time I finally say hello. Introduce myself."

"I guess so, yeah." Anu watched him catch sight of her wedding ring and spotted a flash of disappointment on his face.

"I'm Ryan. I work at the environmental law firm a few floors above your office," he said, politely turning to face Jenny. "You're both at the medical clinic on the tenth floor, right? I've seen you, too, I think."

"We are. I'm Jenny," she said. "And that's Anu."

Jenny took the lead on the conversation. The quintessential confident woman, she excelled at small talk and banter, the ability to remain professional, aloof, yet at other moments transform into a shameless flirt. Anu took a backseat as they discussed the flood in the parking garage, the Canucks' chance at the Stanley Cup playoffs. It only made sense; Anu was married. She'd played the unavailable yet not completely unattractive wingwoman her whole adult life.

After a few minutes, Ryan told them he was on his way to his company's Christmas party at the Pacific Rim Hotel, asked them to tag along. Before Anu had a chance to think twice, Jenny agreed for them both.

They shared a cab. The roads were icy, and the sleety rain turned to snow they were sure would melt before sunrise. Jenny was wedged between them in the middle seat, laughing, telling

Ryan a funny story—one Anu had heard countless times before—about the time she was accused of being a drug runner by the US border guards on her way to Portland.

"They held me in purgatory for *four* hours. Me! Can you believe it? A five-foot nothing half-Chinese girl!"

She brought their driver into the conversation, and as Jenny leaned forward, Anu caught Ryan's eye.

She looked away, but from that point on, she knew what he wanted. What, unless she put a stop to it, he'd inevitably try to do.

They were greeted by a drunken lot of men and women she vaguely recognized from around the building in the hotel's front restaurant. A burst of light off the chandelier made her squint. She thought about leaving, but it was her first night out in who knew how long, and for a reason she wouldn't admit to herself *then*, she decided to stay.

The hours passed quickly, and Anu—who had spent her whole life feeling in control—didn't feel that way at all. She wasn't drunk or hungry or sad or particularly enjoying herself—but she was there, participating in mindless chatter with a dozen new faces. Ryan kept looking at her from across the table. She liked it and wasn't at all surprised when he went to the bar for another round and asked her to join him.

He needed help carrying the drinks, didn't he? So she went with him. When they arrived at the bar, he rested his elbow on the counter, his head in his hand, and started off with broad, indirect questions. She showed him pictures of Kanika on her phone, and they talk about environmental law, his decision to leave "Big Law" and join a boutique firm that fought for the right side, instead of the wrong one. He asked her why she had chosen nursing, and when she didn't have a good answer, just a practiced one, he shifted visibly closer.

"I had a crush on my nurse once. Shoulder surgery. I played hockey."

She glanced past him and found Jenny across the room, with a much-younger man's hand dipping into the small of her back.

"She was at least sixty."

Anu nearly spit her drink in his face as she laughed. "Was her name Florence Nightingale?"

"What? She looked good for her age." He bit his lip. "She took good care of me. And maybe it was also—I don't know—a power thing?"

"That she could euthanize you if you got fresh?"

"Something like that." He leaned in. He was inches away, and suddenly Anu felt more conscious about whether Jenny could see her than how close he was standing. "It's snowing. Wow, it's *really* snowing."

She followed his eyes out the window. He was right. The street outside was covered in a white froth, parallel car tracks running straight through. She moved and stood next to the floor-to-ceiling window, and a moment later, he appeared. Usually, she liked to watch snowflakes as they trickled down, found a good spot, and settled, but tonight they were falling too hard, too fast to keep track of.

"I wonder how long it will last." Ryan wiped the condensation off the window with his cuffs.

She pushed her forehead against the window. It was cold and sent a shiver along the length of her body.

"I can't remember the last time it snowed like this," he said quietly. "Can you?"

She looked over at him from the window, the side of her forehead still pressed against the glass. He was already looking at her.

The moment beforehand didn't build or bloom, crescendo into a perfect storm of tension and sizzle. It was entirely ordinary. He moved toward her, and only at the very last second—just as she began to smell the whiskey on his breath—did she pull away.

She turned back to the window, to the snow piling higher outside, and only then did she think of Neil.

In a flash, something changed. Something shifted within her.

'm going home," Anu said to Jenny's back. Jenny turned around, half-startled, half-drunk.

"What's going on? Here, I'll leave with you."

"Stay, honestly. I'll call you tomorrow." Anu shook her head as Jenny tried to stand up, gently pushing her back in her seat. "Please? Tomorrow." And with a quick kiss on Jenny's cheek, Anu was off.

The Pacific Rim concierge found her a taxi willing to cross the bridge and take her home. It took over an hour, and more than once they nearly smashed into another car, the tires screeching as they gave way to the ice, to the blizzard that had blown in and out and left treacherous walls of snow in its wake.

Ryan had tried to kiss her, and she'd nearly let him.

A few blocks from home, Anu noticed how different the roads looked from only that morning when she had raced off to work. The playground she and Kanika frequented was camouflaged by thick, choppy blankets of snow; the sidewalks and lawns of their neighborhood were buried. Her whole world had been completely transformed.

If she were to graph her marriage, the vortex was their wedding day. The parabola had climbed upward through their five-year relationship, but then overnight they were living together—Anu working long hours as a nurse in training, while Neil took pains to climb the ranks at Google, and then went out on his own as an independent contractor.

They were *both* busy, but that didn't matter, and she learned that the good, decent man who Neil was didn't know how to use a toilet brush, launder his own clothes, or wipe the crumbs off the counter after toasting a piece of bread—his one claim to cooking fame. Anu managed the household the best she could between lectures and days at the clinic, and after a few months, instead of getting fed up, she hired a cleaner.

They also had their mothers. An unending supply of everything from *saag aloo* to *chole* stored discreetly in the freezer, surprise Crock-Pots of minestrone with an Indian flare simmering when she got home from a long day.

The truth was, life was never that hard for either of them. So of course everything changed when Kanika came along. They were tired, always so tired, and despite their good intentions, their mothers hovering in the background only made it worse.

"Alone time" ceased to exist. Alone time became being not with each other—Neil with his headphones on in the basement, finishing off a project, while Anu put their daughter to bed. It was Anu finding an hour on a Sunday afternoon to go meet Jenny's latest boyfriend or practice yoga on the lawn, help Monica pick out a light fixture, while Priya came over because she insisted Neil needed her help to "babysit."

Constantly exhausted, irritated by Neil's feeble attempts at parenting, after her maternity leave, Anu went down to three days a week at the clinic. Priya and Lakshmi would playfully bicker over whose turn it was to babysit, while Anu grew increasingly resentful of Neil's flexible hours, which he chose to exercise to suit his own convenience rather than theirs. The way he would sweep in with smiles, ice cream, and Disney figurines, leaving Anu with what was left.

But wasn't she being unfair? Did any of that give her the right to come so close to kissing another man?

The taxi pulled up beside the pavement in front of their house. When the driver refused to turn up on the drive because it hadn't been shoveled, her guilt evaporated, and the familiar sting of resentment set in. Most of their neighbors' drives were already clear, and one of them had even graciously shoveled the sidewalk in front of Anu and Neil's house. Fuming, she handed a wad of cash to the driver and then started the laborious trek up the snowy drive in her heels.

The front door was ajar. All the lights were on, and Kanika's backpack was open—games, books, crayons spilling out across the foyer. She followed a trail of coats and scarves down the hall, through the kitchen, and up the few stairs to the living room area. Neil was there, of course, with CNN on mute in the background. His legs dripped over the end of the love seat. She rounded the corner, and there he was in full view. One earphone in, his laptop open, a half-empty French press and a china mug wedged between his thighs.

"How was your night?" He didn't look up, and she didn't respond. For a moment, she just stared at him, trying to figure out if this was in fact her life.

They'd been together so long, and for the first time—right in that moment—she wondered why they stayed together. It was more than Lakshmi's and Priya's insistence that they get married so young, make their "modern relationship" a legitimate one. It was more than practicality, that their families wouldn't have approved of them living together—the way other couples their age did.

Or was it?

"Did you have a good time?"

"Did *you*?" she fired back.

He looked up, his face bewildered in that puppy dog "what did I do?" look she was growing to despise.

"You left the front door open again."

"Really? I thought—"

"And there's crap everywhere, and the driveway is—"

"It's still snowing. I was going to do it when it stopped snowing."

She was across the room in four strides and whipped open the blinds. She stepped aside, pointing to the pane glass window as if presenting an award. "The snow will turn to ice if we don't do it right away. Do you know how dangerous that is?"

"It was still snowing the last time I checked."

"What if our mothers show up early and slip? What if the delivery—"

"Anu, it's not that late." He glanced at the clock. "Are you still ovulating?"

"Are you *kidding* me right now?"

She took off her skirt and found a pair of Neil's sweatpants in the front hall closet, pulled them up over her nylons. After locating a pair of winter boots at the back of the closet, a thick wooly coat, and gloves, she shut the door behind her.

The week before, the weather forecast had predicted it might snow. Hadn't she asked Neil to pick up a shovel, just in case? She checked the shed, unsurprised to find no shovel. There were gardening tools, and then she spotted one plastic shovel, a toy almost, that one of the grandparents must have bought for Kanika.

She had to hunch over to use it, but it served its purpose. She started at one end of the drive, and it took four long pushes to clear just a few square feet. Her back started to throb, and she stood up straight.

"Let me do it, OK?" Neil was on the front stoop. He started

walking toward her, and she leaned back over, pushing ahead with the shovel.

"I got it."

"I meant to—"

"I know you *meant* to."

"Anush, quit being a martyr, and let me do it." He was beside her, reaching for the shovel, and she shrugged him off.

"Go away!"

He lunged for the shovel and pulled it out of her hand, raising it out of reach.

"Stop."

He smiled down at her, and she jumped. He just raised it higher.

"*Neil!* You're so"—she jumped again—"*annoying!*"

"I know." He whipped the shovel into the snowbank behind her. "That's why you love me."

He dropped his hands deep into the pockets of the pea coat she had bought him for his last birthday. It was a rich navy blue, threads of coal and burnt almond running through. With his scruff, girly-thick eyelashes, he looked even more handsome than the day she had met him.

"Jesus," he said, watching her face. "Are you crying?"

She wiped her eyes.

"It's just the driveway. Don't—"

"I think you should move out."

His mouth dropped. She didn't say anything else, stared at the snow freckling between her feet.

"Quit kidding around, huh? That's not funny."

"I'm not trying to be funny."

"What is this, some kind of test?"

"No." She shook her head. "I'm not happy. Neither are you. I think we should . . . live . . . separately. We should separate." The idea was created, attached to her mind almost as she said the words. But now it was there—between her heartbeats as he didn't respond, stared at her in pure exasperation—and it stuck.

"Look, let's go inside and talk—"

"*You* want to talk? When have you *ever* wanted to talk about anything remotely serious?"

"Try me. Let's talk. What's this about, then? I'm a slob? I'm lazy? I know, OK? But—"

"I almost kissed someone tonight."

That shut him up. He nodded slowly, his face wound into a tight scowl. He started pacing and then waded into the snowbank to fetch the shovel. A moment later he was back.

"It was just some guy who works in my building."

"*Some* guy."

"It was nothing. Nothing actually happened, OK? I don't even know him."

"You say you almost kissed someone tonight, but nothing happened?" He shook his head and then let out an unfocused, muffled howl. He turned around, whipped the shovel into the opposite snowbank. "What the *hell* is that supposed to mean?"

"It means, Neil . . ." She paused. "It means, something is wrong. Something is wrong with *us*."

"Don't you dare say that. Nothing's wrong—"

"There is. Why would have I put myself in that situation if things between us weren't totally messed up? We're always fighting or snapping at each other—and if we're not, then we're just not speaking. Things *aren't* like they were before."

"What's changed, then?" His eyes were red, his throat hoarse. "Me? *You?*"

She didn't know how to answer him. Had she changed, or was she just tired of expecting him to? "I don't know."

"You don't know, and you're ready to call it quits?"

Wasn't she ready? Wasn't *this* the only move that made sense?

"Fine. *Fine!*" He stomped away from her, leaving a track through the snow. "I'll play along. I'll sleep on the couch tonight. How 'bout that? And I'll see you in the morning after you've changed your goddamn mind."

He slammed the door, and she wondered if it woke up Kanika. She found the shovel and continued to plow, inch by inch, through the snow. The idea of their separation started to ferment, thicken from an idea into a way forward, a way to be happy again.

Morning came. She didn't change her mind, and three weeks later he moved out.

chapter nine

❧

RYAN: Anu, I've left you a thousand messages. Please pick up? Please, let's talk about this.

RYAN: You've got it all wrong. It's not what it looks like, honest. Just answer me, would you? I need to talk to you.

Anu woke up in her own bed with her temples throbbing. She pawed at the nightstand for her phone and a glass of water, but neither were there. The room spun as she sat up, and it took her a minute to notice that Imogen was in the bed next to her.

Both of them had their clothes on from the evening before, and Imogen was still wearing her shoes, too. Her mouth hung open, and she'd managed to get makeup all over Anu's white pillowcase. When Anu tried to gently prod her awake, she just groaned and rolled away.

Massaging her forehead, Anu tried to assemble the pieces of the evening before. After the taxi back to Ryan's house, she distinctly remembered rummaging around for all her clothes, bags, and books, anything she'd left there in the past few months, while Imogen used a designated-driver app to find someone to drive them, in Anu's car, back to her house.

There, it got blurry. Cheap wine drunk straight from the bottle. Laughing or crying—or was it both?

Jewel playing in the background. Was Imogen old enough to know Jewel?

Anu slipped out of bed and took a shower, and by the time she returned to the bedroom, Imogen was awake.

"How are you feeling?"

"I'm not sure," Anu said honestly. In fact, she felt so hungover, she didn't think she was capable of feeling anything.

Imogen nodded and then played on her phone as Anu towel-dried her hair. It was both odd and comforting to see a virtual stranger in her bed. The oddest part was, Imogen didn't feel like a stranger at all.

Anu made them both breakfast, fried eggs and tomatoes and toast, and while they ate, they made a plan to go out again the following weekend, once Kanika was back with Neil. After, she insisted on calling Imogen a cab.

"Anusha," Imogen said, leaning against the door as they waited, "I get it."

"What do you get?" Anusha asked, even though she knew what she was talking about.

"How you're feeling." The weight and tilt of her words sent a shiver down Anu's spine. She didn't know if Imogen was talking about some guy who'd hurt her or something else. "But fuck it, right?"

Anu nodded, searching Imogen's face, wondering what she was trying to say.

Anu didn't have time to feel sorry for herself until later that evening—after she'd cleaned the house, bought groceries for the week, and picked up Kanika. After she spent the afternoon taking her daughter to dance class, for a haircut, and then out to their favorite sushi restaurant on Granville.

After putting Kanika to bed, she sighed as she sank guiltily into the couch; it was the first time ever that she wasn't looking forward to the week ahead with her daughter.

This one, she wished she had for herself.

She'd been putting it off, but after making herself a cup of tea, she texted Jenny, who was in the middle of a Tinder date.

Less than twenty minutes later, Jenny was knocking at her door.

In the basement, well beyond Kanika's earshot should she wake up, Anu cried her eyes out—and Jenny, usually about as sympathetic as a lamppost, let her.

"Don't say it," Anu said, reaching for the tissues.

"Don't say what?"

"Anything."

"I haven't said a word."

"Fine. Say it."

"Are you *sure*?"

Anu nodded.

"He's a jerk! He's a monumental *jerk*, Anu. A real phony suave motherfucker, and I have no idea how you never saw it."

"You and Monica both—"

"Despised him."

"*Despised*," Anu repeated, still processing. "Why didn't you tell me?"

"I *tried*. And we thought you'd figure it out. We wanted *you* to figure it out."

Anu tried to imagine what would have happened if she hadn't gone out the evening before, had instead stayed home at Ryan's house while he "worked late" with Tammy.

Would she have figured it out? Anu was not sure she would have.

Anu sat up. Instead of blowing her nose, she threw the tissue at Jenny's head. "You should have told me."

"Well, back then, you should have told me."

Jenny grew quiet, and Anu knew she was thinking about Blair. Monica and Anu had never warned her that his odd, often sketchy behavior could have been a sign that he was hiding something, like a *wife*, although Jenny didn't actually blame them for that. Anu and Monica had been young, too, even more inexperienced than she was. They had been oblivious to the red flags.

Evidently, Anu was still oblivious.

"I wish I had been with you last night." Jenny shook back her hair. "I would have made you punch him. And if you didn't, *I* would have."

"What would that have accomplished?"

"It would have made you feel better, for one." Jenny shrugged. "So has he called you?"

Anu nodded and handed Jenny her cell phone. Ryan had left several messages, and Anu had ignored all of them. Each plea that it "wasn't what it looked like" and that they were "just colleagues." But her favorite line, which had come only the hour before, was "Whatever happened last night, can't you just forgive me?"

After listening to all of Ryan's voice mails, and commenting with Jenny-like sarcasm on every single line, she threw Anu's phone decidedly on the couch. "It's over. You shouldn't call him back."

"I wasn't going to."

"Then congratulations, Anu. You're officially single again."

Single.

Anu's heart fell, and perhaps noticing that her friend was on the brink of tears, Jenny closed her mouth on whatever she had been about to say next. She scooted in closer on the couch and let her head fall on Anu's shoulder.

Anu had never really been single. In high school, sure, but that didn't count. None of her friends had had boyfriends back then; they were too busy at band or choir practice, studying for university entrance exams, at drama club, or at one another's houses watching *The OC* or *Friends*. And those first six months after Neil had moved out, before she gave in to Ryan's advances, had been a whirlwind. It was all temporary-custody agreements and meetings with lawyers, accountants, and their mortgage broker; it was spending every waking moment fully dedicated to Kanika, ensuring she didn't suffer. It was ignoring her mother's nagging voice saying that their breakup was a giant mistake.

She glanced around the basement. It was unfinished, and the far half of the room was cluttered with boxes, recycling, and clothes that she and Neil had meant to start sorting through right before the separation. The other side, where she and Jenny were sitting now, was furnished with the IKEA furniture she and Neil had bought together right after the wedding, which had fit perfectly in their old apartment. Now it all lived in the room where they'd imagined Kanika would one day hang out with her friends, maybe her younger siblings. Where she'd drink her first can of beer, maybe have her first kiss. Even though that scenario was more than a decade away, Neil had refused to install a door at the top of the stairs.

"You think I'm going to let some little bugger be alone with my daughter?" he'd asked Anu.

Wiping her nose, Anu let her body fall closer into Jenny's. A sadness washed over her entire body.

"Hey, hey." Jenny frowned at her and then pinched her nose. "Don't be a grump, Anu. We can be single together."

"I guess we can."

"I can finally teach you how to use Tinder."

"Tinder? Isn't that just for sex?"

"It can be." Jenny eyed her. "Maybe for you, it *should* be." Jenny reached into Anu's front pocket, and when she started pulling at her phone, Anu swatted her hand away.

"Come on! It'll be fun. . . ."

"Fun for *you*," Anu muttered. "I haven't even been single for a day."

Jenny slid down from the couch onto the shag rug that covered the concrete floor. Beneath the coffee table was a loose stack of newspapers, magazines, flyers, and junk mail Anu had never bothered to throw away, and Jenny pulled out a magazine from the top pile.

"Is this what I think it is?"

Jenny smoothed down the edges of the page. It was their nursing school alumni annual magazine, and they mindlessly flipped through its glossy pages full of job adverts and information on new treatments and equipment, news about the latest graduating class.

"Check this out. Have you read it yet?" Jenny said, pointing to the community news section. "Quinn got married. Thanks for the invite, *Quinn*."

Anu stared blankly at the blond wedding Barbie on the page, swooning just next to her Ken. "God, I hated Quinn."

"Monica says you actually liked her until you saw her trying to flirt with Neil." Jenny hesitated. "Have you told her about Ryan, by the way?"

"Not yet. She'll feel so bad for me, and I don't want to ruin her honeymoon."

Jenny held her gaze a beat longer and then broke off contact.

"Have you spoken to her today?"

Jenny shrugged. "Just in passing . . . anyway. Weren't you in the magazine once?"

"I've been in it three times."

"Three, really?"

"Engagement, twenty eleven. Wedding, twenty twelve. Kanika's birth announcement, twenty fourteen. That's three times."

"I've never made it in. And think about it. I've had a more exciting life than *you*. No offense—"

"None taken."

"I've been to Everest base camp, trekked the Annapurna circuit and the West Coast Trail. I've been to every single continent."

"You learned how to scuba dive at the Great Barrier Reef."

"And I screwed my diving coach, too."

Anu snorted. "What was his name? Jimbo?"

"More like Dumbo." Jenny shook her head. "That guy had his oxygen cut off one too many times."

Anu stared harder at Quinn's picture, at the woman who was perhaps the most unlikable, irredeemable person she had ever known, on display as if getting married was some sort of achievement. Like she'd won some sort of award.

She couldn't quite remember, but Anu wondered how she had felt when she saw her own picture in there. Had she felt *proud*? What had it achieved, anyway?

Her and Neil's marriage had been about consummating a five-year "modern relationship" that Priya said was beginning to look inappropriate, and turning Anu into an honest woman. Their marriage had meant they were finally allowed at twenty-three to spend the night in the same bed, touch each other beneath the duvet without leaving their undergarments on.

It was impossible to imagine an alternate reality without Kanika; she didn't want to. But a tiny part of her couldn't help but wonder what life would have been like if she and Neil hadn't gotten married so young. What if Priya and Lakshmi had just let them be, and they'd dated and had sex—even tried living together first?

Would their relationship have run its same course? Or would they still be together?

"It doesn't make sense, does it?" Anu said, flipping to the next wedding announcement. "We celebrate people getting together, not themselves as real people. Their accomplishments, their flaws—"

"You're preaching to the choir here."

"Where was your announcement for Everest? Why is our *marriage*, our *children* the only fucking thing that's allowed to define us?"

"You don't have to convince me. I've been saying that stuff for years." Jenny not so gently swatted her on the arm. "About time you realized it."

Anu closed the magazine and then ran her palm along its smooth cover. By its account, Anu had excelled at life; her milestones were achievements worth celebrating.

A lump formed in her throat. She was, by all accounts, a grown-up.

She flipped the magazine over. The inside back page was hot pink and blank. She grabbed a pen and starting writing.

Role model to Kanika
Family-oriented
A loyal friend

"What are you doing?"
She ignored Jenny, continued pressing the pen to the page.

Controls urges
Lives life in moderation

"Oh, I forgot." Jenny giggled. "You're a grown-up."

Financially responsible
Chooses a suitable life partner

Anu laughed out loud at the last one, gently scribbled it out.
"I guess you can't say that one anymore, can you?" Jenny said.

Anu nodded, setting down the pen. She had pulled the wool over her own eyes when she had agreed to marry Neil at the tender age of twenty-two, when neither of them had done anything in life aside from what their mothers expected of them. She had done it to herself again when she threw herself into a "serious" relationship with the next guy who looked at her. How could she not see it?

Staring at the list, she wondered what else she was missing. What else she needed to see.

chapter ten

꧁

IMOGEN: ANU! How you feeling, girl? Your Tupac rapping skills have inspired me. We're going to this club I know on Saturday. Dress hot.

ANUSHA: Ugh, all right.

ANUSHA: Wait. What do you mean by hot?

IMOGEN: Backup-dancer-in-a-music-video hot.

She heard the rap music from across the parking lot where Monica, now home from her honeymoon, had dropped her off. Anusha had canceled her plans with Ms. Finch to go into the school and finish building the set for Kanika's holiday play, and instead had spent that afternoon with her two best friends.

Shivering, Anu zipped up Monica's leather jacket and flipped up the collar to cover her neck from the wind, and she regretted wearing Jenny's miniskirt. It was almost December and the first time she had left the house so ill-equipped for the weather.

"Hot damn, Anusha," she heard Imogen say as she appeared around the street corner. "I barely recognized you."

Imogen was wearing her thigh-high boots and fur coat again. Tonight, her hair was in a high ponytail, long red tendrils hanging straight down her back. Her lips were painted red.

"Thanks." Anu grinned. "You look great, too. Wait. Did you walk over? We could have given you a ride."

"It's no bother," Imogen said, taking her by the arm. "I don't live far from here."

A hundred feet away from the club, Imogen stopped short, shook her head. "I'm too sober to go in there."

"Were you out somewhere before?"

"No." Imogen smiled and let go of Anu's arm, then pulled a joint out of her bag. "Just me, my indie depression playlist, and a few bottles of wine . . ."

A few? How exactly was she sober, then?

She watched Imogen expertly light the joint, inhale until the end glowed amber, and then blow the smoke out of her nose.

Anu's stomach clenched as she watched her. She had hated the smell growing up, the way it seemed to stink up every parking garage, alley, and party. But still, for the first time, she wondered why she'd never tried it.

"Here, give me that."

Imogen smiled, took another inhale, and then passed the joint over. Anu tonged it with two fingers. Taking a deep breath, she summoned all the courage she could muster and stuck it in her mouth.

"Ow!"

Something sizzled and popped, and suddenly the joint was laying on the ground. Her lip was throbbing, pulsating like all hell. She could hear Imogen laughing, in near hysteria, as she picked up the joint from the ground.

"You stuck the wrong end in your mouth! You are *too* cute, Anusha."

Anu's cheeks heated up as she nursed her raw lip.

"Have you ever smoked before?"

Anu shook her head.

"Not even a cigarette?"

Again, Anu shook her head.

Imogen giggled, a new sort of giggle, and Anu couldn't tell if the weed had hit her already—or if Anu's inexperience was really that funny.

"Here, let me try again." Anu took the joint and carefully placed it on a part of her lip that wasn't sore. As Imogen relit the end of it, she sucked hard and fierce until she burst into a coughing fit.

"Not bad. Not bad." Imogen held on to the joint until Anu composed herself and then handed it back. "Now, try again. Breathe in like you do in my class. *Ujjayi* breathing. Come on now."

This time, Anu didn't cough so much, and they passed the joint back and forth until there was nothing left. Imogen let the butt fall to the ground and then slowly stamped it out with the heel of her boot.

"Did you go to Charlie's class this morning? *Vinyasa* two?"

Anu nodded. "I like yours better, but she's pretty good, actually. I've been to two of her classes now."

Imogen kicked at a loose rock. "And you're doing OK?" She paused. "About Ryan, I mean."

"We weren't dating that long."

"That's not what I asked."

The rap music throbbed in the background, and Anu glanced toward the club. "I'm doing OK, yeah. Thanks for asking."

There were a few people smoking outside, a big guy with a clipboard hovering by the entrance. Anu wasn't standing that far away, but oddly, it felt like those other people were in a different universe.

"You should buy it," she heard Imogen say. "It would be good for you."

"I told you, I don't know the first thing about running a yoga studio."

"Yeah, but *I* do. I've worked there for a year and a half. I just don't have any money, so I can't buy it. Do *you* have any money?"

"Some." Anu nodded. "And I'd be lying if I said I haven't thought about it, but . . ."

"But what? What's holding you back?"

There was nothing holding her back, except that dreadful, aching throb of responsibility.

Yoga is a hobby, Anu, not a profession.

Don't you want a job that will give you health benefits?

What kind of wife and mother teaches yoga?

Teaching yoga—one day running her own studio—was the only dream she had ever had, and her parents had crushed it right out of her. Could she run a yoga studio if she wanted to?

She could change the name, repaint the walls, give the studio more ambience. She imagined the front room flooded with twinkle lights, ferns, and basketry—from ideas she'd found and filed away on a secret Pinterest board. She had saved them for a time when she and Neil could afford to renovate the basement, but they were even more suited to a yoga studio.

"There's a lot holding me back," Anu said finally, because objectively, the idea was preposterous. She had a daughter and a mortgage, and a husband from whom in the new year she'd need a divorce.

Without realizing it, she found herself telling Imogen all of this, every thought flowing in and out her head. How her life was chock-full to the brim, but with *what*? Working twenty-six hours a week like a robot, her mind always elsewhere? Tiptoeing around Neil, and now Ryan, too? With carting her daughter back and forth from extracurricular activities? Building the set for her school play?

"This is what I spend my days thinking about, you know?" Anu's eyes were focused somewhere off in the distance, past the parking lot, on a nondescript warehouse. "Don't get me wrong, I love my daughter . . ."

"But she isn't enough."

"No, I didn't say that."

"You don't have to say it."

Anu pressed her lips together and let the haze she was feeling absorb her.

A new question appeared in a distant quadrant of her brain, seeping its way to the front. She wanted to be free to do *what*, exactly? Live life on her own terms? Be the sort of woman she admired or was even envious of?

To be a stupid kid and not a grown-up at all and ready to embrace whatever the world threw at her.

"All right," Imogen said after a while, and when Anu turned to look at her, she realized she couldn't see straight. That Imogen's face had morphed all out of proportion. "I'm feeling good. Let's go inside."

chapter eleven

✤

ANUSHA: I smidked a jomnt

JENNY: Is that . . . Punjabi?

MONICA: No . . . No, it's not. You OK, Anu?

Everyone inside seemed to be a mix of ages. Some Anu swore looked young enough to be in high school, while there were others who seemed far too old to be there.

Everything was a blur by the time they stumbled to a corner of the dance floor where Haruto and his friends were dancing, some of whom she recognized from the week before.

Had it only been a *week* since she was out last, catching Ryan with his bloody associate? It might have been the weed, but it felt like an eternity had passed.

Haruto and Imogen disappeared, but Anu was feeling too good to care. Someone, one of the women, passed her a bottle of beer, and she let her eyes close as she swayed to the beat. She liked the bass, the way it sent shock waves up her arms and down her legs, reverberating through the base of her spine.

"Having fun?"

She opened her eyes and spotted a familiar face standing just in front of her. He was bobbing up and down, perhaps in an attempt to dance.

"I'm Jake, remember?" he shouted over the music, stepping in a bit closer to her. Big green eyes, a round face. Like a Ken doll. "I met you last week. At my brother's birthday."

"Oh, yeah." Anu nodded in recognition and closed her eyes again. They felt so heavy. It felt so good. "Nice to see you."

"You can't see me. Your eyes are closed."

Anu burst out laughing. She had never found anything funnier in her entire life. When she stopped, she found Jake's hands heavy on her hips, and she didn't move them. Instead, she turned around and set her hands on his.

"I like this song," he said into her ear. She felt him breathing hard, nudging closer with each step as they danced until his body pressed against hers. The lights were harsh on her eyes, but she kept them open.

When the song changed again, she glanced back toward the group to find they'd all disappeared. How long had they been dancing? How many times had the songs changed? She turned around. Jake was smiling at her lazily. She wondered if he was high, too.

"Where did everyone go?"

He shrugged. "To get a drink, I think."

"You didn't want one?"

He hesitated and then shook his head. "I wanted to stay here with you."

Again, this made her laugh. He moved his hands up from her hips to her forearms.

"Do you wanna go somewhere quieter?" he screamed into her ear, and she winced from the pain. Still, she nodded and let him lead her away from the dance floor by the hand. "That's better," Jake said, sitting down on a ledge. They were near the toilets, but suddenly her feet were tired, and so she sat down. Jake put his arm around her, and it felt nice. Weird but nice. His face was so close to hers that she tried not to look at him. She knew if she did, he'd kiss her.

He was stroking the outside of her thigh, massaging it. Was that normal? Was that how guys tried to hook up with girls? The thought of it made her giggle.

"What's so funny?"

She pressed her hand over her mouth to suppress the laughter, and the edge of her lips began to throb. "Ouch!"

"What happened?"

She stuck out her lower lip and crossed her eyes, just revealing a dark red lump on the end of it.

"You don't have mouth herpes, do you?" His hand was on her chin now, tilting her face upward. "Not that I would care."

"You're cute," she said unexpectedly without thinking, because he wasn't even her type. She kept her eyes down and gazed at the stamp of an X on the back of his hand.

He turned it over. His palm looked sweaty, glistening in the strobe lights. "You're cute, too."

She was mere inches away from kissing him and was surprised by the fact that she wanted to. She wanted him to lean in. Oddly, she wanted those small hands all over her.

His eyes closed, and then hers. Neil's face appeared. His naughty grin. His leather jacket. She didn't want him there. She pushed him away.

Jake kissed her, and her lip throbbed from the burn, but in a good way, and she let her mind and limbs spin away from her as they made out on that ledge in the club by the toilets.

It didn't feel good necessarily, but *different*. Surreal. Like it wasn't really her. After a while his lips moved from her lips to her ears and her neck, and she opened her eyes.

Jake was probing, but without confidence. Anu glanced down, and she became conscious that his hands, with large black X's crossed over the length of them, were sliding higher and higher up her thighs.

The haze was clearing. His mouth moved all over the place, making her whole neck extremely wet. Disgustingly wet.

"You have a different stamp than I do," she heard herself say. Hers was small, illegible red ink, and his was . . .

Another song change, a song she must have heard earlier that evening, and all too suddenly she was conscious of the terrible music, her slippery neck, the smell wafting over from the toilets. She pulled away. His lips were glistening, like he'd just taken a sip from a water fountain.

"Jake." Her voice caught. "How old are you?"

He stared down at her meekly. She dropped his hands.

"You said Tim's your brother, right? And he turned twenty-seven last week?"

Jake nodded and shifted his knees away. "Tim's my older brother." Older brother.

"So you're . . . what? Twenty-six? Twenty-four?" She shook his arm until he looked at her. "Twenty-*one*?"

He dropped his gaze.

"Jake, tell me right now. How old are you?"

He sighed, audibly. "I'm . . . eighteen. Fine, I'm eighteen."

He was eighteen?

Eighteen?

Her head throbbed as she dropped it into her hands. "Oh . . . my . . . God . . ."

"Anusha—"

"You were in a bar last week. You're in a bar *now*."

"I snuck in last week. Tim helped me," he said, his voice improbably high and rushed. "And here . . . well, here they let you in underage but . . ." From the corner of her eye, she saw him tap one of the X's on his hand. "It's so the bartenders don't serve you."

Her mouth gaping, Anu stood up, suddenly sober. Incredibly sober. Jake was eighteen? She had made out with a *teenager*?

She felt him stand up beside her, and he tentatively rested his hand on her shoulder.

"I'm sorry. . . ."

"It's not your fault," Anu said, pressing her hands over her mouth. It wasn't his fault. He was a boy who had seized an opportunity.

She was the opportunity.

"So this means you were born in . . . what year, exactly?"

"Two thousand one."

Anu felt like she was going to be sick. In 2001, she had been twelve years old. She and Monica were learning how to apply mascara, stalking the boys they had crushes on on instant messenger, and had just gotten their periods.

She was overcome with nausea when it came to her: Technically, she was old enough to be Jake's mother.

She couldn't find Imogen, so she texted her to tell her she was leaving. What had she been thinking, going out? *Why* had she smoked a joint and then bloody *kissed* Jake?

There were no cabs in sight, so she called one—but the operator said it would be at least fifteen minutes.

"Do you mind if I wait with you?" Jake asked tentatively. He hadn't brought his coat outside with him, and he was shivering in just a T-shirt.

"Sure."

They waited in silence, an awkward silence, for several long minutes. Anu couldn't bring herself to look at him, see him in the sobering light of the streetlamp.

"It's really not a big deal," he said after a while. "I'm an adult. If you're old enough to vote, you should be old enough to drink."

She couldn't remember if she'd told him how old *she* was or that she had a daughter. Surely, she had. Maybe he didn't care.

"I'm going traveling for a while," he said, after another minute passed. "I leave in the spring. Europe first. I've never been. Maybe Southeast Asia after that. I'll be gone for six months."

She forced out a smile and glanced down at the pavement. Her boots were covered in muck, the black now appearing almost brown.

"I've seen all these pictures on Instagram from everyone's travels, thought maybe it's about time I see it for myself."

"That's nice." Her voice was curt, and she felt bad. He was trying to be nice, trying to make conversation; it wasn't his fault Anu had acted like a fool tonight.

She cleared her throat and then looked over at him. "Europe. Awesome. You'll have fun."

He smiled widely, baring his teeth, and Anu felt rather tender toward him, oddly almost motherly.

"Have you been?"

She shook her head.

"I bet you'd have fun, too."

She shrugged and wiped her nose, which had started to run, with the back of her hand. They'd been looking up flights to Paris when Anu threw up on Neil's laptop, and she figured out she was pregnant. They were always planning to go after they'd had another child, when the kids were old enough to leave with the grandparents while they had a romantic holiday. Of course, that wasn't going to happen now.

But it wasn't like she hadn't traveled. As a kid she'd flown with her parents to India every second summer like clockwork—a few weeks in Chandigarh with Lakshmi's side of the family and then another few in Ludhiana with all of her dad's relatives.

Over the years, she'd traveled around Canada a bit—especially the beautiful western coastline. Hiking. Camping. Skiing. Anu went to Las Vegas the year she and Monica had both turned twenty-one, although they'd blown all their money shopping and couldn't afford to go out in the evenings. And Neil had taken her to Mexico for their honeymoon. Since then, they had been back to the same resort twice, both times with their parents and Kanika.

Despite being invited along, each time she'd turned Jenny down on her exotic monthlong trips abroad. Now she wasn't sure why. Because it would have worried her parents? Because Neil would be home with Priya, working and missing out?

It was Anu who had missed out.

She couldn't look Jake in the eye when he awkwardly hugged her goodbye. Resting her head against the glass, she kept her eyes inside the car. On her skirt, sticky from beer and sweat. Her grimy boots. The pink swell of gum stuck on the passenger seat.

Should she feel ashamed? Wasn't this—what happened tonight— the definition of being some reckless adolescent?

But she didn't feel ashamed, not even a bit. She had smoked a joint and then made out with a stranger. Jake's age aside, she was oddly rather proud of herself. She felt better than she had in months, even years.

Had Jenny been right all along? Did she need to be single, to "live a little"?

She was struck with a surprising pang of jealousy as she imagined Jake, on his own, traveling the world. Why hadn't Anu left

Vancouver when she still could? Why hadn't she ever gone to Europe, gone on a yoga retreat like she'd always dreamed? The joint had fully worn off now. She rested her palm against the car window, the glass pane moist and warm.

If she could turn back time, would Anu have gone? Would she have had a different sort of life?

But the more burning question, the one that overloaded her with guilt just thinking how tempting it sounded, was: If she could have a do-over, if right now she could just leave everything and everyone behind, would she?

chapter twelve

MONICA: I'm sorry I didn't tell you sooner. I just . . . Well, with things ending with Ryan and all. But now that you've moved on with a TEENAGER (LOL!!!), we figured you could handle it.

ANUSHA: A) Thanks for telling me. How long have you known? B) OMG. Shut. Up.

JENNY: She's known since the honeymoon. Neil texted Tom a few dirty messages that were apparently meant for her.

MONICA: Jen wtf I told you we didn't need to tell her that part!

ANUSHA: Dirty . . . messages?

Anu threw her phone on the coffee table. It hit the edge and bounced down to the floor, and when she bent to pick it up, she noticed a new crack in the top-right corner of the screen.

"Shit."

She slumped back into the couch, tracing the crack with her fingers. She'd taken two Tylenol and drunk three glasses of water since she woke up, yet she still had a hangover.

The fact that Neil had a new girlfriend suddenly made her headache a lot worse.

Flipping over her screen, Anu tried to remain calm. Neil had made her feel so terribly for bringing Ryan to the wedding, yet he had been seeing some other woman the whole time? Sending her *dirty* messages?

The Neil Anu knew didn't do stuff like that. He hadn't ever once done or asked Anu to do anything even remotely adventurous.

Kanika was away, and so she let herself sulk for the next four hours with a bad made-for-TV movie while surfing the Internet, pinning images of mandala lights and indoor-water-features meditation corners on her new yoga studio Pinterest board as the ideas appeared. Ignoring text messages from her dad and even Monica, she started to let herself become sucked in by the idea that her dream of running a yoga studio could still be real and she could allow herself to want more.

Her landline started to ring, and the volume of it startled her upright. No one ever called her home phone anymore. She reached for it. It was an unknown number. It was likely a telemarketer, but for some reason, she answered anyway. "Hello?" she said, a trace of irritation in her voice. "Can you tell me who this is?"

"Can you tell me why you never answer your telephone?"

She swallowed hard. *Lakshmi.*

"Hi . . . Mom."

"I am here, too," Kunal said.

"Hi, Dad."

"I knew she would answer," Lakshmi said.

"Your mother had a thesis," Kunal interjected. "You would answer if we blocked our telephone number. Evidently, this thesis is valid, Anu."

He was using a tone with her, one she didn't hear often—the one that meant this was serious. She swallowed hard and pulled her legs onto the couch. She contemplated simply hanging up.

"You've stopped answering our phone calls and now even our

texting messages?" Lakshmi sighed, and Anu could sense her mother was shaking her head at the phone. "I have not heard your voice in— How many weeks, Kunal?"

"Three, nearly four—"

"Four weeks!" Another sigh, one carefully crafted to evoke the feeling of guilt in its recipient. "I am lucky Neil still answers our calls. Otherwise I would not hear our Kanika's voice, either."

Anu prickled at the mention of Neil's name.

"We phoned over there this morning. Did you drop her early this week?"

"*No,*" Anu said, taking pains to relax her voice. "No, Mom. It's Sunday. She went over yesterday evening, same as always."

"Today is *Sunday?*"

Kunal laughed. "Your mother is a student now. Every day is both a workday and a holiday."

"Then this is my first holiday since Anu was born. And your father is my butler."

"Can you believe it, Anu? Thirty-four years as a mathematics professor, but my most difficult job has been making sure your mother eats a proper breakfast."

"Choco Pops *is* proper—"

"Lucky it is sugar. The calories are empty."

"How can a calorie be 'empty'? I am not idiot. A calorie has to be *full.* Otherwise it would not be a calorie—"

"Oatmeal is more nutritious."

"Nutritious but boring. Tell me, my dear husband, am *I* boring . . . ?"

They went on like this for a few more minutes, momentarily forgetting Anu was listening in. She'd always known that their marriage was one to look up to. But right now she couldn't help but resent it. She couldn't help but wonder even if her parents—her traditional elderly parents—had ever sent each other *dirty* messages.

"Anu," Kunal said after they had settled the dispute, Lakshmi having agreed to limit her sugary cereals to weekends. "Tell me, *beti*, where have you been? We never hear from you."

"Sorry, Dad. . . ." Anu paused, thinking of an excuse and failing to come up with one. "I guess I've been busy."

"How can she be so busy?" Lakshmi mumbled, as if Anu weren't even there. "Neil and Priya are looking after her daughter half time."

Anu's jaw dropped. *Her* daughter? Only Anu's daughter?

There was a lump growing in her throat, and she didn't know what to do with it. Why was she so surprised Lakshmi would say something like that, *think* something like that?

They'd been gone only four months, yet she'd forgotten what it was like. This feeling, as if she'd been pinned down on the floor with a boot flattened to her chest. She'd forgotten why she was almost relieved when they left.

Would she have dated Ryan if they were still living nearby, hovering around, supervising her life, judging her every move? She wouldn't have. She wouldn't have found Imogen and the yoga studio or tried weed or kissed a stranger in a club.

Still, she wouldn't have done anything.

"Anu?" her dad said softly. "Are you there?"

Her breath hitching, she wondered what they'd say if she told them she regretted having always obeyed them. Coming home early to study, to sit nicely on the couch with her legs crossed and her back straight, like a *good* Indian girl.

Dating and marrying the appropriate man. Buying the right house. Choosing the *right* profession.

What if she told them that she should have gone to Europe and pursued yoga when she'd had the chance? That she should have gone after her dreams.

"Yes. I'm here."

"You are acting very strange."

"Am I?"

"What is going on with you, *beti*? What is this new attitude?"

She didn't know what to say to them anymore or how to be the good girl who never disobeyed, biting her lip whenever she was tempted to say something they wouldn't want to hear.

"*Beti*," Kunal continued, "we love you very much."

They loved her, but didn't they know how much it hurt? Obsessing, obtruding, berating—that was the way so many Indian parents loved.

Was that the way she would love Kanika, too? Trampling on her until her daughter didn't want to share her life, didn't even want her around. She took a deep breath, wondering where to go from here.

Until she moved to England, Lakshmi hadn't had her own life, and so she forced her way into Anu's. Knowing that history tended to repeat itself, Anu imagined herself in ten years, even twenty— single, biding her time between yoga classes, days at the clinics, and drinks with Jenny and Monica . . . while she waited for Kanika to come home. Kanika to smile. Kanika to tell Anu about *her* day.

"Anu?" Her dad's voice.

The silence stretched between them. The distance was palpable.

It wouldn't be easy, but she wanted to buy Mags' Studio. She *wanted* to go traveling through Europe. Having a responsibility to raise her daughter didn't mean she couldn't pursue what she wanted and not let her sense of responsibility rule her life.

"I'm sorry, but I have to go."

"No," Kunal said sternly. "You must say something. We must discuss."

"I love you guys," she said, smiling, happier than she'd been in weeks. "And I know it's not what you want me to say, but I really do have to go."

After the call, she breathed in and out slowly three times, just like Lakshmi had taught her. Kunal and Lakshmi were five thousand miles away and they weren't ready to hear it all—not yet. But Anu knew what she wanted, didn't she? And finally, she was ready to go for it.

chapter thirteen

✿

ANUSHA: Hi, David. Margaret Barton (Mags) gave me your phone number. I'm planning to make a formal offer to take over the lease on her studio, and she said you might be able to handle the legal side of this for us? I'd love to give you a quick call when you have a minute. Thanks!—Anusha Desai

s this your version of a rebound?" Jenny asked, less than a week later. "Because I would much prefer you went to Vegas, rather than spontaneously bought a *yoga studio*."

"It's not spontaneous. I've wanted this for a long time."

"Why don't you come with me to Chile next week?" Jenny asked. She'd been looking forward to her pre-Christmas trip to Santiago for months. "You get along with my sister. Come with us."

"I don't want to go to Chile, Jen," Anu said as they squished into one compartment of a revolving door. "If I'm going to go anywhere, it would be Europe. I've never even been to London."

"Oh, look who's here," Jenny said as they circled into their building.

Straight ahead, Ryan was standing in line at the Starbucks in the lobby.

Of course he would be there, and of course he'd be with a woman. Ryan wasn't faithful, but he sure was predictable. He couldn't do a thing without his post-lunch coffee. Anu should have taken the back entrance.

"Coffee, Anu?"

"I'm good," she whispered, making a move for the elevator.

Jenny put her arm out to stop her. "Tell me you're not still avoiding him."

"I'm not."

"Didn't you say at lunch you wanted a chai latte on the way back?"

"I changed my mind—"

"Anu," Jenny chided, "I thought you said you were over him."

"I am. I want to be." Anu shrugged. "It's just easier not to think about him or see him and pretend the whole thing never happened."

"Did you love him?"

She shook her head. At the word "love," she thought of Neil and then, irritatingly, Ms. Dirty Messages.

"Anu, it did happen. You were humiliated, and it's OK. He took a meat pulverizer to your confidence and pasted its chunky bits all over the wall and—"

"Thanks, Jen. That's very vivid."

"You're not the only woman who's ever been cheated on. You're not the only one who's ever felt like a fool."

Anu turned back to the window. Over the years, more than one guy had screwed around on Jenny. Monica, too. It was part of the game, the tricky back-and-forth of dating men in the city as ambitious as themselves. The game Anu never had to play.

But didn't she need to? Didn't she need to be *stupid* for once? Experience everything she had missed out on, even if it hurt?

"So what are you going to do?" she heard Jenny ask.

Anu exhaled sharply as she watched Ryan. Her cheeks reddened when she realized that it wasn't even a woman he worked with. He was chatting up a stranger, a woman he'd met right there in line.

She was at a crossroads, an opportunity before her to be bold and brave, be in charge of the course of her life. Her anger rose up, flashing hot and fierce. She had really cared about him. Like a total idiot, she had believed him when he said that he'd never settled down because he was married to his job, that he'd never found a woman like Anu.

What other lies had he spewed? What other bullshit had she gulped down as he wined and dined her over several months, convinced her that what they had was something real, something *special*.

She could admit she was naive—but she had never deserved this. And that rat bastard had never deserved her.

She marched through the lobby and could almost hear some empowering, upbeat song about feminine power in her ears as she stormed toward him, Jenny on her heels. She hadn't done anything. She hadn't even broken up with him, just walked away like a coward, like she was nothing without him.

But she was someone. She could be *someone*.

He turned around, coffee in hand. He cocked his head to the side as she caught his eye.

A deep breath and then another one. How dared he? How fucking *dared* he? She stopped short and held his gaze.

Had she truly cared for him, or had she only cared that he wasn't Neil?

"Anu . . ." He stepped toward her.

"Ryan."

He was inches away, and as his lips curled upward into a smile—those perfect lying lips—she punched him square in the mouth.

"Damn, girl!" She could hear Jenny hollering behind her. "You got him *good*."

"Anu, what the fuck?"

Her whole right hand was on fire, and there was coffee everywhere, even on her.

"Are you out of your mind?" the woman next to him yelled.

Anu glanced at her and momentarily felt bad—not for Ryan or her in particular, but for whatever pathetic soul he would screw over next.

"Oh, you poor thing," the woman said to Ryan, and that was when Anu noticed the trickle of blood on his nose, the cuff of his shirt.

"Here." Anu grabbed a tissue from her purse and shoved it at him. As he wiped away the blood, for the first time she noticed people hovering nearby—including the building's security guard, Ralph, who had worked in the building longer than she had.

"Well," she said to Ryan, "I'm going to go now."

"I'm sorry," he said into his hands. "You know that I'm sorry."

"For cheating on me? *Lying* to me?"

He nodded. He was still not looking at her.

From behind, Jenny yelled, "For assuming Anu would never figure out you're *completely* full of shit?"

"Screw you, Jenny," Ryan mumbled.

"Screw *you*, Ryan." And with that, it was Jenny's turn, and she punched him so hard, Anu thought she heard something crack. He stumbled backward and then dropped to his knees.

"Jenny!"

"That's for fucking around on my best friend!" she yelled, Anu tugging her arm back as the crowd drew closer, and Ralph glared at them.

"Jenny, we gotta go *now*." They walked briskly through the lobby, avoiding eye contact with everyone. "Are you trying to get us arrested?"

"It was my turn!"

"Nice right hook, though. Boxercise?"

"Jackie Chan movies."

"Clearly, I need to watch more Jackie Chan."

They pushed through the revolving door. It had started to rain, and Jenny stayed beneath the overhang, but Anu stepped out into the street. Her hand was on fire, but the cold rain against her skin helped. She shut her eyes and, laughing, looked up into the sky.

Anu knew the financial risks. She knew that having a daughter would make running a business all the harder, but that she was going to do it anyway.

"Hey, Anu?" Jenny said after a while.

"Yeah?" Anu opened her eyes, smiled when she noticed that her best friend was standing next to her, also sopping wet in the rain.

"Are you done 'catharting' yet?"

"Why?"

Jenny nodded her head toward the building. "Because the security guard is looking at us."

Anu turned around. Ralph was indeed staring. "Let's take the service elevator?"

"Yep," Jenny said as they hurried toward the back entrance of the building. "I'm way too hot to go to jail."

chapter fourteen

✿

NEIL: Mom and I both have plans tonight. Any chance you want to take her a day early? No problem if you're busy we'll find a babysitter.

ANUSHA: Sure that's fine. I can pick her up around 5.

NEIL: Perfect, thanks a lot.

Anu pulled into the driveway and killed the engine. She knew what Priya had planned. For years, every Friday night, Priya and her best friend, Jayani, would go to watch a Hindi movie at the Indian theater in Richmond—something with Saif Ali Khan or Shah Rukh Khan or Priya's favorite, Deepika Padukone.

But Neil?

He wouldn't go out of his way to hire a babysitter unless he had important plans, like a date with Ms. Dirty Messages.

Anu stared through the sitting room window. The blinds were closed, and she wondered if his new girlfriend was in there. She knew that it wasn't likely, that there wasn't a chance he had told Priya he was dating anyone, but Anu couldn't help but wonder in what ways Ms. Dirty Messages was sneaking into his life.

What did he have planned for her, on their Friday night out on the town? Dinner and a movie? A weekend away somewhere—

shacked up in some hotel room in Whistler or near the beach on Pender Island?

She grabbed her purse, her hand still throbbing from the punch that afternoon, and flung open the car door. She was happy to see Kanika a day early but wished she wasn't making it easier for him to move on. All she wanted to do was go home and ice her hand on a carton of Ben & Jerry's in front of the TV.

Gathering her strength, Anu climbed the porch steps and knocked on the front door. Her stomach tightened when Neil appeared on the other side of the door. She'd barely seen him since Monica's wedding—halfhearted waves from across the driveway or through the car window. In her head, she'd imagined he'd fallen apart even more without her—red-eyed and disheveled—but in real life, he looked exactly the same.

If possible, he looked even better than she remembered.

"Hey," he said, "come in."

She nodded and followed him to the kitchen. They sat down at the table, the one she used to eat at several times per week when they were dating, and he gestured toward his cup of coffee.

"Want one?"

She shook her head, surprised by how civil he was acting. The last time they had spoken, he could barely stand to be in the same room with her.

"Kanika's downstairs with Mom. They'll be up in a minute."

"Do you want me to wait in the car?"

"No, it's fine."

He had been so angry with her for dating Ryan, but now he was with someone else and so it was "fine." Except that she was now single, and even though she didn't want to get back together, she wished Neil was, too.

They sat in silence for a while, and Anu glanced around the

room. It was spotless, as if Priya had all the time in the world to cook and clean and dote on her son and granddaughter. Even before she stopped working, when Priya worked full-time at Auntie Jayani's Indian Bridal Shop on Main Street, the house was spotless. Anu had never quite figured out how she managed to do it all as a single mom. Her husband had passed away when Neil was only a baby—some sort of cancer, Neil told her once. He'd been vague on the details.

"So how've you been?" Neil asked.

She looked back at him. His eyes were trained on the floor, his shoulders tense and hunched against the back of the chair.

She wasn't sure how to answer the question. "Fine, thanks. You?"

"Fine."

This . . . *silence*. The awkwardness. It felt worse than when he had been desperate to get back together, even when he had hated her.

"Hey." His voice was tentative as he sat forward in the chair. "Can I ask you something?"

Her heart lurched.

"Are you fighting with your parents or something?"

"Oh." She shrugged. "I guess you've been speaking to them."

He nodded. "They call a lot when Kanu is here. Other times, just to chat with Mom."

Annoyed, she reached for his coffee cup and downed the coffee. It was lukewarm, milky, just how he liked it, and if he was startled by this intimate action of sharing a cup, it didn't show on his face. "So you really need me to take her tonight, then?"

He looked at her strangely. "Your parents are worried about you. . . ."

She wondered if he was worried about her, too.

"They said you don't take their calls anymore."

She didn't answer, furiously biting at her bottom lip. "I've been really busy. That's it."

"I figured. That's what I told them this morning when they called a few hours ago. I mean, you and Ryan—"

"You told my parents about Ryan?"

He pressed his lips together, and her heart dropped into her stomach.

"I thought they knew, Anush."

She wasn't even dating Ryan anymore, and Neil had fucking told them?

"I swear, Anush. I thought they knew."

"Like hell you did!"

"I did, all right? You're a grown-up. I didn't think you had to lie about these things."

Of course she had to lie, and she couldn't even fathom what her parents must now think, knowing she had been dating—*sleeping*—with somebody else while still technically married to Neil. What horrible, sexist insults would Lakshmi want to say to Anu about her running off with a new guy instead of fixing her marriage? And her father—sensible and stoic. Now he wouldn't be able to look his daughter in the eye.

She glanced at Neil and couldn't tell whether he looked smug or sad. Her face beamed hot, and so she took a deep breath to calm herself down. Three counts in. Three counts out. Afterward she was still angry, but not quite as much as before. She leaned against the wall, letting her fingers fall to graze its grainy surface.

"I'm sorry," he said. "I really am."

She nodded stiffly. Her parents knew about Ryan.

This was a fact she could not change, and now, like the fucking grown-up she was supposed to be, she needed to deal with it.

"Do not apologize to her," Priya said, startling them both as she walked into the kitchen. How long had she been standing around the corner?

"Somebody needed to tell them, and I did not have the heart," she said, switching to Punjabi. "Poor Lakshmi. I hope this news isn't too hard on her. . . ."

In moments like these, it was hard to believe that Priya used to love her, used to wrap her arms around Anu's waist, and, in Punjabi, tell her that she'd become the daughter she never had.

And Anu had thought of her like a mother, in a way, maybe always would. The morning after the wedding was the first time she had called Priya "Mom"—and Neil did the same with her parents. She didn't recognize the Priya standing before her, berating her, chastising her, but she supposed Priya didn't recognize Anu, either.

Priya continued lashing out at Anu—about her lifestyle, her decision to "break up a happy family." Anu looked at Neil, pleading, but whatever he was feeling didn't show on his face. Even now it was overwhelming, each time it hit her that Neil was never on her side. Neil would always choose his mother, pick his relationship with her over their marriage.

She loved Priya. She had been more than happy to have her nestled right next to them in their happy little life. It was not like she wanted him to choose. But he did anyway.

"Auntie, perhaps your next daughter-in-law won't be so disappointing to you," Anu said softly, almost regretting it the moment the words left her lips.

Priya stopped short, resting her hands on her wide hips. "*Beta*, what is she talking about?"

Silence, and then a beat later, Neil said, "I don't know, Ma."

Anu stared at the ground, at a single speck of dust on the floor as the guilt set in. She shouldn't have said anything. It was so petty and unlike her, so why had she said it?

"Neil," Priya barked, back to English now, "what is the meaning?"

"Mom, can we talk about this later?"

"Are you seeing a woman? I *knew* it. And you didn't tell me? Is this is where you are so late in the evenings?"

"Tit for tat, hey, Anush?"

Anu felt ashamed, red in the face, and she was about to apologize when Neil snapped at her. "Jesus, you're immature."

She froze, setting her hands on the counter, the right one still throbbing. "Immature?" Anu stood up straight as he stared down at her, waiting for her to hit back—and she could.

She could be mean. Neil was the one who used to leave the front door wide open in the middle of winter, who would forget to pick up his daughter from day care unless Anu stapled a reminder to his goddamn hand. *Neil* was the reason she kept putting off having another baby; a husband like him was like having a second child!

She could lash out. Right now she could reignite how much he had hurt her and blame him for everything, cut away at the thin thread left hanging between them.

She opened her mouth, but the fight was gone.

Right now she didn't feel angry or sad or betrayed. It was all gone. There was nothing left. This life—she didn't want it anymore.

Neil could have it.

"You're right," Anu said quietly after a moment passed. "I'm immature and irresponsible, and I think I'm going to go."

He was still staring at her, more gently now, hands on his hips. If she passed him by on the sidewalk like a stranger, she'd still think he was handsome. She would always find him handsome.

"Sure." He nodded, eyes searching her face. "I'll go get her bag."

"No, don't bother."

"Why?"

"Because *I* am going. Alone."

Another pause. "So you'll back for her tomorrow?"

She was about to say yes, but then she didn't. She shook her head.

It hung in the air, a dull silence you could have hacked through with a knife.

"I need to go away for a while," she said, coming up with a plan as the words came out of her mouth. "I'm going to go travel around Europe for a few weeks. And . . . finally take that yoga course."

"Are you serious? You're going *now*?"

"Well, not right now." She checked her watch. "Tomorrow, maybe. Isn't there a direct flight every evening? I'll take it tomorrow."

Neil looked at her as if he couldn't quite believe what she was saying, and she was not sure she believed it, either. But the words were out, and they made sense, didn't they? This was what she was too afraid to admit to herself.

She didn't have to be a grown-up and tow around the heavy, hurtful baggage that came with it.

She thought she could start over by leaving Neil, finding a new guy—but maybe it was more than that. Maybe the truth was, she needed to start over with herself. A clean slate. Go back to the beginning, to the life she could have had to begin with.

Neil turned to look at Priya. It was more shock on his face, on *her* face, than anything else. Anu could no longer make sense of whether she hoped they would try to stop her.

"You're *leaving* her?" he whispered.

"Don't say that. I'm coming right back. I just need some time—"

"For what. For Ryan?"

Of course he'd assume the only thing of importance that demanded time and energy was either her daughter or the man in her life. Because wasn't that the woman she had always been? The domestic goddess. The attentive woman. The daughter-in-law to be desired.

But that wasn't her. This wasn't all she could be. She wanted more. She could *be* more.

She didn't answer Neil's question. Let him think what he wanted, that Anu was still dating that cheating bastard Ryan and leaving her daughter behind for him. She didn't care what Neil thought anymore.

Anu reached for her purse hanging on the back of Priya's chair, tugging at it, but it got caught behind her shoulder. "Auntie?"

Priya looked up, her eyes moist, and for a split second, Anu wondered if she was making a mistake. But wouldn't it be easier on Priya if Anu wasn't part of her family at all? "Auntie, I need my purse."

Kanika was downstairs, finishing the same Disney movie they'd watched a thousand times before. It was near the end, the scene where Moana and Maui are battling Te Kā. The scene used to scare Kanika. It wasn't so long ago that she would bury her face in Anu's chest, whimpering as Anu stroked her hair until it was safe to come out.

Anu sat down on the couch, curled the end of Kanika's left pigtail. "Mommy has to go," she whispered.

Kanika was distracted. Her eyes were glued to the screen as the green monster arced and threw waves at Moana.

"Did you hear me, sweetie?" She choked on her words as Kanika nodded, pressed her clammy hands around Anu's neck.

She needed to go, and one day her daughter would understand, *wouldn't she?*

"I love you," she whispered, wrapping Kanika tight in her arms.

She soaked in the familiar scent of her daughter's hair. "You're going to stay with Daddy a bit longer this time, OK, baby?"

Kanika nodded, but she was focused on the TV. She didn't understand, and maybe she never would.

Maybe Anu wouldn't, either, but still she got up and walked to the stairs. With one more look back at her baby girl, she left.

chapter fifteen

✿

SARA: Hey . . . just checking in. The holiday concert
is coming up quickly and I was thinking the kids should
probably rehearse in front of the set at least once.

ANUSHA: Hi, Sara. I'm really sorry to do this to you but I'm
actually going to be out of town. I hope one of the other
parents can step in and finish off the set? It's nearly
done—the materials for the snowflakes are in the bottom
cupboard.

SARA: Oh! OK, no worries. We'll figure something out. Have
a great trip! And Merry Christmas!

SARA: Sorry! I mean happy holidays. ☺

W e've got loads of time." Anu glanced at Monica from the
passenger's seat. "Don't look so anxious."

"I know."

Her flight to London—the one she had booked only the night
before—didn't leave for another two hours. And after the overnight flight, what would be ten hours of restless sleep and bad
movies, she'd wake up in a new country. She'd wake up with the
world before her.

The highway was slippery, and Monica drove cautiously, more
than ten kilometers below the speed limit. The mountains faded
behind the fog as the industrial part of the city took form. Con-

crete structures and passages of brown, half-frozen water. Dead, brown grass lined the roads, and even though it rarely snowed in Vancouver, she wondered if it would. If that year, Kanika would have a white Christmas . . .

She blinked hard and then forced herself not to run after that train of thought. Monica's dashboard had a scratch on it, deep and white, and Anu focused on it. She wondered if it was she who had nicked it.

"Thanks for driving me."

"It's no problem." Monica looked at her again, perhaps a beat longer than any driver should have. "I have a viewing nearby this afternoon, anyway."

She knew Monica was holding something back, and so she turned on the radio. When a Selena Gomez song came on—one that Kanika used to listen to on repeat—she shut it off just in time to hear Monica sigh.

"OK, fine. Just say what you need to say." Anu looked over. "Honestly."

A moment passed.

"Honestly?"

Another moment, and then one more as Monica nearly missed the last turnoff toward the airport.

"Honestly."

"Well," Monica said, throwing her a glance, "as of a few days ago, you were running a yoga studio. You took over Mags' lease, right?"

"Yeah . . . and . . . ?"

"So you want to go traveling and feel free of responsibility—which I get, by the way—but at the same time, you just *really* tied yourself down. Like, financially. Like, *physically* to a building."

That was true. Only that morning she'd rushed over to sign on the dotted line at Mags' lawyer's office above a Pizza Hut four blocks west of the studio.

"It's not officially mine until January first."

"Don't you need to prepare?"

"Imogen's helping out. I've hired her as an assistant manager."

Monica didn't say anything, which slightly infuriated Anu. Whether Anu was gone a couple of weeks or a couple of months . . . Imogen could run the studio without her. Even if she was only twenty-one; she knew more about it than Anu did at this point. And that morning Anu had given her the passwords to her brand-new business banking account. Anu could figure the rest out when she got back.

The airport appeared as they curved upward on the ramp, and Anu said, "I can see how you think I'm being ridiculous."

"I never said that."

"And Jenny?"

"Never mind what Jenny thinks. This is about you. We get that. We love you, and we get why you're going."

"No, seriously. What did Jenny say?"

Monica eyed the rearview mirror as she changed lanes. "Jenny doesn't understand why you're going to London if you're mad at your parents."

"London is the first logical place to go in Europe." Anu hesitated, and suddenly she was irritated, unreasonably so. "I'll just crash at their place a few nights and then . . ."

She hadn't gotten that far yet. She hadn't even told them she was on her way.

Monica pulled into the loading zone outside the international terminal, and Anu reached into her purse, pulling out a few random receipts and her travel itinerary until she found what she was looking for.

"What's that?"

It was the back page of her glossy nursing magazine, hot pink, which she'd torn out that morning. Monica leaned over and started reading the items off the list out loud. She stopped. "This is what we were talking about that one night at drinks, right?"

"When I insisted I was such a grown-up. Yeah, it is."

"I don't get it."

"Me neither, Mon. I don't know how to explain it, but when I look at this, all I feel is . . . resentment. *Anger.* I don't want *this* to be all I'll ever be."

"You're not making any sense."

Anu pointed to "family-oriented." "All this means is I have only ever done what my parents expected of me." She tapped on "controls urges" and then "lives life in moderation." "And all that means is I'm boring!"

"You're not boring, Anu." Monica nodded toward "a loyal friend." "And how is that a bad thing?"

"Sure, I'm a loyal friend to you and Jenny. But, Monica, these days I'm not sure I even have other friends. I was so busy in my own boring life, I lost touch with everyone."

"Anu . . ."

"You know it's true." Anu slid her hand down to "role model to Kanika." "And what makes me think I am a role model? How is me turning into Lakshmi and Priya something she would ever look up to?"

"Kanika thinks the world of you. You're her everything, her mother—"

"Right now she does. She's five years old. What about when she's fifteen, twenty-five? She won't want to hang out with me or answer my calls." Anu was on the verge of tears, and she stopped herself as she crumpled up the hot pink magazine page and tossed it behind her into Monica's backseat. "If I don't get on this plane, what is she ever going to admire in me?"

"I'm not going to pretend I understand, but sure." Monica cleared her throat. She wouldn't look Anu in the eye. "Do you have everything?"

Anu nodded just as Monica reached for Anu's itinerary sitting by the stick shift between them.

"It's OK. It's on my phone."

"Take it anyway," Monica said, but right before she handed over the paper she pulled it back, her eyes flicking over the page. "Wait. . . . You bought a one-way ticket?"

Anu opened her mouth, closing it again when Monica caught her eye.

"I thought . . . Didn't you only take a few weeks off work?"

"Yeah," Anu said. "But . . . I don't know."

"I get that you're lost. But none of this makes sense. *Fuck*"— which made Anu wince, because Monica swore so rarely—"Anu, what about your daughter?"

"Didn't you hear me? I feel like I need to find myself *for* Kanika."

"You keep telling yourself that." Monica nodded, wrapping her sweater tighter around her chest. "And go. With no plan or return ticket. No idea about when you're coming back."

Anu rolled her eyes. "Of course I'm coming back—"

"Can you promise me that? Can you swear, on your *life*, that you will?"

Anu didn't answer, and she still didn't answer a minute later when she got out of the car and grabbed her suitcase from the trunk, and Monica drove away.

· · ·

There is this baking show," Kunal said, looking at the Persian rug instead of Anu, "your mother and I have been enjoying. The Brits indeed love their cake."

"Really." Even though the fireplace was on, Anu was freezing, and she pulled a wool blanket tighter around her shoulders.

"They find very creative ways to make cake, *hah*, Lakshmi?" Kunal looked to his wife. "Perhaps we can create a television show for Indian sweets."

Lakshmi, fixated on her cold cup of tea on the end table, ignored him.

"Gulab jamun. Jalebi . . ."

A pause, and feeling bad, Anu said, *"Ras malai?"*

"Amitabh Bachchan would be the host, clearly."

"Too old," Anu said, briefly forgetting she was supposed to be fighting with them. "How about Shah Rukh Khan?"

"No. He is much too busy producing action movies in which he stars opposite women half his age." Kunal vehemently shook his head. "Bachchan or *bust*."

"With catchphrases like that, why don't you host?"

"Not a bad idea. What do you think, Lucky?" After Lakshmi didn't reply, he continued. "I might need an assistant. Anu, would you like to audition?"

"You're going to make your own daughter audition?"

She and Kunal went into preproduction mode, brainstorming ideas for their TV show, while Lakshmi sulked on her side of the couch. It had been more than three hours, and her parents had yet to acknowledge the elephant in the room: What the hell was Anu doing there? Not during lunch—soup and sandwiches whipped up by Kunal while Lakshmi studied and Anu showered. Not while they washed the dishes, listening to a BBC Four radio program that her dad said he'd grown to enjoy.

Not in the living room, perched on those uncomfortable moss green couches, while everyone sipped tea and Kunal and Anu made a feeble attempt at conversation.

"Lucky," her father said, after they'd run out of sweets to list, actors to audition, "it is already four o'clock."

Lakshmi nodded, standing up slowly. "I must take shower."

"Do you have plans tonight?" Anu asked them.

"My professor is cooking dinner for all of the students. It is a Christmas party." For the first time that afternoon, she met Anu's gaze. "She is not married, you know."

Not married.

Two little words were all it took to set Anu off, to make her muscles tense and her eyes narrow. Lakshmi always loved to point out when a woman over a certain age wasn't married, and usually that age was about twenty-five.

"Jenny has broken up with that nice young chap?" she liked to say whenever Anu shared details about her friend's life. "She is *much* too pretty to be single."

"Why doesn't Anu come along?" Kunal said. "Silke is very hospitable. A very lovely woman."

Lakshmi nodded slightly in agreement. "I will let her know. I am sure there will be enough food."

"It's OK. You guys go," Anu said.

"It is a Christmas party—"

"Mom, I'm really tired."

Lakshmi, silent, disappeared around the corner, and another wave of guilt washed over Anu.

Could she manage a dinner party with strangers? With her

parents? She was tired and wanted to groan at the very thought of having to spend an evening with a smile glued on her face. She had come all this way to spend her time involving herself not in *their* lives but to get her own.

"Come." Kunal stood up and offered his hand to pull her off the couch. "Staying awake now will help you beat the jet lag."

"Dad . . ."

"*Hah, beti.* Please?" He smiled at her, and her muscles started to thaw. "You have come all this way. And your mother is so excited for the party. She will be very sad to cancel."

Face-to-face, maybe she couldn't lie, maybe she'd never be able to disobey them. Her father's gentle, pleading eyes—how could she say no? Gathering every ounce of strength, she let go of her father's hand and pushed herself off the couch.

"Good girl," he said, winking. "You will make your mother so happy."

Even though she didn't want to be, Anu really was a good girl. It used to be enough for her, but now she fucking hated it.

She threw on her best outfit and a bit of makeup, folded her hair into a messy bun. Silke's house was only a short bus ride away, and it neighbored a wide-open green space that Kunal called the Clapham Common. *The* Clapham Common.

How very British.

They turned onto a side street. The sky was getting dark, and whether it was a coincidence or not, all the houses—cute, very English—dotting the lane were covered in fairy lights. Kanika would have loved this, Anu thought, and a moment later, she heard Lakshmi say the same thing out loud.

Silke greeted them on the front stoop. Her mother's professor was about forty and unmarried, yes, but she was also a lot of other words Lakshmi could have used to describe her. What about warm? Boisterous? Accomplished? Her walls were covered in artwork and degrees, photographs of her and other women in front of the Sydney Opera House, clad in rain gear at the height of Machu Picchu. Her name was on a stack of academic journals on the coffee table— society and the law, gender politics, reproductive justice.

But she wasn't married. So, to Lakshmi, what did all the rest even matter?

There were several bottles of wine open in the kitchen, and Anu stayed close to the makeshift bar while she did her best to mingle with other guests. There was Silke's brother, Theo, and the blond woman next to him whose name she forgot instantly; Pauline, who lived next door; a smattering of other students in Lakshmi's class—all international—who had also opted not to return home for the holidays.

Anu scarfed down dinner, and by the time Silke was cutting up the banoffee pie, she was exhausted. Her parents were seated at the other end of the long table, and without saying anything, she slipped into another room.

There was a couch, empty and enticing. She sat down, and just as she let her head drop back on the cushion, a nearby floorboard creaked.

"It's Anusha, right?"

She looked up and found Silke's brother standing in front of her.

"Would you like some?" He was holding two plates of pie and extended one toward her. "It's going fast."

"Thank you . . ." Anu took the plate, still looking at him.

"It's Theo. . . . We met earlier—"

"Of course, yes." She smiled apologetically. "You were with"—

she caught sight of his hand, noticed the absence of a ring—"your partner? The blond woman? Sorry. I can't remember her name. I'm pretty jet-lagged."

"She's not my— Did it seem that way to you?" He sat down next to her, and Anu caught a whiff of his cologne. "That's Silke's friend from rowing."

Anu sat up on the couch, suddenly aware that she was alone with a man and that her parents were in the other room.

"So how is your visit so far? I overheard your arrival was a bit of a surprise."

"Yeah . . . I guess you can say that."

Theo brought a forkful of pie to his mouth and stopped it just shy of his lips. "How lovely."

Anu snuck a glance in his direction, and her stomach lurched when he caught her.

"This is great pie," she said quickly.

"Have you tried it?"

"Oh . . ." Why did he make her so nervous? Why had she left her wineglass at the table?

"Go on, then."

She smiled and then took a bite. It was good. *Really* good. She was not sure she'd tasted anything like it before.

"You seem to be enjoying it."

"I am."

"Good. I made it."

"Are you a chef?"

"I dabble."

Dabble. The way he said the word, weirdly, made her stomach flutter. She adored English accents, but who didn't? Which North American woman *wouldn't* get nervous around a guy who looked and sounded and probably even smelled like freaking Jude Law?

She looked over, just as he took another bite of his pie. He was younger than she had first thought, although he was clean-shaven, so it was difficult to tell.

"How old are you?"

"I'm thirty-four. Would you like to see my passport?"

"Sorry." She shrugged. "I was just curious."

Curious or cautious?

"Not a bother."

She muffled a smile. "So, Theo, when you're not *dabbling*, what do you do?"

"Coincidentally, I chose the only field that Silke didn't excel in."

She glanced around the room. "Let me see. . . . You're a fisherman?"

He grinned, shaking his head.

"Bullfighter?"

"Have another guess."

She took a bite of pie. "Photographer?"

"How did you know?"

"I don't know. It was just a guess. Silke has such beautiful photographs, yet she's in most of them."

"They're not all mine." Theo pointed to a wild-looking landscape. "That was taken by our mother, same with that one," he said, motioning toward the misty beach scene next to it. His eyes moved across the room, to a cluster of eight-by-eleven photographs near the fire, some of Silke, others of women she didn't recognize. "Those are mine. I mostly photograph people."

"They're beautiful."

"It's really the subjects that are beautiful. My job is to bring it out."

Had the house just gotten hotter? There was a fireplace off to the side, roaring. Anu leaned away from it.

"Enough about me. What about you, Anusha? Tell me about you."

I'm a mother.

She glanced down at her plate. Here was where she would usually pull out her phone and proudly show off pictures of Kanika, her pride and joy. The very center of her universe. The existence of her daughter and her infinite qualities would anchor the conversation, always the starting point to learning about Anu.

"You can call me Anu if you want. Most people do."

"So what do you do, Anu?"

She was a mother. She was about to say it, but then she didn't.

"Guess."

"I reckon you're an academic like Silke and your father."

She shook her head. Was she still a real mother even though she'd left her daughter at home for Christmas?

Theo narrowed his eyes and then dropped his gaze to her chest, her arms.

"Model?" He flashed a smile. "Call me cheesy, but I had to."

Anu blushed. "Good line."

"Good guess?"

She shook her head. "Nope, and you have one left, so make it count."

He leaned forward onto his elbows, and she could smell his cologne again. He was studying her, and briefly she was tempted to ask what on earth it was he saw. "Entrepreneur?"

She was about to say no and then remembered the yoga studio. Her grin widened. "How could you tell?"

Anu wasn't drunk, but the next glass of red—her third of the evening—certainly took the edge off. She tried not to think about Neil and Kanika back home, or whether her parents had noticed the way Theo barely left her side the rest of the evening, laughed at her terrible jokes, kept finding excuses to touch her arm.

He told her about his photography business, the one that paid the bills, kept him traveling much of the year. Conferences, music festivals, the occasional freelance job for some red-carpet event or the other. About growing up in Germany—and, for brief periods, Turkey—and then staying in London after university: a city as diverse and ambitious as himself.

He liked to talk, and right then she was enjoying listening. After all, he *did* sound like Jude Law.

Much later, she found herself on the back terrace alone with him. Others had joined them at first—for a cigarette, to stargaze or marvel at Silke's work space in the back shed—but now it was just the two of them. They were side by side on a bench, snuggled beneath a canvas blanket. Anu kept her hands warm with a mug of mulled wine. She had lost track of her parents; they had been in the kitchen chatting to Silke's rowing friend the last time she checked. A few times, Anu could feel her mother watching her.

Anu heard the door slide open, and they both turned to look at the patio door. Silke had exchanged her striking silk pantsuit for a pair of flannel pajamas.

"I'm going to bed," she said casually. "The sitting room is yours, if you'd like."

"Wait. What time is it?" Anu glanced at her watch. "Are my parents ready to go?"

"Everyone's left, but it's no bother. I told Lakshmi Theo would drive you home."

Anu's stomach suddenly felt odd, unsettled. They had left without her?

"I'm so sorry. I'll go—"

"Don't be daft. You can stay as long as you'd like."

"Your lips are blue," she heard Theo say. "Shall we go in?"

She squatted down by the fire to warm up as Theo hugged his sister good night, said something to her in German. Was it about Anu? She heard the floorboards creak from the stairwell, and a beat later she felt Theo just behind her. He crouched down next to where she was sitting and extended his hand toward the fire, only embers now.

"Can I show you something?" He reached for his phone and held it out in front of him. "I was in Budapest last week"—he scrolled through his camera roll and then angled the screen toward her—"for this. I'm not exhibited in galleries often. . . ."

She inspected the photo. It was black-and-white, of a woman maybe her own age in an unimposing courtyard. Her legs stretched out in front of her, her head tilted up to the sun, eyes closed, arms out behind propping her up. Anu couldn't help but stare. Her pose was striking. Her shopping bags were casually discarded by her feet, with leafy greens and round-shaped bread having fallen out on the pavement.

The woman looked free. So pure. Briefly, Anu wished she were the woman in the photograph.

"You seem to like it."

"Like it . . ." Anu touched his forearm. "Theo, I love it."

"It's my favorite piece."

"Do you . . . know her?"

He smiled, and Anu found herself blushing. "She's my sister."

"Ah."

"Silke is my sister from my mother's side," he continued, as if anticipating Anu's next question. "We grew up in Germany." He glanced back at the photo. "Selma is my younger sister, from my father's side. She lives in Turkey."

Anu turned back to the fire, inching away from him.

"I haven't had a drink in hours," he said. "I can drive you home . . . if you'd like?"

She knew exactly what she would have *liked* and blushed at the thought.

How was it that Jenny, Imogen, and other women so easily let themselves do what they liked? It wasn't a generational thing. Most of the women she knew—older or younger, Indian or otherwise— hadn't waited until marriage, no longer believed that sex and love had boundaries. Why did she?

"Anu, what is it?"

"I"—she swallowed—"I'm not sure."

"About me?" His hand had found its way to her inner forearm, and she watched his fingers trace small circles on the flesh.

Was it about him? Would he be just another Ryan—a man who worked hard and loved harder, whose passion would lead him to stray, make him unable to be faithful to anyone but himself? Or maybe he would be more like Neil, kindhearted, more likely to walk on the moon than purposely hurt even the smallest cell in her body.

But Theo didn't have to be one or the other, did he? Could she let him just be *tonight*?

He moved his hand up her arm and then turned her to face him. Eyes already closed, he leaned in, planted the most gentle of kisses just below her ear.

"I'm not sure about . . . myself."

Her whole life, she had been proud of her modest, even prudish ways—but what had controlling her urges ever accomplished?

Theo's eyes moved to the fire, and slowly he backed away from her. She wished he wouldn't. She wanted him. Right then she was hungry.

She reached for his hand. She got up on her knees, crept toward him, and sat back down.

An entrepreneur, a traveler, a free spirit.

She kissed him softly at first and then harder, and his hands came up to her face, gently guided her closer. One knee over his legs, and she was straddling him. He was hard against her, his hands tugging through her hair, circling her neck, her waist, her ass.

She was a heroine in her own right. A risk-taker. A woman, Anu realized, who was about to hook up with a total stranger.

chapter sixteen

❧

NEIL: Glad to hear you've arrived safe. I've promised Kanu that we'll take lots of videos of the holiday concert for you. The set looks great, by the way. I didn't realize you made it until Ms. Finch told me.

NEIL: I hope you're having a nice trip. You deserve it, Anush.

can't believe we fell asleep."

"It's OK, Anu, really."

"It's *really* not OK."

There was a group of teenagers smoking outside the pastry shop. They looked like stage actors—young faces caked in makeup and odd, ill-fitting clothes. One of them was also of South Asian heritage, and she was twirling her long black hair with one hand, texting and smoking with the other. Her coat was too small, refusing to cover her flat brown belly and pink crop top.

For the love of God, it was winter. If Kanika ever tried to leave the house like that in December, Anu wouldn't try to stop her; she'd laugh.

"Anu?"

She didn't answer, instead watching the group shuffle down the road to perch by another storefront. Anu had been sitting in the passenger seat of Theo's car for the past five minutes watching them, trying to work up the courage to get out.

Did *they* ever simply not go home some nights? Were they that stupid?

"I had a lovely time with you." He was gripping the steering wheel, and Anu could tell that he wanted her to leave.

"Me, too."

She'd had a lovely time with her Jude Law look-alike. They'd made out like teenagers, and when she couldn't bear that any longer, she'd slept with him. She hadn't regretted it the night before, and even now, she didn't exactly *regret* it.

She just wished she hadn't done it in plain view of her parents.

"So . . ."

He was watching her now. She was *annoying* him.

He killed the car engine and didn't muffle his sigh—as she was sure he intended. "Look, Anu. You're thirty, are you not? Don't you have a kid?"

A kid. The way he said it made motherhood sound so impersonal. Last night, maybe that was the way she had made it sound.

"You're visiting your parents for the holiday and thought you'd have a bit of fun. I do not see a problem."

She turned to face him. There were bags under his eyes, and with a day's stubble, he suddenly looked much older than thirty-four.

He didn't see a problem because he didn't know her—yet intimately he knew her in a way only two other men ever had. In a way that, she realized, didn't even matter.

"Theo, I'm Indian."

"That's crap. A lot of people are Indian." He smiled. "There's a billion of your lot. You honestly believe you're the only one having a shag?"

She smiled back at him, trying to figure out whether what he said was funny—or if it offended her.

"You'll be fine." He leaned over and planted a dry kiss on her forehead. "Now, off you go."

Standing there on the curb like a fool, she watched him drive away. When she turned around, the teenagers were at the far end of the block, waiting for a streetlight to change. One of the guys had tucked his hand into the jeans back pocket of the South Asian girl, who was pretending not to notice, huddling arm in arm with one of the other girls.

When Anu was that age, she'd been proud of the fact that she was a virgin, that she had yet to even kiss somebody. She was saving herself, she thought then. She was better than her friends, her peers, because she had the discipline not to be tricked and then trapped by those urges, those instincts.

It all sounded so ridiculous now.

The door was unlocked, and upstairs she found Kunal reading the paper in an armchair. Anu wondered if he'd been there the whole night, if he had waited up like he used to—tutting at his wristwatch when Neil brought her home more than five minutes late.

"Hi, Dad."

He let the paper drop a few inches. His wrinkled brow appeared and then the top of his reading glasses. "Hi, *beti*."

Was she still his *beti*? Did he still think of her as his good little girl? Did she need him to?

She flopped down on the couch opposite him, and he set down the paper on the coffee table.

"Your mother is studying in the kitchen."

She could lie to her parents outright, just like Monica used to before she met Tom and took a stand. Before Tom, if Monica wanted to stay out all night or meet up with a guy she was seeing, she'd tell her parents she was sleeping over at a friend's or working late for a client who didn't exist. She'd come up with elaborate excuses about cars breaking down, her phone running out of battery or data. Once, Monica had told them she was late because she'd helped a nurse deliver a baby on the train that was stuck underground between the Waterfront and Burrard Street stations; the next day, she'd even pretended to be surprised when she didn't see herself on the local news.

"Hungry, Anu? We have already had breakfast."

"No . . ."

But she didn't know how to tell a lie like that. She had never tried.

"Lucky, sweetie," Kunal called out. "*Ohhh*, Lucky. Anu is home. *Aaja.*"

A beat later Lakshmi appeared around the corner—a glass of water in one hand, a textbook in the other. She didn't greet Anu or even look at her as she sat down next to Kunal. "Have you eaten?"

"I'm not hungry."

"*Hah.*"

But the truth was, she did lie to them. Not the way Monica used to: Anu's lies were fewer and farther between. Subtle and more by omission.

Good idea, Dad. I should be a nurse. It is a great career for a wife and mother.

We're trying to save up for a new house right now, OK, Mom? That's why we haven't had another baby.

I've asked Neil to move out. I don't love him anymore.

That last lie had been the hardest to tell. How else did you explain divorce to a generation who largely didn't get to choose whom they married, overwhelmingly stayed together regardless of love? Where families picked their children's spouses from a lineup, chose their future based on horoscope, height and weight, skin color and caste?

Why hadn't she ever told them the truth? She loved Neil; she always would, but Anu didn't want to be his mother, his caretaker, or his housekeeper. She didn't want a life like Lakshmi's or Priya's: the life of an Indian housewife, in which everyone and everything mattered but her.

She wanted a life for herself, and her parents needed to accept that.

"I slept with Theo."

Anu watched her mother's face as she spoke, and for a long, deep moment, no one said a word.

"Did you guys hear me?"

Slowly, Lakshmi set her textbook on the end table. "What is there to say?"

Kunal reached for Lakshmi's hand. Was he trying to stop her? Prompt her?

"I will say that Neil called us this morning. That Kanika is missing you very much."

"Are you trying to make me feel guilty?"

"Do you have *reason* to feel guilty, *hah*, Anu?"

"Neil goes to three or four conferences a year, and you say, 'Oh, Neil, you work *so* hard,'" Anu says, imitating Lakshmi's accent. "'Stay on a few extra days and relax, *nah*? Have a *holiday*.' Mom, do *I* ever get a holiday?"

"Take holiday, Anu. Nobody is stopping you. But abandoning your child—"

"I did not abandon her. I'm taking some time away."

"For Theo?" Lakshmi spit. "For *Ryan*?"

"For *me*."

"Enough fighting for now, *hah*?" Kunal looked between them. "Perhaps we are, as the kids say, all a bit *hangry*?"

Lakshmi started at him in Punjabi. Anu didn't catch what she was saying.

"Say it in English, Mom. Would you *please* just say what you're thinking?"

"Anu, you must understand," Kunal said, interrupting them both. "Your mother and I realize times have changed. It *is* different. But we are still getting used to this change, *hah, beti*? You must be patient."

"When Kanu is grown, then Anu will learn this *patience* business. You will understand when your daughter hurts you like this."

"How am I hurting you? Mom, this is about *me*—"

"When Kanu is old enough to realize what is happening, what will you say?" Lakshmi asked, her voice hard. "Who these men are? Why she was raised in broken home?"

"Crazily enough, Mom, I might just tell her the truth. Maybe unlike you, I'll have an honest conversation with her before she's *thirty*."

"Unlike *me*?"

"Anu," Kunal snapped, "*enough*."

"Yes, unlike *you*. I'm sorry my life choices are so very hard on you, but they are *my* choices. And I'm proud of the fact that I was brave enough to leave an unhappy marriage and *try* dating someone else and go traveling by myself, to start a new business—"

"What business?" Kunal was glaring at her now, too, his arm wrapped protectively around his wife's shoulder.

Anu grimaced and sat up on the couch. "I . . . I am running a yoga studio. I took over a lease—"

"*Kya?* When?"

"Last week."

"Last *week*."

Now he wouldn't look at her, either; and she fumbled through an explanation: meeting Mags, the feeling of completeness, her plans for the business—as vague as it still was. The longer she spoke, the more Kunal seemed to withdraw.

"You say you want a divorce," he said after she was finished. He seemed to be chewing his words, considering their taste and texture. "This costs money. Traveling, *this* costs money. Tell me, was this business so important that you will risk your family's financial security?"

"Dad, it's going to be fine. . . ."

"You were hiding this from us?" A pause. Kunal unwrapped his arm from Lakshmi and dropped it to his lap, palm facing up. "Like you are hiding your relationship with . . ." He trailed off as his hand clenched into a fist, as if he were physically incapable of saying his name.

"It's Ryan, Dad. And that relationship is over. It's been over for a while."

"You left this Ryan character. Just like you left Neil?" Lakshmi said. "So suddenly. Like you weren't even thinking."

"Don't you understand? Separating from Neil was the first time I was thinking," Anu said, trying to keep her voice calm. "That I did something for *myself*. Mom, I did everything you and Dad ever wanted. I came home early. I never drank or dated around. I chose my career because you said it was 'fitting for a mother—'"

"*Nah*—"

"And Neil and I only got married so young because it's what you and Priya wanted us to do. You wanted a wedding to plan, grandkids to babysit—"

"And why do you think I came to London?" Lakshmi's face was

red, and she threw Kunal's pleading hand away from her lap. "To finally complete an education, years after my child? Your father says times have changed, *nah*? Just for you? For women your age? I am a nani and therefore half-dead? Can I not do as I like?"

Anu's cheeks burned. "Sure, but—"

"Being a mother is hard, Anu. You cannot make snap-snap decisions and think there will be no consequences for Kanika!"

"I've only ever thought of her. I'm a good mother."

"If you are so *good*," Lakshmi said evenly. Slowly. "What exactly are you doing here?"

Twenty-four hours ago, sitting on this very couch, she'd asked herself the same question. Finally, she had the answer.

"I'm here," she said, taking a deep breath, "to tell you that I now run a yoga studio. That I slept with Theo. That I dated a man named Ryan for three months, and that from now on I'm going to start dating whomever I want."

She caught Lakshmi's eye, daring her to keep speaking.

"I'm here to tell you that I'm going traveling for a while and that I don't know when exactly I'm coming back. That from now on, I'm going to live my life, for *me*."

"Mothers do not have such luxuries."

"Well, maybe I . . ." She trailed off, but her words had startled them all. Of course she wanted to be Kanika's mother.

But right now the responsibility of it—the weight of her whole damn life—was just too much for her to shoulder.

"Anu . . ." Kunal's voice cracked. She'd hurt them. She wasn't used to this, and so she stared at her feet as she stood up from the couch.

"I'm going to go," she said to her toes, to the Persian carpet. She looked up. "I know I've disappointed you. But I'm not sorry about my decisions."

chapter seventeen

Twelve years earlier

Next, two Scotch on the rocks," Anu said, handing out her tray of drinks to a group of uncles. One drink remained, and she turned to her dad. "And Scotch neat?"

"Thank you, *beti*." Kunal took a gulp, and Anu's stomach churned just watching him. It smelled foul. She couldn't even imagine how it *tasted*. "Excellent. What brand is this?"

"Brandon said it's called . . . Glenfiddish?"

"Glenfiddich, *hah*." Kunal scanned the lawn, shielding the sun with his hand. "Brandon is here? I have not yet been introduced."

"Yeah, he's been here the whole time." Anu gestured behind her toward the porch, where Auntie Jayani had set up a bar beneath the awning. Her eldest daughter, Sonia, was newly engaged to a fellow doctor she'd met in the emergency ward, a *white* guy. Sonia wasn't the first of her family friends to marry a non-Indian, but close to it, and watching some of the aunties and uncles react and process the news had made this particular engagement party a bit more interesting.

There was a spectrum of families in their community—from Auntie Jayani and her husband, very modern, sometimes even criticized as "too modern," to Monica's parents at the other end, who were traditional and religious and would probably have disowned Monica if she'd ever dated someone white. Or dated anyone at all.

Anu followed her dad's eyes around the lawn, past the house—where most of the women were busy cooking—and toward the bar.

"So where is this Brandon? I should go rough him up a bit." Kunal smiled. "You know, be an *uncle*. Should I tell him I am policeman?"

Anu rolled her eyes. "He's that one. With the black polo shirt."

"*Kaun?*"

"Him." She pointed harder. "Right there. He's pouring a glass of red wine."

"That is the bartender."

"Dad, that's Brandon." Anu giggled. "Auntie didn't hire a bartender."

"No." Kunal gasped. He tapped the uncle beside him, pulling him close. "Prem-*ji*, did you know that is Brandon?"

"*Kaun?*"

"The bartender."

"Bartender? I thought Sonia was marrying *doctor.*"

Anu laughed silently as she watched her dad and his friends realize and exclaim over the fact that the white guy who had been pouring their drinks all afternoon was the man they all had come to the party to meet. She wondered if it was also occurring to them that he was also the only man at the party actually helping out.

"Thank you for the drinks, *beti*," Kunal said, as if dismissing her. "Does your mother need help?"

"Do *you* want to help her?" Anu mumbled as she walked away, although not loud enough for Kunal to hear her.

It was hot for early July. Only the week before, on Anu's eighteenth birthday, she'd had to wear a thick sweater and a raincoat—and now suddenly it was summer. It was even warmer inside, and she found Lakshmi, Auntie Jayani, and the other aunties scrambling around the kitchen—frying samosas and *pakoras*, serving up *subjis* into crockery, setting out chutney. Monica was bent over the sink, elbow deep in dishwater. She'd already been caught.

"*There* you are," Lakshmi said to her.

"I was serving the uncles drinks. Do you want one?"

Lakshmi shook her head, and a bead of sweat rolled down her temple.

"Are you sure?" Lakshmi hovered over the stove, and Anu was hot just looking at her.

"No time." Lakshmi gestured toward a stack of china plates. "*Jao.*"

Swallowing a groan, Anu carried a high stack of china plates across the large kitchen, through two sitting rooms—empty—and into the dining room, where Auntie Jayani always served lunch. As she set down the plates on the table, piled high with desserts, she noticed a tall boy her age lurking at the opposite end.

"Oh. Hi."

He didn't reply, and she considered his face. Tanned, angular, dark eyes, and black lashes thicker than hers, even though she was wearing mascara. She didn't recognize him.

"Do we know each other? I'm Anusha. . . ."

He still didn't respond, stared at her like a deer caught in headlights. She saw his Adam's apple bob out of his white crewneck.

"Are you too afraid to talk to me or something?"

His eyes wide, he shook his head adamantly.

"See, *this* is why I don't like Indian boys. Either you're cocky and unbearable and think you're just *so* good-looking, or you can't string two words together to save your life."

He buckled over coughing, and she rounded the table toward him.

"Are you OK?"

He shot back up, nodding, and she realized he was laughing. And choking.

"Are you *dying?*"

He had a good six inches on her, and she had to reach up to pat his back. She knocked a few times, then harder. He turned to her, shaking his head; then he heaved and a gooey brown chunk splatted on her chest.

"I'm so sorry!" He grabbed a tea towel off the table and lunged for her.

"Get away!"

They scrambled with the towel, and Anu eventually got it from him and peeled off the glob, which she realized was a half-chewed *gulab jamun*. It left a stain. She looked up. The boy was smiling at her.

"Who *are* you?"

"I'm Neil."

"Neil, you just threw up on me."

"I did. I'm sorry?" He pressed his lips together, and an odd sensation floated around in her stomach. Like she was nauseous and had just eaten way, way too much.

"I'm just, like, starving, and had snuck a *gulab jamun* when you walked in, and—"

"And you thought I'd tell on you for sneaking *malai?*"

"Well, in my experience there are two types of Indian girls. . . ."

Anu raised an eyebrow.

"Girls that are tattletales, and girls that are fun."

"I'm *fun*."

"And since we're speaking, I must be a cocky Indian boy who knows how good-looking he is."

She felt herself blushing. "I never said you were good-looking."

"Now you've gone and hurt my feelings, Anush."

Anush. No one had ever called her that before. Halfway between her Western-sounding nickname, Anu, and the Indian mouthful her parents had given her. It was smack-dab in the middle.

Anush, she thought, watching his mouth curl up into a smile. She liked it.

He crooked his head, and she suspected he was looking at the length of her neck, where her pale cotton shirt drooped midchest.

"Why haven't I seen you around before, anyway?"

"I'm from Calgary."

Her heart dropped.

"Auntie Jayani is my mom's childhood best friend."

"So you're just visiting." She reached for the plate of *jalebi* and broke off a sticky orange chunk, popped it into her mouth.

"For now."

"For now?"

"I got into the University of British Columbia, but we wanted to check out the program before moving here."

"UBC?" She tried to play it cool. "I'm starting there in the fall. . . ."

"Arts and sciences?"

She nodded. "You, too?"

"Computer sciences." He inched closer and grabbed the other half of the *jalebi* she'd picked at. "What is—"

"*Aho*. Neil!"

He froze, dropping the *jalebi*.

"You will ruin your appetite," an auntie muttered in Punjabi.

Anu didn't recognize her, either, but she could tell she was Neil's mother. They had the same eyes and lips, and though she wasn't wearing any makeup and had gray strands streaked through her hair, she was absolutely beautiful.

"How many times have I told you not to snack? This is not even our house. Have you no respect?" She turned to look at Anu, and her face relaxed. "Was my son sneaking sweetmeats? It's OK. You can tell me."

Anu hesitated.

"He was, wasn't he?"

"No, Auntie. We were just talking."

"Call me Priya Auntie," the woman said, switching to English. While Anu was slightly embarrassed that the woman had noticed how bad her Punjabi was so quickly, she was more relieved she wasn't being forced to speak it.

"Mom, this is Anusha."

"Do you know, Anusha, how often this boy used to sneak *laddoo*?" She sidled toward Neil and started rubbing his stomach. "He used to be so fat!"

"Mom!"

"Eating ghee right out of the container."

"Ew, *ghee*?" Anu laughed, and she caught Neil's eye. Why was he looking at her like that?

"I did not," Neil said grumpily, trying to hide a smile. "Like, not *that* often."

"So you are a Vancouver girl?" Priya Auntie said to her. "You must be Lakshmi-*ji*'s daughter—you look just like her!"

Anu beamed.

"Pretty soon, I may become a Vancouver *girl*, too, *hah*, Neil?"

"You're going to move with him, Auntie?"

"*Hah*. Where else would I go?" She pulled out a dining room chair and sat on it, tugged on Neil's hand until he was standing close beside her. "Neil's papa passed away when he was very young. It is just us two."

"Oh, I'm sorry."

"But it has been a long time now. And we must stick together, like the musketeers." She tugged on Neil's hand. *"Hah, beta?"*

"Hah, Mom."

"So if he finds a program he likes, we will stay." Priya smiled at her suspiciously. "If he finds something *else* he likes . . ."

"Mom."

"What?" Priya turned to him, switching back to Punjabi. "What did I say that is so wrong?"

chapter eighteen

TINA: Anu, hi! We haven't seen you around school this
week. Monet is DYING to have a playdate with Kanika before
the holidays. Maybe at yours again? I'm totally swamped
RN. . . . Call me back! x

A latte and one of those, please." Anu pointed at a batch of cinnamon rolls steaming up the display window. Her stomach
growling, she glanced at a neighboring stack of scones. "And one
of those. Thanks."

The barista behind the counter was about Imogen's age with
white blond hair and a pimply chin. After he told her he'd bring it
all out to her table, she found a seat at a high top near the back and
plugged in her phone to a nearby power outlet. Although she had
packed in a rush and hadn't even bothered to shower, luckily she
had remembered to swipe one of Kunal's UK phone chargers.

She looked out the window, half expecting him and Lakshmi
to be standing there, tapping on the glass, pleading with her to
come back upstairs.

But they weren't there. They had stood in the front hall with
their arms crossed as she mumbled a goodbye and wheeled her
suitcase out the door, and they hadn't followed her down. Anu re-

staged the fight in her mind as the barista brought out the latte and pastries. Anu swallowed each bite hard as she felt her throat constricting. They were loving, doting, supportive parents—but only because Anu had never given them a reason not to be. Only until she became a single mother, someone who wanted *more* than what good Indian daughters, wives, and mothers were supposed to want.

She wanted to experience London the way everyone on Instagram seemed to. She wanted to see other parts of Europe too—the Highlands of Scotland, a wall of graffiti in Berlin, the setting of Elena Ferrante's Neapolitan novels—and finally do that yoga course.

She opened her group chat with Jenny and Monica. The last two messages were from Anu: one right before she got off the plane, telling them she loved them, and another after she had landed in London. They hadn't replied to either.

They were mad at her, and Anu couldn't really blame them.

She checked the world clock app on her phone. It was late at night in both Vancouver and Santiago. Monica would be with Tom, cuddling in bed with a book or already asleep. Jenny would be out dancing with her sister, painting the town Red Delicious.

She knew they would answer her if she called, but she was too embarrassed. Sitting here in a coffee shop with a suitcase tucked between her legs, she wouldn't know what to say.

She scanned the tube map, followed the blue, red, brown, and pink lines up, down, and around the city. There were so many options. *Too* many options. Fleetingly, she almost wished she had someone to tell her which one to choose, which one she would want.

From what she'd been told by friends who had visited before, there were several ways to *do* London. She could go see all the hit shows on the West End—like *Kinky Boots*, which she'd seen advertised on a tube poster the day before. She could slip on a pair of heels and click them up and down Regent Street, and in and out of Soho boutiques, and shop her way through London. Certainly, she could buy a pass for one of those big red buses that toured around the city. Although that option was a cliché, at least then she wouldn't miss anything.

Sweating, Anu unwrapped her scarf from her neck and hung it on the back of her chair. She tried to imagine how Imogen would do London, if she had the money and the inclination.

She'd buy cheap, trendy clothes and drag Anu to a bar. A club. Force Anu to drink shots of syrupy blue liquid until Anu couldn't see London at all, but *feel* it. She knew it was late in Vancouver, but on an impulse, she called her anyway. After three rings, it went to voice mail.

IMOGEN: Was that a butt dial?

ANUSHA: No, wanna talk?

IMOGEN: I'm talking to you right now.

ANUSHA: LOL. Texting isn't talking. Just answer . . .

Anu dialed again and sighed in relief when Imogen picked up the phone. "Did I wake you?"

"No, I'm up. *Gilmore Girls* marathon." She was slurring her words, and Anu half wondered if she was high or drunk. "Twelve hours and counting . . ."

There was heavy breathing in the background, and the TV sounds in the background went mute.

"Are you OK?"

"Am *I* OK?" Suddenly, she sounded more awake. More like Imogen. "The question is, are *you* OK? What's up? Having fun?"

"I don't know. I just got here." Anu shrugged. "I sort of . . . fought with my parents."

"Oh?"

"And had my first one-night stand."

"*Oh*. Juicy." Even though she was five thousand miles away, Anu could imagine the exact expression on Imogen's face. "Spill the tea."

Anu spilled, but she glossed over the reason she had fought with Lakshmi and Kunal; right then she didn't want to even think about it.

"So what should I do next?" Anu asked, blushing after Imogen's intimate line of questioning about her night with Theo. "I suppose I need to find a hotel."

"A *hotel*?" Imogen scoffed. "Go to a hostel. How else are you going to meet people?"

A hostel? From everything she'd seen in travel guides, horror movies, and on TV, hostels were for twenty-year-old Australian boys looking to hook up or for groups of American girls traveling in Italy on a budget.

Serial killers.

"You don't want to see London alone, do you?"

Anu considered Imogen's question. She had wanted to go on a trip by herself, but did she really imagine that she would be alone the whole time? Getting a stranger to take a picture of her sitting on the steps of Trafalgar Square? Trying out that fancy restaurant in Soho with space pods in the bathroom, saying, "Table for one?"

The short time she'd been imagining the trip, she could only picture leaving. Once she got to her destination, well—that was a blank slate.

"No, I guess I don't want to be alone."

"Then stay at a hostel." Something cracked and then shattered on the other end of the line. "*Shit*."

"What was that?"

"Dropped my wineglass," Imogen said nonchalantly. "Oh, well, I'll sort it out in the morning."

"Are you in Vancouver?"

Anu took Imogen's silence to mean yes, and she tried again not to wonder why even though the studio was closed for the holidays, Imogen was spending the weekend before Christmas by herself and not with her family. But whenever Anu tried to ask about Imogen's past—glean details about where she grew up, her siblings, her childhood home—she expertly switched the subject.

Anu tried again. "You're going home for Christmas?" She was a mother; she couldn't help it. If Kanika tried to skip Christmas when she was that age . . . Although if that situation ever happened, Anu couldn't really say anything. Here Anu was skipping a Christmas herself.

"Are you excited?" After Imogen didn't respond, Anu tried again. "Do you have any holiday traditions?"

"Not really."

"Well, what—"

"Anu, it doesn't matter."

"What doesn't matter?" Silence again, and concern rose in Anu's belly. "Imogen, is everything OK?"

"I'm drunk right now, so actually yes, everything is fabulous."

Drunk. Imogen seemed to drink to excess quite a lot, although Anu supposed a lot of people her age went through a binge phase. She wondered if they binged by themselves.

"I'm fine, OK? I'm taking the bus home on Christmas Eve."

Fine. Anu knew that tone. She'd said that word countless times just like that, and it wasn't ever the truth.

"Now, go have fun," said Imogen. "Don't do anything I wouldn't do." And she hung up before Anu had a chance to say anything more.

chapter nineteen

✿

ANUSHA: Hi, Neil. Just checking in. . . . How is Kanika? How was the concert?

ANUSHA: And how are you?

(three hours later)

ANUSHA: You must be busy. Sorry. If you're home tomorrow I'd love to call her. . . . Let me know what you think.

Anu took a deep breath and pushed through the door, which was hidden in a back alley between a microbrewery and a "cold brew only" coffee shop in Dalston, one of London's cooler neighborhoods. Inside, there was a long, narrow hallway, and she emerged on the other side in what appeared to be some sort of religious shrine. There were almost as many Buddhas or Ganeshas or Lord Shiva statues as students sitting on bean bags in the waiting room, and there were garlands of marigolds strung about in every which way, like they would be during a special function at temple.

Was this place serious?

It wasn't just culturally appropriating yoga, Hinduism, and Buddhism; it was making a mockery of them. The space was warm, and she hastily took off her coat. Here and there, she had visited studios that had culturally insensitive aspects that irritated her—like that one on Vancouver's east side that kept the Bhagavad Gita—a holy script—in the women's washroom. But *this* place was so outrageously offensive, it was almost funny.

"Welcome. *Nooh-maah-sti.*" A fit blond woman appeared in front of her as if out of thin air. She was wearing stylish patterned leggings and a canary yellow yoga bra, and when she bowed low to Anu, her hands in prayer, her six-pack didn't bulge out over the elastic band like it did for most women. Like Anu.

"Are you here for the six thirty p.m. *vinyasa* flow?" The woman looked Anu up and down but couldn't hide the look of disapproval. Anu, here in her fading joggers from the Gap and an old T-shirt with a bleach stain, surely wasn't her average customer.

"Maybe," Anu said, stepping forward and lifting her chin higher. "But I also wanted to sign up for the yoga seminar that starts on Boxing Day. Your website said to come in to inquire."

"The seminar?" The woman pursed her lips at Anu. "The seminar is quite . . . *strenuous.* Ten days back to back. Six hours a day . . ."

Anu forced out a smile. "I'm up for the challenge."

"I reckon it's booked up." The woman nodded. "Or very nearly. You might want to start with today's class to get you started." She wiggled a manicured finger at Anu. "You can follow me to sign up. It's only twenty pounds."

Anu hesitated, annoyed that she needed to somehow prove herself to enroll. The seminar was advertised online as intermediate and as a course even some beginners would be able to manage.

"Coming?" The woman looked back at Anu, and Anu hesitated to follow her to the sign-up sheet, but she did anyway because Blissed Out Yoga was her last shot. Besides sightseeing, she'd spent the past five days in London looking for a yoga seminar or retreat anywhere in the UK that wasn't already booked up or started soon enough.

It was nearly the Christmas holidays, they all told her. She was either too late or too early. Of course she was. This should have occurred to her sooner.

The woman never bothered introducing herself to the class, and so Anu started thinking of her as Alexa. After all, she sounded exactly like Jenny's irritating smart speaker. That Alexa had lasted a week and a half before Jenny, tearing her hair out, returned the damn thing to Best Buy for a full refund.

This Alexa . . . well, Anu wasn't sure she would be able to get through an hour-and-a-half class. Everything seemed wrong. Some of the students had self-proclaimed to be brand-new, yet Alexa was encouraging them to push themselves into deep backbends and forward folds, moving everyone in and out of poses at an alarming, even dangerous rate.

"Breathe in and *tone* those bottoms, ladies," she said during a disturbingly long hold of bridge prose. "Isn't that why we're all here?"

Anu's eyes rolled far back in her head, and she wished Jenny and her entire yoga-skeptic worldview was here to laugh at this with her. These sorts of teachers and studios were the reason yoga culture had started to get a bad rap. It wasn't like Anu had a problem with white people doing yoga; the more, the merrier. What she had a problem with was studios like Blissed Out that packaged up all yoga like it was a good workout class or some sort of hipster status symbol.

Finally, the class was drawing to a close. Alexa instructed everyone to lie flat on their backs for *shavasana*, breathe deeply into their relxation. Anu heard something fall to the ground, and she opened her eyes and chanced a look at the front. Alexa was fetching an acoustic guitar from the corner and bringing it back to her mat.

Was she kidding with this? Anu had often been to classes where teachers chanted *om* several times toward the end or mantras, which were meant to aid with meditation—but *this*?

Anu tried not giggle as Alexa started strumming on the guitar. She could hear a few others chuckling near her feet, too. The melody sounded a bit like a Coldplay song, but then Alexa started to sing. And it wasn't the lyrics to "Yellow" or "The Scientist" or "Viva la Vida." It was in Sanskrit, the words to a religious hymn Anu knew well, and Alexa had remixed it with freaking Coldplay.

Anu coughed, pressing both hands flat over her mouth to keep from laughing. The past few days, whenever Anu had thought about Mags' Studio waiting for her at home, her stomach sank. She'd been terrified, utterly overwhelmed by the reality that her dream was ready for her, and quite possibly, Anu could fail.

But if Alexa could do *this*, if a fraud could run a yoga studio, surely anyone could. And realizing this, Anu wondered if she had flown so hastily to Europe not to pursue something but to escape what was waiting for her at home.

Anu stretched as she stood up from the mat. She knew every single butchered, mispronounced word Alexa was singing. Anu had been singing them since she was a little girl.

"Please stay seated, class," Alexa said in a singsong voice, still strumming on the guitar. Now it sounded a lot like "Clocks."

Anu continued rolling up her mat, and a beat later, Alexa stopped playing.

"For those of you who are *new* to this, I must say, it's very important to lie down for a while. It gives your body a chance to rest after such a tough workout."

Anu's eyes widened. She bit her tongue. *Tough workout?* Yoga was never intended to be a tough workout; it was to prepare one's body for meditation.

Anu raised her hand, and after a moment, Alexa stopped singing.

"Thank you, class. You may stay seated, and I can take questions."

Anu remained upright, her hand high.

"Yes?" Alexa flexed her palm against the guitar strings. "What's your question?"

"I wanted to know more about the song you're singing right now."

Alexa stiffened. "How about I tell you all about it when you take my seminar?"

Anu narrowed her eyes as she picked her mat up off the floor. So she had "impressed" Alexa enough to be allowed to take the seminar?

"I think we're all curious, though," Anu continued, and a few others in the class nodded as they, too, sat up from their mats. Alexa's face was getting redder, but she kept her cool as she set her guitar to the side.

"I'm singing 'Om Jai Jagdish.' It's a mantra. Can I continue now?"

"I thought it was a hymn."

"Mantra . . . hymn. Potato, patato."

"Sorry, no. A mantra is chanted to prepare the body for meditation. What you're 'singing' is a religious hymn that Hindus *only* sing during *aarti*, a *pooja* where we offer light to our dieties." She gestured to the stereotypically Hindu artifacts plastered around the practice room. "So I'm thinking I'll skip the seminar. Thanks. I'm not a big fan of potatoes."

Anu heard a giggle behind her, and she snuck a look. It was another woman about Anu's age, also of South Asian heritage. The woman gave her a discreet thumbs-up, and Anu smiled in return, her head held high as she walked out of the room.

Old Anu, always so sweet and polite, would have never called out somebody else's bullshit. Jenny and Monica would have been proud of her. Hell, Anu was proud of herself.

Suddenly deflated, Anu realized that her mother would have been proud of her, too. Lakshmi had been the one to introduce her to yoga. Anu had resisted for years, rolling her eyes whenever Lakshmi meditated or prayed or practiced yoga in the corner of the living room, where she'd set up a small shrine. Lakshmi had never forced her beliefs on Anu or insisted she come to temple or pressured Anu to join her for a yoga class.

One day it simply clicked. Anu had found it on her own.

I t was dark outside by the time she took the London Overground back to her hostel, her train car crowded with merry, tipsy Londoners on their way to or from some Christmassy thing or another.

Maybe it was time to leave. Time to travel somewhere new. Surely, she could find a yoga retreat somewhere in Italy, maybe in Greece. It had been less than a week, and she couldn't go home yet, could she? She couldn't go home without having accomplished any of the things she'd come here for.

Her dorm room was messy and, yet again, entirely empty. She'd found the female-only hostel on TripAdvisor, and although her roommates seemed like fun from the belongings they kept on leaving everywhere, Anu had barely even seen them. Anu was always fast asleep by the time they stumbled home, and in the morning—Anu up and ready before nine a.m., her shoulder bag packed for a day of sightseeing—they were still passed out cold in their bunk beds.

And so all week Anu had done London on her own. She ate

mouthwatering masala prawns and black dal at the bar in Dishoom. She walked the South Bank and wandered the streets of East London taking photographs of the vintage shops and graffiti, spent way, way too much buying the clothes all the fashionable Londoners seemed to wear. She went to all the sights, the museums, the tours—and after nearly a week, there was still more to do.

The bed just beside hers was typically littered with clothes, books, makeup, and bottles of cheap neon-colored bottles of conditioner. Anu turned to her own bed, which was perfectly made. Her backpack and belongings were neatly folded into the locker beneath her bed.

Anu had all but told her parents and Neil to screw off, and at the age of thirty, she was traveling and living life like everyone else seemed to.

Still, she didn't know how to be like these other girls. She hadn't even met them.

Tomorrow was Christmas Eve, and Anu would yet again be alone. Everything would shut early, the hostel receptionist had said. London would turn into a ghost town, and she'd find herself back here at the hostel with nothing to do. No one to spend the day with. Her parents hadn't called her, and what would it say if she called them first, that she was happy for them to continue running her life?

She swirled into a pool of pity when she remembered she did know someone. Theo. Hazily, she tried to recall their conversation—him utterly charming, disarming, while Anu sat there doe-eyed and took it all in. She felt silly wondering, but maybe he wanted to see her again. She pulled out her phone and clicked on his contact details; he'd saved them in her phone while they were still in bed that morning. Didn't he live close? She could have sworn he said he lived in East London.

"There you are. We keep missing each other."

Blinking, Anu looked up. It was one of the girls from her dorm, the one she'd seen sleeping in the messy bottom bunk just opposite. "Hey."

"It's Marianne. What's your name again?"

"Anu." She smiled "From Canada."

"Kiwi over here," she said, just as Anu was about to guess out loud that her accent was Australian. She sat down next to Anu. "What are you doing? Texting a guy, are we?"

Laughing, Anu set her phone down on the bed. "I was thinking about it."

"Tell him to come out with us." A comb appeared from the floor, and Anu watched Marianne as she teased the back of her thick black hair. "You should change. We're leaving in twenty."

"Leaving for where?"

Marianne threw her a glance as she grabbed a bottle of hair spray from the sideboard. "Where do you think?"

Anu glanced at the clock on the wall. It was getting late, and she hadn't eaten dinner or decided where she was going the next day. She was exhausted from her day of sightseeing, shopping, and yoga, but then again, she didn't want to be alone, either.

"Text him. Come on," the girl said as if they were best friends. The familiarity of it made Anu smile. "You can bring him back here. We won't even watch."

Anu laughed, grabbed her phone. "I don't know. It was a one-time thing—"

"So make it a two-time thing."

Anu hesitated as she watched Marianne peel herself from the bed and scrounge through the pile of clothes on the floor between them.

It would be nice to see him again, wouldn't it? To be close to someone? To share London with *someone*?

ANUSHA: Hi, Theo. It was great meeting you the other night! I'm staying in Shoreditch. Would you like to get together??

Get together.

The words sounded so lame, like she was setting up one of Kanika's playdates, but she didn't know how else to imply what she meant. She typed and retyped the text, and then without thinking about it anymore, she pushed SEND. Marianne ushered her to hurry up, and so she dragged herself off the bed and dug through some of the purchases she'd made in Soho the evening before. A coat very similar to the one she'd seen on Marianne's bunk earlier that week. Boots with laces and all sorts of nylons and tights with interesting patterns and colors. A skirt so short Anu doubted even Jenny would wear it. Tops that looked like dishrags on the hanger but surprisingly managed to narrow Anu's waist and hips.

"That one," Marianne said as Anu pulled on a slinky red shirt. "With the skirt, the boots. I *love* it. I love it so much, I kind of hate you."

Anu laughed, not sure if she was being serious. She didn't have time for foundation, and so turning to the mirror on the back of the dorm door, she went heavy on the eye makeup and then picked out dark pink lipstick.

"Perfect," she heard Marianne say as Anu reached again for her eyeliner. "Ready?"

Anu nodded and quickly dabbed a touch of black eyeliner behind her right ear. When she turned around, Marianne was staring at her intently.

"What was that for?"

Anu hesitated, reaching for her coat and purse. "It was nothing. You'll think I'm crazy."

"I'll think you're crazy if you *don't* tell me."

She followed Marianne out of the dorm and down the hall. "It's something I've picked up from my mom. A superstition." She glanced over, wondering why she felt the need to say all this—explain herself—to a perfect stranger. "A black mark is an imperfection, or so she thinks. It wards off the evil eye."

Marianne snorted a laugh. "Is there someone out to get you?"

Anu didn't respond as they continued down the corridor, past the Italian guy asleep at the front desk who had checked Anu in earlier that week. She snuck a look at her phone. Theo hadn't texted back.

"It's kind of like the story about the black cat," Marianne added. "We're not supposed to let it cross our path, right?"

Anu laughed. "Right."

What was Lakshmi doing at that very moment? Anu imagined her hunched over her textbook by the fire as Kunal—who seemed to be the one cooking now that Lakshmi was back in school—made a simple dinner of dal and rice. Did it feel like a holiday without her there?

"Are there more?" she heard Marianne say. She sounded interested, not dismissive like Ryan had been when she had explained the superstition.

"A few." They stopped short outside the door to the common room, which muffled the rowdy sounds inside. "We're not supposed to touch our feet to books or paper, out of respect. Taking or giving anything in threes is unlucky. Um, what else? Oh, don't open only one eye in the morning—whatever that's supposed to mean. If you shake your leg, you'll lose money—"

"That's a harsh one."

Anu nodded. "And my mom also used to do this . . . thing . . . every Tuesday and Saturday night to ward off the evil eye. Or, as she calls it, *nazzar.*"

"What sort of thing?"

"Well, we'd stand around the stove. She'd put chili and mustard seeds and salt in her hands and do this"—Anu moved her wrist in small circles—"over the flame, and then *blow* on us."

Anu watched Marianne's face, which remained stony, transfixed on the door. What was she thinking, saying all that to her? Someone outside of her culture?

"Anyway," Anu ventured, pedaling out her feet, "should we get the others?"

Blinking, Marianne nodded. She moved to open the door and then stopped. "It sounds like your mom is doing everything in her power to protect you."

Taken aback, Anu could only shrug.

"Wanna know what my mom does?" Marianne laughed as she pushed on the door. "She buys me condoms."

Marianne chose a club on Redchurch Street, and everyone followed. There was a group of them, and Marianne introduced them so quickly, Anu barely had a chance to learn their names. There were three women from Brazil, two from South Africa, and another from Sweden. Anu was the only one who wasn't drunk already, and she half-wondered whether she should be for this. They were all so *young*. But then how did they project such confidence?

How did they charge through the streets, arms linked and voices high, like they had the authority to be there?

Anu was at the back of the group as they waited in line, and so she was the last to pay the cover charge, have her bag searched, and check her coat. She was surprised by how long it took to get in, the level of security—especially considering the club wasn't even that full. She walked into what appeared to be the main area, lit up with blue and green strobe lights, black leather booths circling an empty dance floor.

Had they ditched her? There were a few people by the bar, and so she headed in that direction, adjusting to the low light. Out of the corner of her eye, she spotted one of the South African girls walk into the restroom, and she relaxed, shifting her purse to her other shoulder.

OK, they hadn't ditched her.

As she moved farther into the club, she realized how big it was, and she appeared to be on one of several levels. She didn't have to use the restroom, so she picked a spot by the edge of the dance floor near the bar—where everyone would surely see her when they came out.

Nobody was dancing, but that didn't surprise her. The music— if you could call it that—was god-awful. Pulsing, whiny techno that made her feel like an extra in a sci-fi movie. She checked her phone. Theo hadn't texted her back, and it hit her that he wasn't ever going to. In retrospect, she didn't even like him that much; he was conceited and had talked only about himself. Still, she couldn't help but feel like a fool.

As she waited for the others, she checked Instagram, once in a while flicking her eyes toward the restroom, but the girls seemed to be taking their time. She refreshed her feed, and her stomach dropped as a new photo appeared, posted just a minute earlier by Tina, one of the moms in Kanika's class.

It was a photo of Kanika and a dozen other kids, posed in front of the backdrop Anu had built for the holiday concert. *Of course*. It was still afternoon in Vancouver, and the day of the concert. Right now the concert would be over, and they'd be back in Kanika's classroom, the kids hopped up on the sugar they were never allowed to eat on a regular school day. All the parents would be there, too. Some grandparents. The art table by the window would be covered in the large snowflake tablecloth Anu had bought at a craft sale that fall and gifted to Ms. Finch. It would be covered by juice and water and coffee, a potluck of treats and desserts and savory snacks.

Neil would have left work early to go, picking up Priya along the way. Would he remember to take photos? Was Kanika asking where she was? The curiosity bit at her, pulling at her skin until she felt a shiver run up from her arm and down her spine.

"India or Pakistan?"

Anu looked up, startled. She hadn't noticed being approached, the beefy guy in the thin white T-shirt creeping up next to her and setting his hand on her wrist. She recoiled away from him and crossed her arms.

"India or Pakistan, love?" he repeated, smirking. "Usually, I can tell."

"*Excuse* me?" She was tempted to tell this asshole she was from Canada, and because of Partition instigated by *his* bloody ancestors, her family was from both present-day India and Pakistan.

"You should smile more," the guy said, still smirking. "And tuck that phone away. You'll have better luck."

She rolled her eyes and couldn't contain a sigh. Without saying anything, she turned to walk away, but he grabbed her again by the wrist.

"Don't touch me," she said, whipping around, jerking her arm away.

"Doll, come on. The jig's up." He laughed, leering at her. "Where's your boss?"

"What?"

"No boss. Is that right, hun?" He tried to sidle in closer, and again Anu inched farther away. "I could be your boss."

"Look, you're making me uncomfortable," Anu said, summoning her courage. "I need you to leave, or I will."

"Babe, I mean no offense—"

"Do *not* call me 'babe.'"

"This is business. I'm all business—you'll figure me out in no time, love. What's your rate?"

He stared at her again, and because of the way his eyes fell on her bare arms and chest, the slight snarl of his nose and lips, something clicked.

"If you come work for me, I'll make sure you get double."

And then the reality came crashing down around her.

He was a pimp and thought she was a *prostitute*.

Fuming, she pushed his hand away again. Her face was hot, and she wanted to punch him because of the way he was sneering at her.

"You're a dick." She could hear her voice crack as she shouted at him over the music. "A complete dick—you know that?"

"There aren't many that look like you." He drew his tongue across his teeth. "Really, where are you from . . . ?"

He trailed off just as Anu felt a pinch on her arm and then spotted Marianne's jet-black hair off to the side.

"*There* you are," Marianne said loudly, eyeing the guy. "Who the hell are you?"

The guy hesitated, his eyes skirting between Anu and Marianne.

"*He* is leaving," Anu said, shooting daggers at him with her eyes. "Or I'm going to get security."

The guy scoffed at her as he hulked back to the bar.

"What was that about?" Marianne asked her after he left.

Anu could feel all the blood rushing to her head. Was she crying? It felt like it. Her chest was heavy, and she couldn't bring herself to say out loud what had just happened.

"Anu, what is it?"

Was it because she had been standing alone in a club? The way she was dressed? The revealing neckline, the bare arms, the skirt so short it could have been underwear? Of course she had the right to dress that way. She could wear whatever she damn well wanted. But what right did he have to approach her like that? Make those judgments? Say those disgusting things?

"What—"

"Nothing." Anu met Marianne's eye. "It was nothing. Please, drop it."

"OK." Marianne looked taken aback and, a beat later, grabbed her by the hand. "We're upstairs. Come with me."

Hand in hand, Anu let Marianne lead her upstairs. There was a second level full of tables, only half-full, and then a third. Another DJ up here played "music" similar to that below, and there were even more strobe lights. Here, the dance floor was full, and she spotted the rest of the group at the far edge. Among them was the South African girl who she had seen go into the bathroom; Anu must have missed her coming out.

The scene looked exhausting. The high heels and collared shirts and cheap cologne and throbbing music. The blank expressions. The fog machine.

They weren't in the eighth grade. They weren't at a fucking Rihanna concert.

And for God's sake, it was *Christmas*.

Anu tugged on Marianne's hand at the top of the stairs, stopping short.

Did Kanika mind that she wasn't around for the holidays, and did Neil remember to buy her the Lego set she'd wanted for Christmas, which Anu hadn't had a chance to purchase yet?

Would she be celebrating the holiday with Priya, Neil, and Ms. Dirty Messages?

"Look," Anu said, staring at the ground. The confidence, even the calmness, she'd felt after yoga had completely dissipated. "This isn't really my night."

"Whatever that guy said, fuck him."

Anu shook her head. "It's not just that."

The lump in her throat was growing, constricting her breathing. She was in London. She was here, finally here, so why was she still missing out? Why did playing this part feel so wrong, too?

She felt Marianne's hand in hers, and the simplicity and kindness of the gesture made her want to cry. Anu wondered if Marianne, who was as far away from New Zealand as it was possible to be, ever felt alone. If she ever missed her family.

"You're sad."

It wasn't an accusation or a judgment. Just a fact. Anu nodded. She was sad. The pictures she'd snapped of perfect London were nothing like the memory she'd carry.

This London, the one she was living in—it was lonely. And it didn't love her back.

"Here," Marianne said, pulling her away from the light. In the corner, she reached into her bra and slyly pulled something out.

There, their backs to the dance floor, Marianne opened her hand. In it were two white pills, unimposing, no more than the size of an aspirin. Marianne discreetly popped one into her mouth and then glanced at Anu.

"What is it?"

Shrugging, Marianne pressed the remaining pill into her hand. "You want to be happy, don't you?"

Anu *did* want to be happy. It was the reason she had always tried to please her parents. Why she followed her heart and married Neil at the age of twenty-three. Why, years later, she had left him and was now taking over a yoga studio.

And it was the reason she was standing here right now. To find that sense of happiness that had always eluded her, hovering, reminding her of the youth she'd never had. The memories she never got to make.

The pill was heavy in her palm, whatever it was. Maybe it would make her happy. It would be a reprieve, an escape. Maybe everything she'd wanted London to be.

But she pressed it back into Marianne's palm because it wouldn't be the answer.

chapter twenty

MONICA: Hey . . . your phone must be on silent. Anu, call us ASAP.

Back in the dorm room, she crawled under the covers fully clothed, her makeup still intact. Rolling to the side, she was almost surprised to find the cold concrete wall—and not Neil nor Kanika nestled in beside her. Warm limbs like hot water bottles beneath the sheets. The smell of Neil's deodorant. Kanika's pineapple shampoo. Crumbs on the pillow because Neil loved to eat his toast in bed.

He hadn't texted her back after she'd asked about Kanika's school play. She'd missed it. And for what? For *this*? To attend some terrible yoga class? Get hit on in a bar? Fall asleep on the bottom bunk of a dorm room?

She kicked her cold feet against the wall. What was she doing here? What kind of woman left her whole life behind on a lark?

Something vibrated by her elbow. It was Monica calling, and surprised by the outreach, Anu answered.

"Hey," Monica said. She was wearing a gray sweatshirt she'd had since high school. "Jenny's here, too."

Half of Jenny's sunburned forehead materialized on her phone. "Anu, hey."

"Hey, guys." Glancing at the tiny image of herself in the top-right corner of her phone, Anu dried her cheek with her sleeve, hoping they wouldn't notice, but the eye makeup spread harshly down her cheek. "How was Chile?"

"Good, thanks . . ." Jenny trailed off, and Monica readjusted the frame, until both of them were there sitting side by side. They were at Monica's house in the suburbs, at the kitchen table the three of them had picked out together at HomeSense, right after Tom and Monica had moved in. There was a bottle of sparkling water and a bag of the expensive organic salt and vinegar chips they all loved open on the table.

If she had stayed, she wouldn't have been alone. Even if Kanika was at Neil's, at least she could have been with them.

"I'm sorry for leaving so suddenly the way I did, you guys. It wasn't right. I haven't been myself," Anu said suddenly, the words pouring out of her.

"I tried calling earlier," Monica said, leaning into the screen. "We need to talk."

Anu nodded. "We do. I know you guys are mad at me—"

"It's not that, Anu. . . . Neil called. Priya Auntie started having chest pains during the holiday concert. Jenny picked Kanika up from school and brought her here, and Neil took Priya in. . . ."

"To her doctor?"

Monica shook her head. "The emergency room."

Anu's heart dropped. Priya was in the emergency room? Was she having a heart attack?

She cringed thinking about the last time she had seen Priya, sitting at the kitchen table right before Anu stormed off without saying goodbye. Would that be their last conversation? The last time she was ever going to see the woman who had treated her like a daughter for more than a decade?

Anu shook her head, panicking. *No.* No, she couldn't think like that. Priya would be fine. Maybe she wasn't the healthiest or the most active, but she was only in her mid-fifties. For Christ's sake, she was younger than Anu's parents.

"Do you understand what I'm saying, Anu?" Monica's voice startled her. "You need to come home—"

"Mon, no," Jenny snapped, pulling the screen toward her until only she was in view. "Anu, you don't need to do anything, all right? You're sick of people telling you what to do, what's right—blah, blah, blah. And if you come home because you *need* to, pretty soon you're going to be fed up again and then fuck right off. Who knows, maybe for good."

Anu paused, trying to register what Jenny was trying to say.

Monica pulled the screen slightly back, until only half of each of their faces were in the frame.

"Yeah, I guess Jenny's right," Monica said, although she didn't sound like she believed it. "Everything's in control here. And you know, Kanika loves us. We're fine. It's all . . . fine."

But everything wasn't in control. It wasn't *fine.*

Anu shivered as she imagined Neil at the hospital in the waiting room by himself while the doctors tended to Priya. He hated hospitals. He hated the smells, like iodine and laundry detergent, and the almost blue fluorescent lights. His knees went weak at the sight of blood, at a realistic operating room scene on *Grey's Anatomy.*

Was Tom with him? Auntie Jayani, Priya's best friend?

Ms. Dirty Messages?

And what did Kanika think was going on? Did she understand that her Dadima was sick? And that her mother had left?

"Where is she?"

"In the other room. We're watching *Mulan*."

The movie was decades old now, the graphics dim and outdated, yet Kanika would climb onto Anu's lap anytime they had watched it, and with her small, warm hands clasped around the back of Anu's neck, she'd shake in equal parts excitement and fear whenever the villain Shan Yu appeared on-screen.

"This is my favorite movie," Anu had whispered.

Wide-eyed, Kanika turned to the screen. "Then it's my favorite, too," and for more than a year, it had been.

The tears welled up, and they wouldn't stop. She wanted to be Imogen or Marianne or any other young girl with an infinite list of choices before her, but the truth was, Anu had only two: She could stay, pounding her fists and grinding her teeth through the pain, forcing herself to experience life the way others seemed to live it, or she could go back to her real life.

"I don't need to come home," Anu said, quietly grieving for the woman she never got to be, maybe, or never could be. "I want to."

chapter twenty-one

ANUSHA: Hi, Mom and Dad. Merry Christmas. I just landed
back in Vancouver. Priya Auntie is experiencing some chest
pains and so Neil has taken her to the hospital to be safe.
Please try not to worry. I'll be home in a few hours with
Kanika if you want to call.

She didn't realize how packed the airport could be on Christmas Eve. Every flight to Vancouver was completely booked up,
but she managed to get on a flight to Newark the following afternoon, and then a connecting one to Vancouver. She landed at two
a.m. on Christmas Day, and a forty-five-minute taxi ride later, she
arrived at Monica and Tom's house in Surrey. They had mounted
red and blue twinkle lights above the garage and around all the
windows, and there was a silver Christmas tree on the porch,
sparsely decorated with fake snow and ornaments Anu didn't recognize.

Taking a deep breath, she lugged her suitcase up the steps to
the front porch, and Monica's face appeared in the doorway just as
Anu raised her left hand to knock.

"It's OK. She's stable," Monica said immediately, letting her in.
"But she needs surgery."

Anu dropped her bag without meaning to.

Surgery?

"It's called an angioplasty. It's noninvasive, but she'll be in the hospital a while." Monica picked up her bag and led her inside. Once the door was closed, Monica threw her arms around her.

The physical contact was overwhelming. Anu cleared her throat and gently pulled away. "How's Neil holding up?"

"Tom went in for a while to keep him company, but he said Neil didn't seem to want him there."

Anu nodded. "I'm sure he didn't. Neil doesn't handle this kind of stuff well. He shuts down."

She followed Monica into the kitchen. Jenny sat at the kitchen table, picking at a store-bought gingerbread house.

"Hi, Jen."

"Hi." Jenny smiled at her, met her gaze. "Kanika's sleeping."

"Maybe let her sleep," Monica said as they joined Jenny at the table. "It took a lot to tire her out."

Anu smiled at the half-collapsed, half-eaten gingerbread house. She knew exactly which parts her daughter had decorated. She reached for a chunk of the roof that was a mash of red and green icing, Smarties, and sprinkles and popped it into her mouth.

"Thank you." She smiled at her friends, but she couldn't look them in the eye. "For all of this. For stepping in when I . . ." The tears formed, and both Jenny and Monica slid closer toward her on their chairs. "I don't deserve you guys. I really don't."

"Oh, quit being dramatic. You do, too, deserve us." Jenny pulled away and then Monica. "And even though you've been a pain in the ass lately—"

"Jenny!" Monica exclaimed.

"—we're going to be here for you as you figure this all out."

Jenny's smile turned into a giggle, and Anu smiled in return.

"We've all had pain-in-the-ass stages," Monica said. "Remember that summer Jenny counted her calories and by extension *ours?*"

Anu smiled. "I hated Jenny that summer."

"Remember when Monica first started dating Tom, and we barely heard from her for, like, *six* months?" Jenny asked.

Monica slapped Jenny's arm, and for a moment, it was like it was before.

"Still, I'm truly sorry about the way I left. I don't know . . . I don't know what happened. I still don't understand it all."

"We know, Anu."

They smiled at her, smiles of true friendship and forgiveness.

"Look who's awake," Jenny said quietly, and her tone made Anu spin in her chair, and her heart skipped a whole beat.

D o you have enough Magic Markers, sweetie?"

Kanika nodded as she pressed furiously into the paper with a blueberry-scented marker. A moment later, she set it down and reached for a yellow pipe cleaner.

"Glue?"

"Nope," Kanika said, forcing its wiry end into the corner of the page. "I'm going to braid it in!"

The morning had come and gone, and back at their own house, Anu had laid out everything in their craft closet on the kitchen table. It was Monica's suggestion that Anu pass the time with Kanika making get-well-soon cards while they waited for Priya to get out of surgery. Something to occupy their minds.

Anu painted a smile on her face and tried to keep herself animated, but Kanika was quiet and more interested in her art project than in talking to her mother. Anu knew she should say something, anything, about the situation. That she needed to explain what had happened and why Anu had disappeared the past week, put into words something a five-year-old could understand and deserved to hear.

I'm sorry for leaving you.

Was that how to start it? She was sorry. But how could she make her understand that while Anu was sorry for leaving *her*, she wasn't sorry for leaving. She had needed to leave. That trip—whatever it was—Anu had *needed* it.

Her phone buzzed on the table, and Anu lunged for it when she saw Neil's name and face appear. She had taken that picture of him at Kanika's third-birthday party. He had been dressed up like a dinosaur, his face painted a bright green. After the separation, she had never bothered to change it.

"Hi . . ." She quietly slipped into the dining room, sliding the glass door behind her. "Neil, how are you? How's . . . ?"

"It's so nice to hear your voice, Anush."

Her chest hurt as they let the silence hang there. He didn't answer the question, and for a moment, all she could hear was him breathing and she could picture him there, slouched in a bland, barren waiting room chair, his right leg shaking. Fleetingly, she was there, too. She was holding him. She was there for him, and his burden was her burden. His pain—it was hers, too.

"Neil . . . I—"

"How's Kanu?" he interrupted.

She realized she had been holding her breath. "She's fine. We're home."

"The surgery is scheduled for tomorrow morning. The doctors have been in and out all afternoon. I . . ." He trailed off. He was incapable of saying anything else, and she knew better than to press him.

"Have you eaten?" she asked finally. When he didn't respond, she continued. "Please, eat something, Neil. Can I bring you dinner? A change of clothes? Anything?"

"I'm fine. No." She could hear him pacing now, something vague and intimidating beeping in the background. "You're home. You're with Kanu—that's all I need."

It wasn't all he needed. It couldn't be. Neil was in pieces, falling apart with every second Priya was lying in that hospital bed. She wanted to insist, pry her way into the situation further, show up at the hospital with an armload of things he wouldn't even need, and hold Neil so he didn't feel so alone. But that wasn't her place anymore. And didn't he have a woman in his life now? That was *her* place.

"I'm not sure how long Kanu will have to stay with you. Her school backpack and snowsuit are at my house. You'll have to—"

"I will—"

"The key is under—"

"Neil, I know. Please, don't worry about anything else right now."

Was Ms. Dirty Messages holding his hand right now? Making sure he ate, slept, and showered? Gritting her teeth until his soon-to-be ex-wife got off the phone? Anu was struck with a pang of jealousy and then felt terrible about it. She had no right to be jealous, and overwhelmingly she had the urge to hang up the phone.

"So you'll tell me if you need anything? And keep me updated on how Mom's doing?"

He was silent, and she realized that once again she'd slipped up. That she'd called Priya "Mom."

"Give Kanika a big hug for me," he said quietly before hanging up. "From me and Mom."

Five minutes later, Anu returned to the kitchen and found Kanika hunched over her greeting card. She sat up startled, smiling, and Anu noticed that she'd glued some of the popcorn they'd been eating—warm, buttery—onto its surface.

"Was that Daddy on the phone?"

"It was." Anu pulled out the chair closest to her and sat down. Kanika sat forward on her seat.

"Is Dadima going to die?"

Anu didn't have an answer for the question, although she was tempted to blurt out no to calm her own nerves rather than her daughter's.

The year before, Kanika had come home asking questions about death after her friend's grandfather had passed away. The simple fact that something—anything—could happen and change everything, wreak havoc on the normal, and turn consistency to chaos had been just beyond her grasp at the time. Anu explained to her that death, that people sometimes leave and never return, was the reason she'd never met her other grandfather—Neil's dad, whom she would have called Dada or Dadaji, if he were alive.

At the time Kanika had been satisfied by the answer and distracted by the neighbor's cat prowling on the back fence; she'd scampered to the window to watch it.

It was different now, of course. Kanika was older, would be six in the spring, and it wasn't just a nameless, anonymous human who was leaving the world—it was quite possibly her grandmother.

Kanika's eyes were wide as she looked up at Anu. They were searching her, even testing her, and Anu let the weight of it press her firmly into the chair.

If Priya wasn't sick, if Monica and Jenny hadn't called, would she have come home? Would she have spent Christmas in a hostel? Would she have turned up at one of London's four airports, pointed at the departures screen, and said *that*. She'd go there. She'd take *that* life?

"Is she, Mommy?" Kanika whispered. "Is she going to die?"

Reaching for Kanika's hand, Anu tried to imagine what Lakshmi would have said to her in a moment like this.

Lakshmi was never one for confrontation, for tension or discomfort. She never spoke of sex, safety, and relationships because she didn't know how, and she never knew of Anu's innermost thoughts and adolescent fears because she didn't know what questions to ask.

Like continents, the generation between them had drifted until they were miles apart, and the only way to cross was by a lie. Anu omitted all truths that Lakshmi wouldn't approve of while her mother picked and chose what she wanted to see.

Anu loved her mother, missed her more than she could express—but she didn't want to be her. She wouldn't ever put up a wall between herself and her daughter.

"Do you remember that song in *The Lion King*?" Anu said, shuffling closer to Kanika. "About how dying is part of the circle of life?"

The Disney reference semed to have disarmed Kanika, and her shoulders visibly relaxed.

"Everybody will die one day, sweetie. But I don't think it's Dadima's time. Not yet."

Was it the right thing to say? Was she *too* honest? She couldn't tell. Kanika wasn't giving anything away.

"It's not her time, Kanu, because there's still so much for her to do, so much to see—"

"Like my dance recital this summer?"

Anu beamed, squeezed Kanika on the arm. "Like your dance recital. And what else?"

"My birthday party?" Kanika climbed out of her chair and onto Anu's lap. "She has to come to my birthday party."

"All your birthday parties, Kanu." Anu wrapped her arm around her daughter. "She wants to see you grow up and go to your first school dance—"

Kanika giggled.

"—and she'll tease you when you have your first *kiss*!"

Kanika threw her head back, laughing, and one of her pigtails hit Anu on the mouth. "I will *never* kiss anybody but you and Daddy." She paused, mulling this over. "And Nani and Nanaji and Dadima. And *maybe* Auntie Monica."

"What about Auntie Jenny?"

"I guess Auntie Jenny. But I don't like that shiny stuff on her cheeks."

Anu smiled, twirling the pigtail in her fingers. "Mark my words, Kanu. One day you'll want to kiss somebody, and when that happens, we're going to tease you"—she tickled Kanika's ribs until she squealed—"*so* much!"

Kanika tickled her back, and pretty soon they were chasing each other around the house and up and down the stairs. Later, side by side, they fell breathless on the living room floor. Her daughter's chest rising and falling as she chattered at the empty room—about what, Anu had no idea—she watched her. Studied her. Fell in love with her beautiful, spirited daughter for the millionth-and-a-half time.

This was her life. And now, for the first time, she could understand why she so desperately had wanted to be home: She couldn't imagine a life anywhere else.

chapter twenty-two

LAKSHMI: I do not understand why you are not letting me come home to help. I can finish classes online. Beti, this is difficult time for you—many balls on your plate!

KUNAL: Your mother has mixed metaphors. She means too many balls in the air OR too many things on your plate.

ANUSHA: Mom, really, you don't need to come home—I can manage!

LAKSHMI: You must correct my English, dear husband, while I am sitting next to you in bed?

How come *I* have to drink apple juice?" Kanika pouted. "I want what you're having."

"You want some wine?" Jenny held out her glass. "Go ahead. Try it."

Kanika eyed it suspiciously, leaning in. Her face hovering just above the glass, she sniffed hard and then made a face that sent Anu, Jenny, and Monica into a fit of laughter.

"*Eww.* Grown-ups drink that on *purpose?*"

"They sure do."

Kanika sighed sarcastically, imitating the way Jenny often did. "I don't understand grown-ups."

Anu had promised her daughter she could stay up until midnight, but as expected, Kanika was fast asleep on the living room floor hours before the New Year. After putting her to bed, Anu grabbed another bottle of wine from the fridge and settled in next to her friends on the couch.

"Cheers," she said, toasting them. "To a brand-new year of . . ."

"Friendship," said Jenny

"Family," added Monica.

"And . . . forgiveness?" Anu smiled at each of them in turn, and they nodded, clanging their wineglasses against hers.

"Imogen didn't want to come?" Monica asked. "I was excited to meet her."

"No offense, but if I was twenty-one, I wouldn't want to spend New Year's with three thirty-year-olds and a baby, either."

"Kanika's almost six, Jen," Anu said.

"If it's too young to drink, it's a baby."

"It?"

"You know who was too young to drink . . ."

"Ha-ha. I made out with a teenager. Get a new joke, Mon." Anu winked at her. "And don't worry. You'll meet Imogen soon. At yoga. This week, maybe?"

"Yoga . . . ," Jenny groaned.

Imogen had seemed interested in coming over for New Year's, but then had canceled at the last minute without giving a reason, despite Anu's insistence that she wouldn't be intruding.

Anu had seen Imogen a few times already since coming home, preparing for reopening the studio at the kitchen table while Kanika played in the other room.

Scheduling. Payrolls. *Budgeting.* These were foreign concepts Anu had never thought about when agreeing to take over the damn place. And it didn't help that she had blown through more of her savings than she'd expected in London. Eating out. Roaming charges. Two last-minute flights. That Oxford Street shopping spree, on which she'd spent more than she'd ever admit on clothing she'd never have the courage to wear out in Vancouver.

She and Neil had always been money conscious, frugal even, yet that month Anu would barely make her half of the mortgage payment. She would have to dip into her savings account to pay her bills, and it was Anu's turn to pay Kanika's monthly fees for swimming and dance lessons. Kanika had grown several inches since the year before, and soon she would need new sneakers and a raincoat, a whole new wardrobe of summer clothes. Of course Neil would want to pay half as his share, but he was a contractor, and with Priya sick, he would be on unpaid leave indefinitely. She couldn't ask him now. She *wouldn't* ask him.

Without even crunching the numbers, Anu knew she couldn't afford any of the updates and renovations she and Imogen had dreamed about. All of it would have to wait. They would have to reopen the studio that week without changing a thing.

Imogen had turned surly when hearing the news, prompting Anu to think that her disappointment was the reason she had skipped out on New Year's. But she couldn't help but wonder if it was something else. Anu kept having this nagging, clawing feeling that Imogen was going through something. But whenever Anu tried to get personal, or even asked her how she was feeling that day, Imogen would laugh or make a joke and then change the subject. Typically aloof, Imogen had even been vague when Anu asked her about her own Christmas holiday with her family. Had she brought Haruto? Was she close to her parents? Anu knew Imogen was also an only child, but that was the extent of her knowledge on Imogen's family.

"So," Anu said, trying her best not to worry about Imogen, "what should we do tonight?"

They all looked at one another and shrugged. Usually, they didn't *do* anything when they got together. They talked. They teased. They drove one another crazy.

"We could watch a movie?" Monica ventured.

Jenny shook her head. "No. I'm not in the mood."

"Board game?"

"What are you, twelve?"

"Excuse you," Monica snapped. "Board games are super trendy. Everyone plays them—"

"Dorks—"

"Well, what do you want to do, then?" Monica threw back her wine.

After taking a big sip, Jenny laughed. "We could play Tinder."

"*Play* Tinder?" Anu asked. "Is that how you say it?"

Jenny pulled out her phone from her back pocket. "I don't know. I think I've swiped through every single guy in Vancouver."

"That can't be." Anu glanced at Monica. Neither of them had ever tried the app, and they only ever watched Jenny swipe and text from over her shoulder. "Doesn't it give you new matches every day?"

"A few, yeah. But I've been off and on Tinder since it was *invented*. I've seen everyone there is to see."

Anu and Monica looked at each other for a second, not quite sure which way to steer the conversation.

"Can you *stop*?" Jenny sat up, glaring at the both of them. "I'm not a charity case. I have *zero* problems getting dates. Hell, I have a date tomorrow."

"With who?" Anu asked.

"His name is Ahmed. I met him at the bank."

"Who meets guys at the bank?" said Monica.

Anu sat back on the floor, letting her weight fall onto her hands. "Jenny, that's who."

"You know who should be on Tinder . . . ?"

"Me?" Anu shook her head, thinking back to Theo, to— Oh, Jesus, she couldn't even remember the eighteen-year-old's name.

"Yeah, Anu. Let's do yours," Monica said. "We can help you make a profile. Well, Jenny can. I don't know what I'm doing."

"You're telling the girl who had a one-night stand less than two weeks ago to go on *Tinder*."

"Yes. I am."

"You can't punish yourself forever," Jenny said.

"After London . . . I feel like I need to calm down a bit. Tinder wouldn't be good for me right now."

"But this is harmless," Monica said. "This is about keeping your options open. It's like window-shopping."

"It'll be *fun*," Jenny said, and Anu sighed.

"Fun for you guys. I don't have time to date. I don't have time to . . . go *window*-shopping."

Over the past week, all she had time for was getting back into a routine with Kanika, checking in on Neil and Priya, and chatting with Imogen on speakerphone as they prepared to reopen the studio.

Lakshmi kept offering to come home and help out, but Anu refused. It was time to be a grown-up, and grown-ups didn't go crying to their mothers for help when life got tough. No, they figured it out for themselves. And would she even want her mother close by after what they had said to each other?

Jenny scooted off the couch and slyly grabbed Anu's phone from where it was sitting by the wine bottle. "What's your iTunes password? I'm downloading it."

"Jenny," Anu said firmly, "I said *no*."

Jenny held her stare, and Anu couldn't tell if she was upset. A beat later, Jenny turned to Monica and batted her eyelashes.

"What is it you were telling me, Mon?" Jenny looked at her quizzically. "Neil's girlfriend is *desperate* to meet Kanika?"

Anu's mouth dropped.

"Jenny," Monica whined, "you are *such* a bitch!"

"His girlfriend wants to meet *my* daughter?"

Monica threw another look at Jenny, shaking her head at her before turning to Anu. "That's what Tom heard from Neil, but I don't know if she ever actually met her because, well, it was before everything happened with Priya Auntie. . . ."

Anu glanced up the stairs. Had her daughter met this woman? Did she *like* her?

Wincing, Anu realized that even if Kanika hadn't met the woman already, one day she would. Kanika would sometime soon wake up and find that woman in her kitchen, with Neil's arm around her. Anu swallowed hard. Neil was going to marry that woman, wasn't he? He wasn't the type to fool around. If he was with her, he must really like her. Maybe he already loved her.

Anu stretched her legs out in front of her, staring at them. She could feel tears threatening, the swelling in the back of her throat. Was this how Neil had felt? Had he stopped breathing when he'd seen Anu and Ryan? When he'd imagined their life together, without *him*?

"Anu . . ." Jenny's voice. Anu looked up and saw that Jenny felt bad. Monica, too. Anu smiled, pushing past it all.

She needed to be a grown-up.

She needed to get her shit together and simply handle it.

In a few weeks, it would be a year since she and Neil had separated. The fact that their marriage was over was hardly new. What had she thought, asking Neil to move out: that they could live separately and lead separate lives, and he wouldn't move on?

Surely, by now Neil had fallen in love with Ms. Dirty Messages. The fact was a foregone conclusion, and the perfect, undoubtedly *beautiful* couple would buy a house together and get married and have babies—and hell, so could Anu if she wanted to. She could go on a thousand first dates and send her *own* dirty messages.

"How much does Tinder cost?" Anu asked, spinning toward Jenny. "I'm on a budget."

Jenny's face lit up. "It's free!"

chapter twenty-three

✿

Damien. 28 y/o. Physicist, foodie, and pheromones.

Happy New Year, Anusha! You're my first match of 2020.
Maybe it's a sign? ☺

By the time Kanika woke up, Jenny and Monica had dragged themselves home, and Anu was at the kitchen table drinking coffee, staring at a text message from Neil. Priya had finally been discharged from the hospital, and he was ready for her and Kanika to visit.

"She may want you to sit with her as she sleeps," Anu said, eyeing her daughter in the rearview mirror as they drove over to Priya's. "Is that OK?"

Kanika nodded, clutching the get-well-soon cards she'd made in her hand, crafted with everything from neon glitter to macaroni.

Priya's best friend, Auntie Jayani, was standing by her red hatchback on the driveway when they pulled in. She squinted at them, one hand shading the dull sun from her eyes. Anu couldn't remember the last time she'd seen her, from a distance—perhaps—at Priya's Diwali party. She pulled Anu in for a hug and then Kanika, and Anu remembered out of the blue that she was the reason Anu and Neil had met in the first place. More than twelve years earlier, they had met at Jayani's daughter's engagement party.

It was cold outside, so they didn't chat long, and Anu waited for Auntie Jayani to reverse off the drive and disappear around the corner before going inside. The door was unlocked, and as Kanika pulled off her boots on the front bench, Anu crossed the front foyer and peeked around the corner.

"Hey."

Neil was bent over the kitchen sink, his large hands lifting a saucepan to the dish rack. He turned at her voice. "Anush, hey."

Anu could tell that he'd been crying, and it took everything not to run to him.

A beat later she felt Kanika brush past her hip as she flung herself into Neil's arms.

Her heart hurt as she watched them together. The way Neil pushed past the fatigue right there on his face, brushed his daughter's hair behind her ears. The way he was near tears as he wrapped his arms around her shoulders.

"Should we see Dadima?"

Her get-well-soon cards pressed against her chest, Kanika nodded and followed Neil down the corridor toward the den, where Neil had set up a bed for Priya. Anu couldn't do anything but watch and, after she composed herself, finish the last two dirty dishes sitting in the sink. The rest of the kitchen was clean, as were the living room and bathrooms; Auntie Jayani must have cleaned up. Anu paced from room to room and eventually forced herself to sit down.

Her phone dinged, and she glanced at it. It was a notification from Tinder, a message from Damien, the first of several guys she had matched with the evening before after Jenny had signed her up.

She deleted the notification without reading the message; at work the next day, she knew Jenny would take the intiative to reply to it.

Jenny had been the one to write up Anu's profile and choose the photo, a selfie Jenny had taken of the two of them at Sunset Beach Park the previous summer. Anu had initially protested the selection: A pair of giant Armani sunglasses covered Anu's eyes, and she'd taken a dip in the water, so her salty, wet hair curled awkwardly around her shoulders. Meanwhile, Jenny hadn't gone into the water, so in the picture, her hair looked great.

Another notification appeared from Tinder, and again Anu swiped it away without reading it. She wondered if she'd ever be ready to be with someone new. Somebody like Neil whom she could trust and build a life with. Someone stable, and age appropriate, who respected her values and culture. Someone she could marry not because she felt pressure to but because it was what they both wanted.

Anu glanced at the end table by the window. The pictures she was looking for were still there: Anu and Neil's wedding photos. There was a montage of them: one of just Anu and Neil, standing next to each other and chastely embracing by the water in Coal Harbour. Two more of the whole family: Kunal, Lakshmi, Priya, Neil, and Anu.

Did moving forward mean letting go?

"Dadima's tired now."

Anu glanced up. Kanika and Neil were standing in the hallway, his hands secured protectively around his daughter's shoulders. He looked better. Twenty minutes with Kanika, and already he looked better.

"She'd like to see you."

"She does?"

Neil nodded, tugging on Kanika's left pigtail. "Kanu, should we have some ice cream?"

"But, Daddy, it's winter!"

Neil took her by the hand toward the kitchen. "So?"

Anu walked slowly, dragging her feet through the seventies shag that still carpeted the hallway. Several times Neil had volunteered to pay for new carpet, and Anu was never sure whether Priya genuinely liked it or was too proud to accept more help than she already did.

She'd raised Neil herself, first in Calgary—where she'd been a cashier, then a manager at the same neighborhood Safeway where she bought groceries—and then in Vancouver, after they moved so Neil could go to the university he wanted. Then she worked at one of the three clothing stores Auntie Jayani and her husband owned on Main Street until a few years earlier, when Neil paid down the last of his student debt and insisted she retire. Anu knew that she had savings and that Neil helped with the rest. It was something they had discussed early and often, even as teenagers.

"I'm going to help my mom out," he'd say over and over, and every time, she replied, "I understand," because she did understand. Priya was her mother, too.

Priya's eyes were closed when Anu walked into the room, and they didn't open as Anu sat down next to her and squeezed her hand. Her face had a gray tinge to it, and her plump features seemed entirely frail, like a tiny speck on the bed. Despite the tube of Vaseline on her pillow, Priya's lips were cracking, dry and white, and there was sleep crusted at the corners of her eyes.

Anu gently touched Priya's lips to the Vaseline. There was a washcloth on the desk, wet, and with it, she gently dabbed at the corners of Priya's eyes.

"I'm awake." A voice, soft and vulnerable. "Thank you, *beti*."

"How are you feeling?"

Priya smiled, and slowly, her eyes opened. "Like brand-new."

"You look brand-new," Anu said, smiling down at her. "Like a million dollars."

"Million dollars." Priya gently turned her head from side to side. "Maybe not. Maybe one million rupees."

Anu laughed, pulling the duvet farther up Priya's arms. "Can I get you anything?"

"*Nah.* This is all I need," Priya said. "We are all *home.*"

Anu's stomach tossed. What did Priya mean by that? Any other day, Anu's words would have been a prompt for an underhanded remark about the separation, their broken vows. But the wall Priya had put up seemed to have vanished. Staring into Priya's eyes, Anu realized how dilated they were. Vapid.

So Priya hadn't really forgiven her. She was heavily medicated.

"Yes, Auntie, we're all home."

"I spoke with your parents this morning. *Neil* spoke. I listened."

"They want to come home. They are worried about you."

"I am glad they will stay. They should make the most of England. I am all right now."

"That's what I told them, Auntie, that you would have wanted them to stay."

"England," Priya repeated, blinking hard at the ceiling. "I would have loved to visit England. . . ."

"When you're better—"

"I was supposed to go, you know." Priya's eyes were wide-open now, and they were trained straight on her. "Neil's papa. He had secured a job there when my *baccha* was newborn. He sent me a picture once, of the house." Her gaze moved back to the ceiling.

"It was so, *so* square, dark bricks, no light. But there were two whole bedrooms, *beti*. Neil was to have his *own* room."

Anu squeezed Priya's hands, trying to bring her back, wondering if she should get Neil. Did the pain medication make her like this?

"And when the letter came, it was like—like I could not believe. This could not happen to *me*, to my boy—"

"Auntie, are you feeling OK?" She scooted forward on the bed. "Do you—"

"And Jayani told me, forget him. Forget England. Even, forget *India*. I will sponsor you and Neil for Canada—"

"Auntie, your husband never lived in England. He died in India, remember? Before —"

"*Nah.*" There were tears now. Bubbling out from the corners of her eyes, pooling, before rolling down the hills of her cheeks. "There was a woman in his office. She had a very rich father."

Anu was frozen next to the bed, her hands against Priya's.

"He left. He said he would come for us, but he never came."

Anu's stomach was bubbling, churning so hard and fast, she wasn't sure she could keep her last meal down.

"It was common thing then. Our Indian men working abroad, leaving their families for some American woman. Englishwoman . . . But I never thought it would happen to me."

He *left*? Neil's father was alive?

"Aunie . . . does . . . does Neil know?"

Priya's eyes closed, and a beat later, she nodded.

chapter twenty-four

ANUSHA: Hi, Aman. I'm the new owner of Mags' Studio
(new name pending). We've recently lost a few yoga
teachers and are looking to hire. I saw your ad. What's your
rate? Call me if you're interested. Thanks.—Anusha Desai

ANUSHA: Hi, Sasha. I'm the new owner of Mags' Studio
(new name pending). We've recently lost a few yoga
teachers and are looking to hire. I saw your ad. What's your
rate? Call me if you're interested. Thanks.—Anusha Desai

ANUSHA: Hi, Jinjing. I'm the new owner of Mags' Studio
(new name pending). We've recently lost a few yoga
teachers and are looking to hire. I saw your ad. What's your
rate? Call me if you're interested. Thanks.—Anusha Desai

Facebook advertising. I'm telling you—"

"You've *told* me already."

"And Instagram. Instagram, too. It needs to be online, Anusha. You think anyone's going to see your *flyers*?"

Imogen grabbed the last stack of posters from her backpack and set them down on the desk with a thud. They'd papered all the coffee shops, grocers, college campuses, and independent shops this side of Vancouver. The paper and printing had cost two hundred dollars, and even that Anu had parted with reluctantly. But it had been over a week since they went up, three weeks since the studio had reopened, and they hadn't made a dent.

Anu didn't fully go through the paperwork before actually buying the place, and only recently had she noticed that Mags had barely broken even the year before she sold it. She paid her teachers the bare minimum someone decent would be willing to accept, and some months didn't even give herself a salary. And even though Anu had bumped up the wages for all the teachers—especially Imogen, whom she was paying a small salary to help her manage everything—several teachers have already jumped ship to other studios, disappointed that Anu's plans for a grand redesign weren't happening.

"The class sizes are just too small," some of them had said, while others hadn't even bothered to give a reason.

Every time Anu walked through the front door, she tried to remember what had prompted her to buy the studio in the first place. How she had summoned up the courage, the audacity, to run a yoga studio when she knew absolutely nothing about it.

Anu couldn't afford the aesthetic changes she had envisioned. She wanted to create something new, find her own purpose, but here she was, trying to keep afloat someone else's dream, a dream that maybe should have been converted into another hipster coffee shop.

Anu turned back to her laptop. She had already gone over with Imogen dozens of times that she couldn't afford advertising or any other changes. It would be irresponsible to deplete her family's savings for the studio; she had a mortgage and a daughter, and she could never ask Neil to take on more than his share, especially now that he was on unpaid leave indefinitely to stay home with Priya.

Priya. Anu didn't often let herself follow that train of thought, dwell on her and what she'd shared with Anu, anymore than she already had. Neil's father had left them, but he never told her. They had been together for twelve years, married for seven of them, yet he had never told her. *Why?* She didn't have the right to ask him anymore.

"Class starts in fifteen minutes," she heard Imogen say, "and no one's here."

Anu glanced at the class schedule open in her browser and noted that only five of the regulars had turned up for early-bird yoga with Imogen that morning. Mags' records—paper records, in a brown binder in the bottom drawer—showed that the mid-morning Wednesday classes typically hosted a dozen. Where *were* they?

"They'll come," Anu said decidedly. "Who's teaching today?"

"I'm here during the day, and Charlie's taking both the evening classes," Imogen said. "You're OK with her locking up?"

"Did Mags let her lock up?"

"She didn't let anyone lock up."

Anu nodded, sitting up straighter in the chair. "Well, I say it's fine. You can make her a key, tell her the alarm code. There's nothing in here anyone would steal, anyway."

"The computer?"

"Good thinking. Would you mind buying a padlock for the top desk drawer? Tell her to stick it in there. Thanks." A beat later the bell on the front door rang, and needing to stretch her legs, Anu raced to stand before Imogen. "See? Someone's here."

"I got it." Imogen stood up, too, and when they moved to brush past each other, Anu knocked her backpack off the desk. "Sorry—"

"Leave it."

They bent down at the same time to pick it up. A few things had fallen out, and Anu's hands found a scarf, a hairbrush, and then something that gave her pause.

She stood up slowly, trying not to stare at the pill bottle, but she couldn't help it. She was a nurse.

It was a prescription antidepressant.

"Sorry." She set down the bottle on the desk, averting her eyes, and Imogen quickly picked it up and stuffed it into the pocket of her hoodie.

Anu wasn't a doctor, but she knew alcohol and/or marijuana and antidepressants didn't mix well together, and in some cases could even be dangerous. Had Imogen stopped drinking and smoking? Anu hadn't seen her do either since before Christmas, but that didn't mean she wasn't. Concern rose in Anu's belly.

"I'm worried about—"

"This doesn't concern you. This is my own shit."

"I know, but . . ." But what could Anu say? This *was* Imogen's business, and she was free to share and discuss it with Anu if and how she liked, and on her own terms. But what if Imogen wasn't talking to anyone about it?

"Tonight. Why don't you come over?" Anu paused, trying to suss out Imogen's reaction. "We can just hang out and talk if—"

"It's not your place, Anusha."

"I know that. I know." She pressed her lips together. "Did your doctor—"

"Yes, I have one, and you're not her. OK?"

"OK." Anu smiled, placing her arm lightly on Imogen's forearm. "But I am your friend. So will you let me know if you change your mind? You can call me anytime, day or night, about anything. Deal?"

Imogen didn't answer, avoiding eye contact as she played with the hem of her hoodie.

"Deal?" Anu asked, and finally, Imogen nodded.

Anu volunteered to sign up the customer for the class while

Imogen changed. Leaving Imogen in the office, she rounded the corner toward the lobby, and standing there in his old newsboy cap and woolly parka was the last person she expected.

"Dad?"

He was beaming at her, and she felt like crying as she ran toward him. He held her for a moment, and the comfort of it was breaking her down. He was home. He had come to see *her*.

"Dad, what are you doing here?"

He patted her shoulder, gently pulling away from the hug. "*Aacha*, so this is the place?"

Anu shrugged, trying to see it through his eyes—the uneven walls, like parchment, the water-cracked floors. "It's a bit shabby, I know."

"Shabby or shabby *chic*?"

Anu laughed. Except for Kanika the week earlier, she'd never been so happy to see someone. "Who taught you that phrase?"

"I heard it on some British television program. No matter, it is very nice studio, Anu. I can see why you are here."

He was making an effort, she could tell. He was the business-minded one, the penny-pincher, the one who grilled Anu every year on her income tax filing, deductions, and registered retirement savings plan. The few times they'd spoken about the studio in the past few weeks, he'd held back—she assumed because he had nothing to say. A studio like this was a terrible investment. It had made no business sense, if any sense at all.

Yet he was here. He'd come all the way here.

Kunal chatted with Imogen as Anu signed in the seven students who showed up, all of them regulars. Imogen seemed taken by Kunal—his fatherly charm, his soft accent—and ended up starting the class a few minutes late. After, Anu took Kunal to a café down the road. She knew her dad would insist on paying, but still she only ordered a drip coffee with milk and nothing to eat—even though the lattes there were great, not to mention the avocado and feta on toast. . . .

"That's all? You're not on a diet, are you?" Kunal asked her after he ordered a full breakfast and chai latte. He patted his stomach. "*Beti*, bellies are very in style this year."

Anu laughed. "I already ate." She didn't bother to tell him about her new routine of not buying things she didn't need. He'd worry, and then he'd offer to lend her money; she didn't want him to do either.

Her whole life she'd taken for granted the fact that her parents were never more than a twenty-minute drive away. Forty-five, at most, with traffic. And except for the few days she'd spent in London at Christmas, this was the most she'd seen of her dad in over six months. Seeing him here, back in Vancouver, back in familiar surroundings, she realized again how much she had missed him and Lakshmi.

"How long are you here?" She was surprised by the coolness in her voice, even the fear.

The waiter arrived with his chai latte. Kunal smiled at him and, after he left, said, "I purchased a one-way ticket."

"Why?"

"Why else?" He took a sip. "You kept insisting that your mother shouldn't come to help, that she should finish her studies, and I agree." He wiped the froth on his lips. "However, you never said *I* could not come help. . . ."

She laughed. "Dad, what are you trying to say?"

"I'm saying, I am a nuisance for your mother anyway as she tries to finish this thesis of hers." He leaned forward, his eyes twinkling. "I am saying, I am still on sabbatical and can be here with you. I can be a help with . . . your life. With Kanika."

"You want to be my babysitter?"

"Why do you seem so shocked?"

"I'm . . . not." She wrapped her hands around her mug, pulling away only when the tips of her fingers started to burn. "It's just that usually Mom was the one who helped."

"So maybe it is my turn. . . ." He cleaned the grit behind his nails with another nail, wiped the end of it down with the same handkerchief he'd been using since she was a girl. "This was my idea. I wanted to come."

"Dad . . ." She felt completely overwhelmed—full of so much gratitude that she was afraid it'd get taken away, that he didn't really mean it. He would leave Lakshmi and come live with her, help her take care of Kanika? Kunal was always a mess whenever her mother wasn't around. A few times, Lakshmi had gone home to India without them—when her mother was sick, for a family wedding—and Anu would go home to find her father staring blankly at the freezer, at one of the meals of biryani or *subji* or dal that Lakshmi had spent weeks preparing and freezing ahead of her departure.

Like so many Indian men in her community, her father was incapable of functioning properly without his wife by his side. Or, at least, he used to be. Maybe people really could change.

"It's a really nice offer, but . . ."

But she needed to handle this on her own and be a grown-up, didn't she? "I took you and Mom for granted before. Priya Auntie, too. I need to do this on my own."

"*Kyon?*"

"Why do you think, Dad? I'm an adult. I need to be responsible—"

"Is accepting help from someone who loves you, in a time of need, not the adult thing to do?" He reached for her hand. "The responsible thing to do?"

"You don't have to do this," she said, even though she wanted him to. Of course she wanted him to.

"This is for you, but also for your mother, Anu. If I did not come, she would have insisted on coming herself." He paused, considering his hands as if they were artifacts to be studied. "You know, only one year before you were born, we were still living in Chandigarh. She followed me here for the job offer. She left her whole family, her friends."

Anu nodded. She knew the story.

"We didn't know anybody in Canada then. There was no family to help her when you were born. We had no money for a babysitter or day care, and so she stayed home. We always planned that she would do her master's degree one day, find a job in her field. But then, when you were older, the universities all said no."

Anu felt a tinge of guilt deep down her in her center. She thought back to her first year at university. Neil had finally asked her out, and she'd been too distracted and *in love* to ask Lakshmi why she decided to audit a few classes on politics. Anu hadn't even said hello the few times she noticed her around campus, too embarrassed by the way she sipped from her giant thermos of chai, mouthed along inaudibly to the words as she studied in the cafeteria.

"All the employers said no, too," she heard Kunal continue. "She studied political theory at college in Chandigarh, but after so many years, does anybody really care what an Indian housewife thinks about women's reproductive rights? About that *Trump*? About anything."

Her stomach churned. "Dad . . ."

"It is true. You know the halfway house where she was working once you got older? They did not pay her for the first five years. She worked so hard like that most days as volunteer. Then she was earning maybe, *maybe* the same as these young girls and boys working in this café."

"I had no idea. Why didn't she ever talk to me about this?"

"Your mother is embarrassed."

"Why?"

He smiled. "You are so brave, Anu. A successful working mother. Such *fun* and *interests* and what lovely friends! Your mother never had such opportunities. She wants you to have this modern life, to be happy. She truly does, *beti* . . . but you must understand. She—*we*— are from a different time. You must have patience as we catch up."

The hypocrisy bit at her, and sitting across from Kunal, she felt both anger and shame flush her cheeks. Why couldn't Lakshmi have sat her down and said this to her out loud?

Everything had gone unsaid, and now it was lying between them—bare and exposed—and her throat tightened, thinking of all the conversations that had slipped by. Replaced with accusing looks and judgment, sly remarks that passed quickly.

"Anu, *beti*." Kunal's hand was on hers, and she squeezed back. "I see what is on your face. You and your mother have the same temperament."

"I'm sorry, Dad. I'm sorry about how I acted in London." She let go of his hand. "I have no excuse."

"I am sorry, too." He picked up his own glass of water, as if in tribute. "Ah, I almost forgot. Your mother sent you something."

Reaching into his shoulder bag, he pulled out a plastic bag and slid it across the table. Unwrapping it, Anu found layers and layers of plastic bags, and then parchment paper, and then a bundle of dried limes, lemons, chilies, and garlic. They'd dried out; some of them were crumbling, each piece tied to the next with a piece of string.

"I told your mother we could buy here, that I need not break customs laws by bringing this into the country, but she *insisted*." He laughed, leaning in closer to look at it. "She wanted to make it herself."

Anu was about to ask what it was, but as she lifted the wreath out of its packaging, a memory slowly revealed itself. When Kunal's friend—his name, she couldn't remember—had opened an Indian restaurant in Langley, hadn't there been similar garlands across the doorway? And when Lakshmi and Priya had dragged her along to the grand opening of Auntie Jayani's newest sari shop on Scott Road, hadn't she seen wreaths of the stuff there, too?

"I know it is a silly superstition," Kunal said, "but it would make her so happy if you put it up. It will bless your new business with prosperity and keep away *nazzar*."

Anu smiled and bent down to smell the garland. Behind the sour tang, she could almost smell her mother. A bit of cinnamon, like Lakshmi had just brewed a cup of chai before she made it. Held the garland against her, for a taste of her Dior perfume.

Staring at the wreath, Anu said, "I'll hang it up today."

"These superstitions she does, these things that seem so silly— they all come from somewhere, Anu. Long ago, do you know why business owners used to hang wreaths like this?" Anu shook her head, and he continued. "It kept the insects away. It is a natural pesticide. And of course the business with no pests will flourish, *nah*?"

Anu laughed. "I guess you're right."

"Your mother . . . is your mother. I am the first to admit she is not always easy. But this, all of this, is coming from somewhere, Anu. It is coming from a good place."

chapter twenty-five

❧

DAMIEN: Hahaha that's the funniest thing I've ever heard.

ANUSHA: Are you saying you wouldn't?

DAMIEN: Are you saying you *genuinely* didn't know you were entering a wet T-shirt contest?

ANUSHA: The way I heard it, the contest was *for* a T-shirt. . . .

DAMIEN: A wet one, though?

Jenny?" Anu looked down the empty corridor. No one replied, and so she went into the break room next door. "Jenny?"

The room was empty, except for a spread of cupcakes, cookies, and squares that patients had brought in, even though Valentine's Day wasn't until the next day. She wrapped up a handful of sugar cookies for Kanika and Kunal in a tissue, popping one of the cookies into her mouth as she continued down the hall toward Jenny's office.

The weeks since her dad's arrival had passed quickly, and pretty soon it was halfway through February and the worst of winter was behind them. He had taken over the basement, or the man cave, as he liked to call it, because he and Lakshmi had rented out their own home for the year. And every morning, he insisted on preparing Kanika's lunch and driving her to school so that Anu could be on time for work at the clinic or, on her days off, be there to open the studio for the first class of the day. Most days, she even came home to him pottering around the kitchen—FaceTiming with Lakshmi while he tried out a new recipe for dinner. And Anu was grateful for him. Every day was a blessing, and she would never again take them for granted.

"I'm off," Anu said, finding Jenny at the nurses' station.

She was texting and didn't look up. "Early?"

She bit off half a sugar cookie and, her mouth full, said, "I'm taking Kanika to Neil's."

"Give me some."

Anu handed Jenny the other half of the cookie and sat down on the chair opposite Jenny. She had time to kill; Kanika had joined after-school choir on Thursdays and wouldn't be out for a while still.

"Wait," Anu said, noticing the pink phone case in Jenny's hands. "Is that my phone? When did you take it?"

"When you were in the bathroom earlier."

"That was two hours ago." Anu grabbed the phone, unsurprised to find that Jenny had been on Tinder. Anu's Tinder.

Annoyed Anu hadn't taken the initiative to use Tinder, Jenny had been stealing her phone for weeks, swiping and messaging guys of her choosing whenever they were together. Until now, Anu hadn't realized Jenny had been stealing her phone behind her back, too. She made a mental note not to leave her phone laying around during appointments.

"You have seven matches right now," Jenny said, watching Anu flick through the messages. "I've deleted a *lot*—no need to lead people on, right?"

"Right . . . So you—I mean, *I* am chatting to all of them?"

"Some more than others. A few you're still in introductory chitchat—you know, where you work, what's your favorite restaurant, that sort of thing."

"And the others?"

"The others want to meet. Damien, especially. The guy you matched with on New Year's. He's away right now visiting family, but he wants to go out with you when he's back."

Anu clicked on her messages with Damien. She remembered him from the few times she'd opened the app out of curiosity or looked over Jenny's shoulder while she was commandeering Anu's phone. He was a few years younger than them, African American, a physicist from California who had settled in Vancouver after doing his master's in the city. While Anu only had the one picture of her and Jenny on her profile, Damien had several.

One of him making a silly face in his lab, white coat, goggles, and all. Another of him skiing Whistler Mountain, a selfie from the chairlift. A third of him at Tofino beach, shirtless, with friends.

"He's hot, right?" Jenny asked.

Anu blushed, swiping away from the shirtless photograph. "That he is."

"He's nice, too."

Anu scrolled up through their message history. It was longer than she'd expected.

"You told him your Byron Bay wet T-shirt story?" Anu furrowed her brow at Jenny. "What if I do meet him? He's going to assume that's *my* wet T-shirt story."

Jenny gave her a look and then reached for Anu's phone again. "He probably won't even remember . . . but anyway, he seems great. I'm going to organize a date for you guys in the next week or so."

"Jenny." Anu sighed at the prospect of meeting a guy. She'd have to plan ahead what she wore that day to work, as most of her work clothes wouldn't be cute enough for a date. She would have to wake up early to straighten her hair and put on makeup, rather than opt for her go-to messy ponytail and tinted-moisturizer look.

Would she lie to Kunal or tell him the truth about what she was doing that evening?

Dad, I'm going on a date.

She shivered just thinking about it. She couldn't say that. She couldn't just . . . *date*, like women her age did—and be honest about it—could she?

"You said you'd try," Jenny said. "I thought you wanted to try online dating."

"I do, in theory." Anu imagined herself with Damien at the Italian restaurant by the water Ryan used to take her to, one Ryan probably took a lot of women to.

They would chat, have a laugh. If they liked each other, they would go out again.

Dating didn't have to lead to anything. It *could* be what Jenny and Monica tried to convince her it was: an experience. A trial and error. A journey, not a destination.

"Don't you want to fall in love again, you know, eventually?"

But falling hurt; she hadn't realized that until recently. Of course she wasn't picturing herself alone forever, building a life—new, interesting—all by herself. But that meant she had to *date*, didn't it?

What she'd had with Neil—for a moment, what she'd thought she could have with Ryan—Anu wanted that again.

"You're going," Jenny said quietly. "Because, Anu, love doesn't just happen like you think it does. Relationships don't just *appear* out of thin air."

There were sugar cookie crumbs on Jenny's desk, and Anu fought the urge to brush them off as she stared at them.

"You got lucky with Neil, Anu. And then you got unlucky with Ryan." Jenny smiled. "The truth is, it usually falls somewhere in between."

Anu got there a few minutes late because Damien had sent another message and Jenny insisted on replying to it before Anu left. Kanika was the last of the choir kids to be picked up, and she was waiting for Anu by the gymnasium door, her small pink gloved hand in Ms. Finch's.

"Nice to see you, Anusha," the teacher said, turning to leave as Anu helped Kanika into her car seat.

"Nice to see you, too, Sara."

Anu hadn't seen Sara since before the Christmas holidays and she had bailed at the last minute on finishing the holiday set of the school play, although she had come close to finishing it. She tried not to read into Sara's unusually cool smile and lack of chitchat.

Initially, Anu had been alarmed by how young Sara was, that Kanika's kindergarten class was her very first since graduating university. But despite her age—no more than twenty-two, Anu guessed—Sara had surprised them all by how confidently she carried herself in front of both students and parents. She was pale and blond, but nothing like the stereotypes that often went along with those features. Kanika's class was diverse, and Ms. Finch had made an effort to pronounce every child's and parent's name correctly, and she had everything from Diwali to Ramadan to Yom Kippur marked on the class calendar—all of which the class celebrated together.

Kanika prattled on about Sara on the drive over to Neil's, and Anu half-listened while she became increasingly nervous. She hadn't seen Neil in what felt like forever; her dad had been the one taking

Kanika to visit these past few weeks. Neil opened the door while they were walking up the driveway, and Anu couldn't help but notice how much better he looked than he had the month before, like he'd been eating and sleeping. Like a woman had been taking care of him.

"Daddy!"

Kanika ran up the porch stairs and flew into his arms, nearly knocking him over. Picking her up, he smiled at Anu, and for whatever reason, she nearly tripped forward up the steps.

She walked inside behind them and immediately noticed the difference. It smelled different. The house had always been full of rich, simmering smells—*aloo gobi* or *rajma*, deep-fried *pakoras* or *dal makhani*. Now it smelled like garlic and tomatoes, something else, too. She couldn't put her figure on it.

"Is Dadima asleep?" Kanika asked.

Neil shook his head, setting her back down on the floor. "She's awake. I think she might even have a present for you. . . ."

Kanika beamed and vanished down the hall. Her disappearance made the house uncannily silent, and Anu wondered why she had gone inside.

Her life had been so busy the past few weeks, it had been easy not to think about him. Every time her mind had wandered, or her heart had pondered questions she'd never know the answer to, she distracted herself—with Imogen or Kanika, an e-mail, a task. But standing here, mere feet away from Neil, all the questions came rushing back.

Did they look alike? Did he give Neil those kind, soulful eyes? His perfect lips?

Had he ever tried to reach out? Did he ever care about his son?

It struck her now that she had only ever seen one photo of Neil's father.

"Where's your dad?"

The question startled her, but then she realized Neil was asking her about Kunal.

"At home." Anu cleared her throat. "I wanted to come see how you and M—Priya Auntie are doing."

"She's been walking around more. She even wants to move back into her room upstairs, but I told her to wait a bit longer."

Anu could tell that he wanted to say more, but that he wouldn't. No matter how many times she told him she was here if he needed her, no matter how many times she volunteered to come over and help, he refused. He didn't want her here. He didn't need her in his life. Why couldn't she just accept that?

Kunal had been the one to fill Anu in lately on Priya's recovery, her checkups with the doctors. Her diet would have to change. Less oil, more vegetables, and she was now on a string of medications and being treated as prediabetic. One day, Kunal drove around to all the community centers, yoga studios, badminton clubs, and recreation centers in Burnaby to collect pamphlets for her. If Neil wouldn't let Anu help, at least he wasn't saying no to Kunal.

"Shit," Neil said. "The stove is on." He moved toward the kitchen and beckoned Anu to follow. The kitchen counter was a mess, but rising above the debris, she could make out a Caesar salad in one of Priya's CorningWare dishes. Thick rigatoni pasta boiled on the stove, a saucepan on the burner opposite full of a rich red sauce. Was that eggplant in there? Fresh basil drying on the chopping board?

Her heart dropped into her stomach as she remembered that tomorrow was Valentine's Day. Was all of this for Ms. Dirty Messages?

He picked up a block of Parmesan and started grating it into a bowl.

And he was cooking?

She swallowed hard. Maybe she was wrong about Neil. Parading this in front of her, maybe he was trying to hurt her.

"Sorry about the mess," he said, moving to the stove. "I was folding laundry and haven't had the time yet." He tapped a wooden spoon on the edge of the saucepan. "Do you want to stay?"

"For dinner?"

"It's the third time I've made it. Mom likes pasta now, apparently."

She squinted at him from across the kitchen, the air coming back into her lungs. The acid settling in her stomach.

"I found the recipe in Nigella Lawson's book." He gestured to the top of the fridge, and she followed with her eyes. There was a stack of books—all Western food or fusion—none of which would be Priya's. "I'm good at pastas now, salads, casseroles, stir-fries. That sort of thing." He chuckled. "I haven't worked up the courage to try cooking Indian food yet."

He reached for the chopping board and then a large chef's knife and started chopping basil. With each downward fall of the knife, it hit her. Neil was cooking.

He was taking care of Priya and running a household.

He was doing it right there in front of her, and still she couldn't believe it.

"Could you pass me the ricotta?" He looked up and smiled, although he was not meeting her eyes. "It's in the fridge."

Nodding, she fetched the ricotta. The fridge was stocked, mostly with healthy food, and the top shelf was lined with the craft IPA Neil liked. The sight of it—the graffiti-like design, the lime green stripe—made Anu so sad, she almost dropped the cheese.

"Thanks," he said after she handed it to him.

She had assumed that it was Auntie Jayani and Priya's battalion of friends on roll call who had been feeding her and Neil, taking care of their house, that he had left his job to be there for emotional support rather than for anything else.

Who was *this* man standing in front of her?

Abruptly he set down the ricotta and pulled out his phone, buzzing now in his hand. "Could you watch the pasta? I'll be a minute."

He went into the dining room, and she tried not to eavesdrop, although just by his tone she could tell he was speaking to *her*.

The jealousy grew unbearable, deep and cutting. Anu had married the Neil who hadn't known yogurt needed to be refrigerated, and this other woman was getting someone entirely different. A man who put effort into his relationship and didn't become as useless as putty as soon as he got home from work.

Anu moved around the counter and hovered over the stove. Using a fork, she pulled a piece of pasta out of the boiling water, blew on it, and put it in her mouth.

Their marriage had never been like this. Sharing. Taking turns. One of them starting the pasta and the other one finishing it.

Could it have been?

Neil was back in the kitchen by the time she had drained the pasta and folded in a touch of olive oil. He took over for her, and she retreated from the stove.

"Sorry about that."

"Was that your . . . ?"

"Yeah." He set down the wooden spoon and looked right at her. "Her name's Paula."

Paula. So she had a name.

"I'm happy for you."

"Thanks." He smiled, moved back to the Parmesan. "I haven't introduced her to Kanika yet—"

"It's OK," she said, cutting him off. "It's your decision." Was she relieved? She was relieved, but the word "yet" haunted her.

I haven't introduced Kanika to her future stepmother yet.

I haven't moved on entirely from you, forgotten the twelve years we spent together—yet.

The pattern on the fake granite counter top was nauseating, zigging and zagging and spinning out right in front of her. She stared harder.

"After everything that's happened, Neil, you deserve to be happy."

She was saying the words—she *meant* the words—but why did it hurt so much?

"You too, Anu . . . So what happened with Ryan?"

She winced, crossed her arms in front of her. "Sorry. I meant to tell you we broke up. It's just with everything going on I . . ."

She trailed off but quickly realized Neil was still waiting for her to speak.

"When did you find out?"

"While you were in London. Tom mentioned it in passing but didn't give any details."

"Right . . ."

"I didn't realize things weren't going well."

"Me either . . ." She gave him a look, and Neil's mouth dropped. "No . . ."

She shrugged. "Unfortunately, *yes.*"

"Damn it, Anush. I always knew he was a bastard."

Anu snorted. "Apparently everyone did but me."

"You trust too easily," he said, still looking at her.

And why was that? she wanted to ask him out loud. Because she'd never had a reason not to trust anyone before? Because as inconsiderate and juvenile and mind-numbingly frustrating as Neil could be, he would never, *ever* have broken her heart?

The pasta was delicious. He'd always been precise, competent when he was in the mood, and Anu knew he would have followed the recipe to the T. Every so often, Priya would set down her fork to grab his hand, squeeze it, while Kanika talked about the latest move she had learned in dance class or her thoughts on Ariana Grande's newest single. If Priya remembered telling Anu the truth about Neil's father, she didn't show it, and for a while, it was like nothing had changed.

It was a normal weekday night, and the four of them were eating dinner. Enjoying a quiet family dinner.

Later, Anu helped Neil clear the dishes and then disappeared to the bathroom while he warmed brownies in the microwave oven. She flipped down the toilet seat cover and, sitting on it, opened Facebook on her phone and typed Neil's name into the search bar. They were still friends, but she had unfollowed him months ago. She scrolled through his home page, but there was nothing she hadn't seen before. A photo of Neil and Kanika at Science World. A random article he had posted about something technology related, one that she didn't comprehend. Anu clicked on his friends and searched for the name "Paula."

One profile appeared: Paula Tsi.

Anu clicked on it. Her profile was private, yet some information was visible. She had graduated from Simon Fraser University in 2010, which by Anu's count meant she was about thirty-two, and her profile photo had been taken on the Capilano Suspension Bridge. Her hands were fastened on the ropes on either side, lush evergreen and rock face and sky all around her.

She knew she shouldn't, but she clicked on the photo. She zoomed in, and in silence, the tears started to roll off her cheeks and onto her lap, her phone, her fingers.

Of course she'd be beautiful.

Paula was smiling at the camera. She had a wide, beautiful, kind smile.

The smile of a woman who deserved a man like Neil.

Anu's hands shook as she stood up and tucked her phone into her back pocket. She flushed the toilet and then ran the tap as she blew her nose with toilet paper, dried her face with a clean hand towel. It smelled like lavender.

Anu couldn't turn back time; she didn't want to. But this—moving on, moving forward—she wasn't sure she could do that, either.

chapter twenty-six

LAKSHMI: Our munchkin will be six in the spring! Is Anu planning big party? I can come home for visit between terms.

KUNAL: Oh, Lucky. Please come visit. I am missing you dearly.

LAKSHMI: Kuku, you are my lovey-dovey doo. I miss you more than Shah Rukh misses Rani in Kuch Kuch Hota Hai.

KUNAL: I cannot fall asleep without you, my honey. My Rani, my queen! Sending all the xoxoxoxox kisses and smooches and cuddles, Lucky Luckhoo chuku.

ANUSHA: Ahem. You know this is the group chat, right?

have an idea, but you won't like it."

Just then a piece of drywall broke off and slid down to the floor, widening the giant hole in the practice room wall. Anu's dream was *literally* crumbling before her eyes.

According to Imogen, some months before Anu took over the studio, Mags had hired a friend to mount an equipment rack. And mount it he had. The rack, although an eyesore, had neatly stored all the mats, ropes, blocks, and blankets they could need.

Of course, it had been mounted on a wall of plaster without the proper brackets and framing, and that morning, Anu and Imogen had come in to find that the rack had succumbed to gravity, ripping a hole in the wall on its journey down.

"I think we should tear down the wall," Imogen continued.

Anu wheeled around. Imogen was sitting on the floor cross-legged, with specks of white dust and plaster all over her orange yoga pants.

"Look how much space is back there." Imogen pointed past her and through the hole. "We don't need a storeroom. Those boxes are full of junk, anyway."

Anu had known Imogen was going to suggest this, but it still irritated her. All of Imogen's grand ideas, including this one, would cost money, and Anu didn't need to be a lawyer to understand that the landlord wouldn't pay to fix it. The hole was Mags' fault—so now it was Anu's.

Fucking Mags. Anu imagined where she was at that very moment, perhaps sitting at some pub outside London, sipping a pint of cider, or in some cozy, obnoxiously English sitting room with tea cozies and crumpets. Meditating, like a virtuous monk, on her sister's back porch.

"I've done the measurements," Imogen said, "and if we had a wide-open space, we could double the class size."

Taking a deep breath, Anu picked up a piece of the plaster that had broken off. "It would be cheaper to fix the hole than redo the room."

"But it's an investment." Imogen stood up, set her hands on her hips. "Did you not hear me? It would *double* the class—"

"Because we're in desperate need of the room, hey?" Anu snapped. She shook out her hair. "Sorry. I didn't mean that. I'm just upset."

The hole in the wall was only the latest setback for the studio, although admittedly the largest. Several of the new teachers she'd hired hadn't work out, and Charlie—the only reliable teacher besides Imogen on the payroll—had quit to join a hot-yoga studio in Strathcona.

Anu was running an unreliable, sparsely populated studio that no one knew about, and she could barely afford to pay the teachers' and Imogen's salaries, let alone one for herself. Sure, Imogen had launched a weekly trial program for new students and charged them chump change, but they'd only secured a handful of new students who stayed on after that. Evenings tended to stay relatively full with drop-ins by university students, but those classes alone just barely allowed Anu to pay the studio's rent.

They didn't have enough students, and in the afternoons, more often than not the classes were empty.

How long could she go on like this?

Anu wondered if this was a sign that she was supposed to walk away. As much as she loved the studio, she'd been thinking this more and more. Now all she'd have to do was pay a contractor to fix the wall, and then she could leave. She'd call Mags, do her best not to yell at her for bolting that bloody equipment rack to the wall, and find out which hipster was interested in the space.

Anu could cut her losses, assign the lease over to someone else, and by the time it had been turned into a coffee shop or a brow bar or a wine store, she would be back on track financially. She could increase her hours at the clinic no problem; the partners would love to have her on full-time. She could go back to saving responsibly.

Imogen lay down full on the floor, extending her arms and legs like a starfish. Her eyes were closed.

"I'm sorry for snapping at you," Anu repeated, and Imogen didn't respond. Anu searched her face for a moment, but just like every other day, it was unreadable.

Anu helped Imogen clean up for a few minutes before leaving

for the clinic, apologizing for not being able to stick around and help more. Despite the hole, the room was otherwise fine, and they'd be able to keep the studio open for classes.

All day long at work, Anu's mind had kept wandering back to the studio, and she couldn't help but wonder what Lakshmi would have done in her situation. Even though Lakshmi had been a mother and wife first, and let everything else had come second, hadn't she been brave? Hadn't Lakshmi accepted the proposal of man who she knew wanted to leave India, move to an uncertain life abroad? At the age of fifty-eight, hadn't she again left, this time for England, to do the master's she'd always dreamed of?

Finally, the workday was over, and Anu found herself sitting in the break room with Jenny, waiting for her phone yet again while reading out loud the pros and cons list of investing in the studio.

"I either need to walk away right now or fix the whole place up and advertise. Imogen's right. Nobody knows we exist." Jenny didn't respond, and so Anu continued. "That means taking out a business loan."

Jenny smiled at something on the phone, and Anu collapsed back on the office chair. "Are you even listening to me?"

"Yes."

"No, you're not."

"Blah-blah, business loan. I'm so confused, blah." Jenny darted her eyes upward. "You're still free this Friday, right?"

"What's this Friday?" Anu deadpanned.

"Your date with Damien!" Jenny practically screamed.

Anu grinned. Of course she knew her date with Damien was on Friday. Jenny had only mentioned it every single day since scheduling it the week before.

"So you're free?" Jenny asked again, missing the joke.

Anu rolled her eyes. "Yes, I'm still free."

"Don't forget. And *don't* wear your mom jeans, OK? You have"—she glanced at her watch—"forty-seven hours prepare. Do you need help picking out an outfit?"

"Your lack of faith is actually kind of offensive." She paused. "And aren't mom jeans in fashion?"

"Yeah, eighties mom jeans are in fashion, like these." Jenny tugged on the belt loop of her high-waisted trousers. "Yours are . . . I don't even *know* what yours are."

Anu laughed, remembering the clothes she'd bought in London. She hadn't worn them since she got back. In fact, most still had the tags on them and sat at the back of her closet.

"I was listening before, you know . . . ," Jenny said quietly, in a voice that forced Anu to look up. "I can't tell you whether or not it's a good idea to invest in your dreams. But I can say that, well, I haven't seen you like this in years, Anu."

"What do you mean?"

"You're energetic. You're passionate. You're *laughing* again and interesting—"

"And not *boring*." Anu finished.

She paused. "You weren't boring *me*, Anu. You were boring yourself."

Jenny was right. It wasn't motherhood and marriage that had bored Anu; it was the way she had mindlessly thrown herself into them. Gone through whatever motion she had thought right, appropriate, and until she left Neil, she hadn't dared to question a thing.

"I can't go into debt to prove something to myself, Jenny. I can't keep making mistakes."

"You know that grown-ups don't appear out of thin air, right? You have to actually *grow*. That means making mistakes, Anu. That's the whole freaking point!"

Anu stared at her, and Jenny rolled her eyes in her Jenny-like way.

"Pretend for a second that the guy you made out with wasn't *eighteen*: Do you regret kissing him or sleeping with Jude Law?"

"Theo wasn't *actually* Jude Law—"

"I asked you, do you regret it?"

Anu looked down at her hands. Although embarrassing, although she wouldn't do anything like that again, there was no question that she'd had fun. "No."

"And do you regret punching that toxic wasteland of a man Ryan right in the schnoz?"

Laughing, Anu shook her head.

"Good, me either." Jenny crossed her arms. "London? Do you regret that?"

Anu had needed to leave to appreciate what she had at home. Anu knew that now, and so she shook her head.

"And was marrying Neil a mistake?" Anu opened her mouth to say something, and Jenny cut her off. "Before you answer, think about it. Think about what I'm asking. Knowing it would end, do you wish you had never married Neil?"

She took a deep breath, summoned the last twelve years of her life with him—the good and the bad.

For a while at least, it had been a marriage, solid and real and supportive. It had brought her joy and pain and, above all else, their daughter.

"No," Anu said finally, "I don't regret any of it."

"So then how were those things mistakes?" Jenny asked her quietly. "I know you went off the rails for a while there, but part of growing up is taking detours, Anu, so you can realize who you are and what you want."

Anu nodded, wringing out her hands. Hadn't she known that all along?

"Your Hallmark yoga crap might be rubbing off on me, but there are no such things as mistakes. You live, you learn, and you move on."

Thinking hard, Anu again realized how right Jenny was. As much as Anu didn't like the woman she'd been while in a relationship with Ryan, hadn't it taught her to trust herself and to follow her intuition? Find self-worth from within and not from others?

Wasn't she happy she had finally confronted her parents? That she was bold enough to go to London to begin with?

And, as difficult as it had been, as hopeless as it often seemed, didn't she want to run the yoga studio? Create something of her own?

An ambition, she realized, she wasn't ready to give up on.

She could be in Vancouver, be a good mother, friend, and daughter, and she could do this, too. She didn't have to leave her family, her responsibilities, to be the woman she wanted to be.

"So," Jenny said, slyly sliding Anu's phone back to her, "what are you going to do?"

"I'm going to bet on myself, Jen. Fuck it. I'm going into debt!"

chapter twenty-seven

ANUSHA: Hi, Mom. . . . Thinking about you a lot these days. [deleted]

ANUSHA: Hi, Mom. Are you awake? I'm about to take a giant leap and could use some advice, maybe . . . [deleted]

ANUSHA: FaceTime tomorrow? Kanika misses you.

LAKSHMI: Yes please.

LAKSHMI: I am missing you both also.

After work, Anu raced over to the studio, wanting to catch Imogen before she started the six p.m. class. She parked her car and then jogged down the block. There was a woman walking toward her on the sidewalk, trying to make eye contact, and Anu hesitated, unable to place her.

"Anusha?" The woman stopped, and Anu realized it was one of Mags' regular students. "Are *you* teaching tonight?"

"Me?" Anu glanced past her down the sidewalk. There were four more people, other regulars, waiting by the studio door. "Is the door not open?"

"No." She sounded upset, snappy. "We've been knocking for ten minutes."

Strange. Imogen was never late. Anu called her as she unlocked the studio, unsurprised to find that Imogen didn't answer her phone. Except for that one time in London, Anu had never spoken to Imogen on the phone. She only ever seemed to text.

Inside, the studio was empty, and the computer wasn't on the registration desk. She let the others in, and after they shuffled downstairs toward the change room, Anu went into the back office.

"Imogen?"

She wasn't there, either. Anu turned around and headed toward the practice room.

The light was on, and Imogen was at the front of the room, dressed in her usual uniform of brightly colored spandex, lying flat on a yoga mat. There were still drywall and plaster all over the floor; garbage bags, a dustbin, and a broom had been left haphazardly around the room, as if Imogen had forgotten about the task right in the middle of it.

"Imogen?"

Anu took another step into the room, but Imogen didn't flinch. Her eyes were wide-open, fixated on the ceiling, and Anu tried to contain the fire building in her belly.

Had she been like this the *whole* day? Not run a single class, the *entire* day?

"What's going on?" Anu glanced at her watch. It was five minutes before the class was supposed to start; if they both worked quickly, maybe they could still make it.

Anu lunged for the broom, started sweeping up the plaster as quickly as she could. But there was white dust everywhere, stuck to the grain of the hardwood. They would need to mop. Christ, where did Imogen keep the mop?

"Imogen, can you help. *Please?*" Anu snapped. Imogen was still lying on the mat, but her chin tilted to the side toward Anu. Their eyes locked. "Your class starts in five minutes."

"So?"

"What do you mean, *so*? So there are people changing downstairs."

"What, like, *five* people?"

There *were* five people downstairs. Anu threw down the broom and stomped toward Imogen. She leaned down and grabbed her hands, tried to pull her up from the floor, but Imogen was deadweight on the floor.

"What's going on with you?" Anu leaned down again, tugged harder, but it was useless. But squatting there, she smelled something. She moved in closer. "Are you drunk?"

Imogen laughed, hard, and from the smell and the deranged look in Imogen's eyes, Anu could tell. She was drunk or high, maybe both.

She grabbed Imogen by the hand and pulled her up off the floor. Gently, Anu pressed the back of her hand against Imogen's forehead, but Imogen swatted it away.

"How much did you drink?"

There was no judgment in her words, only concern. Anu had been so wrapped up in her own journey that she'd missed all the signs. Running around with Imogen to bars and clubs like nothing mattered. Trusting her business with someone who was not only not ready for such responsibility but desparately calling out for help.

What on earth had Anu been thinking?

"I know you don't want to talk to me. But this isn't right."

Imogen swayed to the side, and Anu caught her by the hand to stabilize her.

"I don't understand what's going on here. Why you don't care that—"

"Why should I care about this place, huh? It's not like you give a shit about it—"

"Excuse me?"

"You don't care about this place or what happens to it. I've *heard* you talking to your friends. You're thinking about shutting down the studio." Glaring at her, Imogen lifted her chin and then her torso, resting back on her elbows.

Anu bit her lip, wondering if she should tell Imogen about her plans to invest now or wait until she'd sobered up.

"Don't you realize how lucky you are? How many chances you get? *Jesus*, you don't. You don't get it at all."

There was a noise behind her, and Anu turned. A few students were hovering in the doorway, watching. Anu turned back around. "Imogen, please calm down—"

"You take everything for granted. *Everything*." Her voice was louder now on the edge. "You can just run off to London and buy a studio because you feel like it. And you can fail, too. You have your perfect house and perfect parents and *perfect* daughter."

Anu's face heated in anger. In shame. "I know what I have, Imogen. I know it. That's why I'm *here*. That's why I came back—"

"You don't know shit, Anusha. You can't see a thing, even when it's fucking right in front of you." Imogen stood up, almost tripping over herself, and again Anu was hit with a wave of something strong. Vodka, maybe. Anu reached to help her, but Imogen swatted her hand away and, then smirking, looked at the students in the doorway. "What the fuck are *you* looking at?"

"Imogen!"

But it was too late. The students, all five of them, disappeared from the doorway. Fuming, Anu whipped around toward Imogen.

"They're never going to come back—do you realize that?"

"Why do you care?"

"It's not like you care about this place. For all I know, *you* ripped down the equipment rack." Imogen's mouth dropped, and immediately Anu was filled with regret. She didn't think that; why had she said it? "I . . . didn't mean—"

"You meant it. You fucking meant it."

"I'm sorry." Anu sighed, and all the anger made way for something else. Something worse. "I'm glad it fell down. You see, I've made an appointment with my bank for tomorrow afternoon. You were totally right about everything. I need to—"

"You need to get a clue." Imogen brushed the hair out of her eyes and then backpedaled toward the door. "Good fucking riddance, Anusha."

"Imogen, don't go." She rushed after Imogen, through the foyer and out onto the street. Imogen was already half a block away, walking furiously into the night.

"Imogen!" Anu chased after her, but by the time she'd reached the end of the block, Imogen had disappeared.

chapter twenty-eight

ANUSHA: Imogen . . . I'm really sorry for what I said. For what I accused you of doing. I was upset, and I didn't mean it. Can you call me back? Every time it goes straight to voice mail. . . .

(two hours later)

ANUSHA: Blocked my number already? Look, I'm so sorry. I'll give you some space, but please know that if and when you're ready, I'm here for you. I want you to come back. This is your studio, too.

(two days later)

ANUSHA: I'm not sure if you've gotten my voice mails. . . . Anyway, I want to tell you something . . . what I came by to tell you that night. I'm going all-in. You were right. This morning I applied for a business loan. Mags' Studio is getting a face-lift . . . and I want you there with me.

Jesus, what's wrong with my hair?"

Anu looked up from her phone. Jenny was still hunched over a rounded mirror at the center of a funky piece of installation art, fluffing and smoothing her bangs. In the reflection, Anu could see Jenny's pursed lips spread out to twice their normal size, her cheeks and eyes spread wide. She looked like a cartoon version of herself. In the distorted reflection, her *hair* was the one thing that looked fine.

"We're going to be late."

"Give me a minute."

"I've given you five, Jen. . . ."

Anu wasn't sure when tonight had turned into a double date, but she wasn't complaining. All day, every time she thought about having to meet Damien, go on a date—a real *adult* date—with a handsome, age-appropriate man, she could feel herself start to sweat. So when Jenny had announced after lunch that Damien was bringing a friend for her and the four of them were all going together, Anu had been relieved.

She and Neil had never gone on a proper first date, and by the time she'd had her first date with Ryan, he'd been chasing her so long she already knew him—or at least thought she knew him.

How was she supposed to act around Damien? Coy? Mysterious?

And what had Jenny told him about her? Compared to Jenny's witty, practiced banter online, would he find Anu dull?

At least she looked good today. As instructed by Jenny, Anu had worn lipstick, straightened her hair, and left her mom jeans at home. In fact, after putting Kanika to bed the evening before, she'd torn the tags off all the clothes she bought in London and laid them on her bed. And they weren't as daring as Anu remembered. It was only the miniskirt that she needed to give away.

For the date, she'd put on a new coat and tight leathery jeans, and paired them with one of the tops and blazers she usually wore to work. She didn't look that different, but she felt strangely confident. Even their receptionist at work, a twenty-five-year-old girl who looked like a supermodel, complimented Anu on her outfit.

Eventually, Jenny gave up on her bangs, and they started on

their way. She hadn't been to Granville Island in years, even though it sat right on the edge of the downtown core and she had to drive by it all the time. It was an artists' paradise, chock-full of galleries, boutique shops, and craftsmen making everything from leather goods to glass vases to baskets.

They bypassed the outdoor art exhibit and then the food market, despite the tempting smells wafting out from behind its barn-like doors, and hung a right toward the brewery.

"Do you see them?" Jenny asked as they push through the door.

Anu shrugged, searching the low wooden tables for Damien. It was dark inside, with the wall-to-wall exposed brick.

"Where are they? Do you think they stood us up?"

Anu narrowed her eyes at her. "Why would they stand us up?"

"I don't know. It's"—Jenny glanced at her watch—"six-oh-one. . . ."

"Oh, good gracious, Jenny, they're a minute late!" Laughing, Anu led her toward an empty table by the window. "Why are you acting nervous? Shouldn't *I* be the nervous one?"

Jenny threw her a glare. "I'm nervous for *you*. Your date etiquette is more than a decade old. She's a *teenager*."

"My date etiquette is old enough to have her period."

Jenny laughed, and her shoulders visibly relaxed. Over the years, Anu had heard dozens of stories about Jenny's love life—everything from awkward first dates, one-off encounters with liars who hid their wedding ring in their front pockets, overeager men who Jenny made cry and, once, required a restraining order.

Jenny belonged in a modern-day retelling of *Sex and the City*. She could have written, and often suggested that she should write, her own sex-and-relationship advice column. So why then was she acting like a nervous wreck?

"Oh, my God, they're *here*," Jenny whispered, pulling off her coat. She tugged at her left sleeve, but too hard. It hit the water glass on the table next to her and crashed down to the floor. "Shit!"

"Jenny, it's fine." Anu moved in to help, but Jenny brushed her hand away.

"They're here. Anu, they're here. Just leave it and look up, because—"

"They're here?" Anu laughed, and after letting her eyes stay on Jenny for just a beat longer, she looked up.

She recognized Damien immediately from his pictures on Tinder. Tall, dark, and handsome—an incredibly cute smile. He towered over his friend next to him, a white guy—also very cute—with grayish blond hair and light eyes.

Jenny and Anu stood up to greet them, and Damien leaned in to hug Jenny and then Anu.

"Where are my manners," he said, pulling away. "*This* is my friend Tyler."

Tyler went next, hugging Anu, then Jenny. There was an awkward lull as a waiter came by to clean up the broken glass—Jenny's face turned beet red—and then Damien and Tyler took their seats. Tyler had chosen the one by the far window, opposite to Anu's purse; he must have not realized where they were sitting. For simplicity, Anu switched her purses with Jenny's and took the seat opposite Damien, leaving her chair for Jenny.

"Are you OK?" Damien asked.

Anu opened her mouth to speak, but then closed it when she realized Damien was looking at Jenny, not at Anu.

"Me?" Jenny said.

"Yeah." Damien's eyes flicked to Tyler and then back to Jenny. "Are you OK over there?"

"Uh, yeah. I'm OK . . . over here."

Anu pressed her lips together. She liked to think she had OK people skills, a high emotional quotient, and the general ability to read the room. But this was a room she could not read. Jenny was acting like she wanted to be anywhere but here, and Tyler—well, *Tyler* kept looking at Anu.

The waiter came by, and each of them ordered a pint. Jenny, usually the one to take the lead in all group conversations, stayed eerily silent, and so Anu tried to step up as best as she could. She made small talk with Damien and Tyler—about the weather, the Vancouver Canucks game the evening before, and, after their drinks arrived, the pleasantly bitter aftertaste of the brewery's IPA.

Anu could tell Damien was a gentleman, because he kept trying to bring Jenny into the conversation—complimenting her on her choice of pint (a pale ale), asking her about her day—but Jenny did little more than offer five-word answers and sip rather steadfastly at her drink. Meanwhile, Tyler, a schoolteacher and semiprofessional skier, although endearing, seemed to be paying more attention to Anu than to Jenny.

Maybe that was what double dates were like? Anu wondered.

They all finished their pints, and when the waiter came by to ask if they'd like another, Jenny nodded her head before anyone else could answer.

Jenny was petite, a cheap drunk, and also Anu's ride home that day. Anu kicked her lightly under the table. Jenny kicked her right back.

"Anusha, did I do something wrong?" Damien asked abruptly. "Are you upset with me?"

"Why would be I upset with you . . . ?" Anu trailed off as she realized Damien's gaze was again fixed on Jenny. "Wait. Why did you call *her* Anusha?"

"Because she *is* Anusha."

"No, I am."

"Aren't *you* Jenny?" Tyler said to Anu. "*My* blind date?"

"*She's* Jenny."

"But her profile picture," Damien said, his voice high. "The profile picture is—"

"Of both of us," Anu said, laughing. "Why did you assume it was her? 'Anusha' is an Indian name!"

"Well, I didn't know that. And besides, *she*"—he pointed to Jenny—"is more prominently featured."

"You thought it was me," Jenny said to Damien, which was perhaps the first time she'd looked at him all night. "You thought Anusha was me?"

Anu sat back, taking in the table. Tyler looked just as confused as Anu felt, and Damien and Jenny were just staring at each other. A smile spread slowly across Anu's face as it hit her: So *that* was why Jenny was acting strange. She *liked* Damien. Jenny was annoyed that she'd started to like the guy she was trying to fix up with Anu. She had invited herself along on Anu's date because, secretly, *Jenny* wanted to meet Damien.

"So you're not Anusha, then," Damien said, looking from Jenny down to his hands. No one said anything, and a beat later, his eyes flicked up to Anu. "So I've been talking to you this whole time?" He laughed. "How about that . . . ?"

"Actually," Jenny said, shifting in her seat, "you've been talking to me."

"But you just said you're not Anusha—"

"No, keep up, man. I'm *Jenny*." She rolled her eyes, bumped Anu's shoulder with hers. "Anu sucks at dating, so I was just helping her out."

"By pretending to be Anusha?" Damien asked.

Jenny nodded.

"So she's Anusha, and you're Jenny," Damien said, and they all nodded—even Tyler. "And I was talking to Anusha on Tinder, but *you*"—he pointed at Jenny—"were pretending to be Anusha?"

"I was, but I mean, *I* was the one texting. So, really, you were talking to . . . Jenny."

They were staring at each other again, and their eyes stayed locked even as the waiter brought over the next round.

"Perfect timing," Tyler said, breaking the silence. He caught Anu's eye, and oddly, it made her smile. "I need another drink."

Anu reached for her glass. "I think we all do."

Tyler turned to Damien, moving to stand up. "Should we switch seats?"

"Hang on." Damien waved him off, and leaned forward diagonally toward Jenny. "So why did you come then, to meet Tyler? Are you even single?"

"I am," Jenny said tersely, palming her pint glass. "I am single."

"Are you on Tinder?"

"Yes."

"Then why haven't we ever matched?"

"Because you're twenty-eight."

"So?"

"So I've set my age minimum to thirty."

"What? Why?"

"I don't date younger men."

The table grew quiet. Damien picked up his pint, and in a breath, half of it was gone. He set down his glass on the table, hard. Gently, Anu reached for Jenny's hand beneath the table, but Jenny swatted her away. Anu wanted to laugh out loud and throttle her simultaneously.

"So I guess we should never have met. Is that what you're saying? Because I'm too immature or something?"

Jenny shrugged, glancing out the window. "Or something."

Who would have thought that Jenny could develop a crush on a guy—a real, rare crush—and she, too, could turn into a silly teenager? Anu and Monica were the type to giggle and bat their eyelashes at their crushes, while Jenny, apparently, acted like a jerk.

Why wasn't that surprising?

Tyler caught Anu's eye from across the table, and when he gestured to the door, she nodded in understanding. Slyly, she reached for her purse under the table and then for her coat. "Jenny, I'm going to take off."

Jenny turned, stared up at her blankly. "I can't drive anymore."

"That's fine," Tyler said, also standing now. "I'll drive you, Anusha. It *is* Anusha, right?"

Anu laughed. "Call me Anu."

They barely made it out the door before they burst out laughing, and then they spent the whole drive back to Burnaby replaying the mix-up, trying to sort it out: Anu thought she was on a date with Damien, who thought he was on a date with Jenny, who thought *she* was on a date with Tyler—who thought he was on a date with Anu.

"It sounds like a Mindy Kaling show, doesn't it?" Anu said, dabbing at the tears. She couldn't remember the last time she'd laughed this hard. With Jenny and Monica, it was a different sort of humor: quick, combative. More often than not crude.

This was different. *More subtle*, she thought, watching the city go by. When was the last time she had laughed like *this*?

Her face dropped when it hit her.

It had been with Neil. Kanika was a toddler. They were giving her a bath, and she had pooped everywhere. *Everywhere.*

That was the last time. That was more than three years ago.

"Are you disappointed?" Tyler asked. She looked over, unable to read his face. "I know I have my charm, but I'm telling you, it's hard to be friends with a guy like him."

"Why would you say that?"

He grinned. "I'm straight, but I'm not blind. If Damien is Idris Elba, then I'm. . . . Martin Freeman."

"Oh, come on, I *love* Martin Freeman," Anu said. "*The Office* is one of my favorite shows."

"Damien is Kanye West, and I'm—"

"Vanilla Ice?" Anu teased.

"Ouch!"

"Damien is . . . ," Anu started, "Barack Obama . . ."

"And I'm . . . ," Tyler finished, "Joe Biden?"

"I was going to say Justin Trudeau."

"Trudeau." Tyler laughed again, and Anu had this unsettling feeling that she was starting to like him. Suddenly, she was overcome with the urge to call Imogen and tell her all about the double date, right there in the car before the "date" was even over. Swallowing hard, she remembered their last conversation and the fact that Imogen had been ignoring her ever since she ran out of the studio two nights earlier.

"So are you disappointed, then?" she heard Tyler ask. "That you're on a date with Justin Trudeau?"

"Not at all," she said, pointing out her exit from the highway. "I'm not disappointed."

On that final stretch of the drive, he told her about growing up in interior British Columbia near a ski field, about his class of seventh graders in South Surrey. She told him about working at the clinic with Jenny and her newfound attempt to be an entrepreneur. All too soon her neighborhood appeared, Kanika's school, her local grocery store and gas station. All too soon, she was home.

"If it works out between Damien and Jenny," Tyler said, pulling into the driveway, "we might be seeing a lot of each other, hey?"

"We'll have to tell the story of how they met when we co-emcee their wedding reception."

"And in the hospital waiting room, at the birth of their first child."

"Who knows?" Anu said. "We might be the kid's godparents."

"I'm going to make 'em an offer they can't refuse," Tyler said in a gruff voice, and when it hit her, she burst out laughing.

"The Godfather?"

"The Godfather," she repeated, still smiling. "I got it."

Behind the drawn curtain, Kunal's shadow appeared in the front window. It lingered for a second before disappearing again.

Twelve years ago, she would have been mortified if Kunal had caught her sitting in Neil's car. She would have run in the house, gone straight to her room, and avoided eye contact with her dad for days.

But today?

She straightened in her seat. Today she'd go inside, and over the dinner they prepared together, she'd tell him the truth. She would relay the story of the double date and the mix-up, and it would make Kunal laugh—his full-belly, raucous laugh, the one he usually reserved for his favorite Indian comedian, Johnny Lever.

Would Anu also tell Lakshmi? A part of her wanted to, if her mother was ready to hear it.

"There's one thing I haven't told you yet," Anu said to the dashboard. "I have a daughter. Her name is Kanika, and she'll be six next month." She turned to Tyler, who didn't look at all alarmed by the news. "Her father and I are . . . separated."

He nodded, holding her gaze. "Is it a . . . new separation?"

"It's been more than a year now."

"A year," he said, nodding.

She appreciated that he wasn't asking any more questions, ones she didn't have the answers to.

Is the separation going to become permanent?

When are you getting a divorce?

She couldn't think about these questions without thinking about Paula, and so Anu tried not to think about the subject at all.

"And you have a daughter," Tyler said, shrugging. "That's nice. I like kids."

"Me, too, I suppose."

"Never would have guessed."

Anu laughed. Something about him made her want to let go and laugh even more. He reached his hand across the seat and, without hesitating, intertwined his fingers with hers. They were warm, rougher than she had expected. For a moment, she imagined them elsewhere.

"I'd love to see you again."

He was smiling at her, but her palms had started to sweat and so she couldn't meet his eye.

"Is that your babysitter watching us from the window?"

Anu looked up. Kunal had come back, but disappeared when she started to wave at him. "My babysitter *and* my dad."

"Your *dad*." Tyler gently squeezed her palm. "I have to admit, it's been years since I dropped a girl off and her dad was waiting up."

Right then, she wanted to kiss him, but she didn't. She wasn't ready. And besides, Kunal was probably watching.

chapter twenty-nine

JENNY: OMG I just got home—what a weird night. After you
left, Damien hung around (against my will) and we ended up
talking for hours. Other things ensued. . . . Are you pissed?

ANUSHA: Why would I be pissed???

JENNY: Because he was your date!

ANUSHA: He clearly didn't know that. ☺

Are you *sure* you're going to be OK?"

"*Mommy.*" Kanika rolled her eyes impatiently at Anu, the
same way Jenny did, and Anu made a mental note to tell Jenny not
to do that around Kanika anymore.

"You don't have to sleep here, you know." Anu crouched down
on the front step. "You can stay for cake and presents, and then I'll
come pick you up—"

"I *want* to stay, honest." Kanika smiled, tugged on the straps of
her *Moana* backpack. "Mommy, I'm ready. Are *you*?"

Anu laughed, standing back up. "Well, I have to be, don't I?"

She rang the bell. There was a thundering of footsteps, and
then Kanika's best friend from school, Monet, appeared in the
door. She was wearing a plastic tiara and a gold sparkly dress, and
she had the number 6 painted on each of her cheeks.

It was Monet's sixth birthday, and Kanika's first-ever sleepover party. Initially, Anu thought kindergartners were a bit too young for sleepovers, but Kanika seemed so excited by the idea, she didn't have the heart to say no.

Most of the girls had already arrived, and with little more than a quick hug, Kanika went barreling inside. Anu chatted for a few minutes with Monet's parents, who'd she known well for years, and with a quick glance down the hall toward Kanika, she left.

Tyler had invited her out that evening, but Anu had politely declined and told him she had plans. And she wasn't lying: She had a studio to redesign. On the drive back, Anu resisted stopping in at her favorite sushi restaurant and drove straight home. Her dad's car wasn't in the driveway; he must have already left for his poker night, a tradition he'd had with colleagues since Anu was in high school. As she opened the front door, Anu smiled to herself, welcoming the idea of an evening to herself to sort through all of her ideas.

Anu had swept and mopped up the studio and hung a flat gray sheet over the hole in the wall so classes were still running, and she'd temporarily assigned all of Imogen's classes to other teachers. Should she assign them permanently? They were pressing her to, but still she was holding on to the hope that Imogen would come back.

Imogen was refusing to answer her phone calls and texts, and Anu couldn't find any information about who her family was or how she might contact them, despite spending more than an hour searching on Google. She was worried about Imogen's well-being, her mental health, and half-wished that she had given that eighteen-year-old her phone number when he asked so she could get in touch with her through his brother, who she remembered was friends with Haruto.

Anu had tried calling and texting many times, but Imogen hadn't replied, not even once. She had considered going to the police to try to get help finding Imogen, but she didn't feel like she had cause to involve them.

After making herself a snack of cheese, crackers, and pickles, Anu sat down with her computer and the notepad on which she'd been logging all of her ideas. She had no idea where to start.

Mags' Studio was *vinyasa*, but she wanted to expand. Offer all sorts of classes, if she could find the right teachers, even courses on mindfulness and meditation. Right now the studio attracted the usual demographic: university students, thirtysomething women with disposable time and income, and seniors.

Surely, Anu could reach more. There had to be something more she could do.

The doorbell rang. Anu sat up from her work, and her neck spasmed as she looked toward the front door. How long had she been sitting here, hunched over like this? She stretched her arms above her head, in a modified *talasana* pose, as she walked down the hall.

"Coming," she called out. Anu stretched her hands higher, pointing her fingers in the shape of a gun, until she felt her shoulders release. "Who is it?"

"Neil."

Neil?

She froze, paralyzed on the other side of the door. Neil was here?

Taking a deep breath, Anu opened the door, suddenly conscious of the fact that it was not even dinnertime and already she was in her pajamas. He smiled at her, and she backpedaled as he stepped toward her and into the foyer.

"Kanika's not here," Anu said as he stamped his wet boots on the doormat. "Tonight's the sleepover."

"I know," he said, shutting the door behind him.

"Oh?"

"And your dad mentioned he had a poker night, didn't he?" Their eyes locked for a moment, and Anu's mouth went dry. She leaned back against the wall, shrinking away from him as she realized why he had come over.

He was going to ask for the divorce, the divorce *Anu* had wanted to begin with. Why else would he come over when he knew Anu would be alone?

"Sorry to drop by like this."

She shrugged, unsure of what to say or what to do with her limbs. They all felt heavy and awkward, utterly useless. She managed to cross her arms, staying limp against the wall.

This is what you wanted to begin with. You can handle this.

"Your dad told me your big news," Neil said, still looking at her. "You're redesigning your studio? Congratulations."

"Thank you." She knew he was making nice, making polite chitchat before springing it on her, but still she was pleased he had said this. That, however vague, he was taking an interest. "I took out a loan. Apparently, you and I have excellent credit."

He grinned. "Are those the plans?"

She followed his eyes down the hall, to the mess of papers on the kitchen table. She nodded, walking toward them. "It's more ideas than a plan." She picked up a pamphlet that had fallen on the floor. It was for faucets: a selection of more than thirty in chrome, brass, and stainless steel from a supplier out in New Westminster. The faucets at the studio were covered in rust and, she suspected, more than fifty years old.

"Not all ideas can be glamorous, of course."

She felt him standing beside her before she could see him. He leaned in and tapped on one of the three pictures she'd already circled. "I like these."

"Yeah?"

"Yeah." He was standing so close to her, she could smell him. "They look like ours."

The tension in her shoulders, her chest, faded away, and quickly, she found herself telling him in detail the plans she had in her head, the difficulties she'd had with keeping and attracting students, differentiating her studio from her rivals. Did she want to compete on price? Neil poured them both a whiskey and Coke, and she brought out a bag of Cheetos she'd hidden above the fridge. Would her studio be about paying for a quality experience—routines, teachers, decor—or did she want to take a more minimalist approach? And what would her studio really *be* about? Whom was she trying to lure in? People like herself?

He was pouring them both another drink when she realized how long she'd been talking. Blushing, she pulled her feet up onto the chair cross-legged. "Look at me blabbering on like this."

"It's been a while since I've been blabbered to." He came back to the table. The ice knocked against the glasses as he set down their drinks. "And it's nice to see you like this again, Anush. It really is."

Like this.

She winced, because she knew what he really meant. It was what Jenny had meant when she told Anu—in not so many words—that she had grown dull. Uninterested. Did he think that of her, too? Was that why, at the end, he'd acted like he didn't care about her until it was too late, until she told him to move out?

"You've never asked me why," she said, "why I left for London like that."

Her mind raced as he sipped his drink, his eyes fastened on her. He was waiting for her to keep speaking, to explain herself, and she struggled with how much to tell him.

Should she start from the beginning? She shook her head, dismissing the idea. He already knew that part; they'd fought about it for months. The way Neil got a gold star from their mothers for deigning to be a part of his daughter's life, the way, after marriage, he had become so *freaking* Indian. She wanted a fresh start so badly, and surely Neil understood that was why she had chosen Ryan, a modern man she thought could be a partner.

And then after Ryan, she'd felt trapped in a life crumbling around her, and for the first time in years, she'd wanted to *live*. She sucked out an ice cube from her drink and maneuvered it into her left cheek. It was freezing, burning her from the inside.

Should she tell Neil about the list? How what had started out as a prompt, Jenny's dare to be bold, became something so much more?

Would he want to hear about how what was so freeing at first quickly became reckless? How guilty she felt about what had happened, but that she was learning she could be at home, right here in this life, and still *live*?

"I needed to leave." She chewed the ice cube, cracking the silence between them. "I needed to leave to come home." A bush rustled somewhere beyond the window. "I'm sorry I put you through that. I can't imagine what it was like for you, especially when your mom—"

"Anush." He shook his head, cutting her off. "It's OK."

She wondered if it would ever be OK.

"I'm sorry I blamed you for everything, even for the fact that I became . . ." Her throat was hoarse, and words came up, words she hadn't planned on saying.

"Our mothers?"

She nodded. "But it was my choice to work part-time. To change my last name. It was *my* choice to try to be this perfect mom, the perfect cook, the perfect wife. . . ." She trailed off when she felt her throat constrict. She coughed, clearing it. "You know, on weekends we'd put Kanika to bed, and you were perfectly happy to"—she shrugged—"work or watch a movie or play Warcraft."

He winced.

"And I was furious. Furious at *you* that I had nothing to do. That I'd let go of most of my hobbies, my interests, even some of my friends. That if Jenny and Monica were busy . . . I had absolutely *nothing* to do."

"Anush . . ."

She smiled, knowing it was his way of accepting her apology. That, even though she used to berate him for every tiny mistake, he had never hung something like this over her head.

"The past few months have been a wake-up call, Neil. I've done a lot of things"—she sighed—"that I can't take back." She stared out the window and watched a bird precariously toeing its way across the fence. "But I'm not sure I would take it back, you know?"

"Yeah," he said, "I know." He plucked a Cheeto from the bowl and stared at it. "We started a family so young and had to grow up so quickly, sometimes I think we didn't have time to grow up at all."

Wasn't that the truth? While he looked away, she considered his face. His kind eyes and perfect smile. His slight, rather charming double chin, the way his head was pointing down.

"I don't want you to beat yourself up over what happened," he said. "It's in the past."

"Still," she said, "I shouldn't have just left like that—"

"Really, it was OK. It was only a week, Anush. And anyone who asked, like Kanika's teacher, Sara, I said you were away visiting family. I knew you were coming back. *Kanu* knew you were coming back."

Her stomach curdled. They'd had faith she would come back, even though, fleetingly, Anu hadn't had that faith in herself. "Didn't Kanika wonder why I didn't even call?"

He sipped his drink again, and her cheeks burned. He wasn't answering because he didn't want to hurt her. Of course Kanika had asked about Anu and profoundly felt her absence.

Anu was her mother. Her *mother*. Anu considered how paralyzing it felt—often, it still felt—to be so far away from Lakshmi. She was *thirty*. What must Kanika have felt? Anu wanted to cry just thinking about it: How much pain must she have caused?

"Anyway," Neil started, pushing his glass to the side. He flicked through the pile of papers in front of him, a stack of business card templates, the neon green class schedule of a rival studio Monica had surreptitiously plucked from its front desk.

"Anyway," she repeated.

Now he would ask for the divorce. Now one hard conversation was out of the way, and another one was about to begin. She kept waiting for him to say something, but he seemed to be distracted, fixated on the schedule.

"What is it?"

He rubbed his hand along his jaw, squinting at the page. "I was just thinking. . . . Those nights when Monica and Jenny were busy, after Kanika went to bed, when I was"—he shook his head—"doing whatever I was doing . . . you never went to a yoga class, did you?"

She shook her head, unsure what he was getting at. "No. Most studios don't have have classes later in the evenings on Fridays and Saturdays."

He leaned forward, nodding now, spreading his palms and fingers wide on the table. "You want to distinguish yourself, don't you? Anush, that's *exactly* my point."

He poured them another whiskey, and then one more after that. Neil's point had struck a chord in her, and pretty soon the ideas wouldn't stop coming.

Why couldn't she hold classes on weekend nights, just because nobody else seemed to? She could brand them "Ladies' Nights In." Charge double and throw in a glass of wine or coconut water at the end, a mindfulness session, leave the space open afterward for women to socialize. Weren't her adult friends always complaining to her how hard it was to meet other like-minded women outside of work? It was exactly what they needed.

She asked Neil aloud why her business had to conform to the same old yuppie demographic at all; they had enough studios pandering to them. She could hire wellness professionals and use the room to run courses on mindfulness, meditation, and breathing for any age group. Or even family-friendly beginner yoga classes, maybe weekday afternoons when the usual yoga crowd was at work or in class.

And what about yoga classes just for kids? Neil asked. On her laptop, he pulled up an article he'd found on Twitter a few months back on the benefits of yoga and mindfulness for children, how some more progressive schools were even implementing them as a form of detention. What if Anu held kids' yoga classes in the late afternoon, those few hours right after school? She could market them to schools in the area directly.

Neil logged in to the admin page of the website Imogen had created, and in a few clicks, he linked everything to the studio's social media accounts to increase SEO—which, Neil explained, would increase traffic to the website. She was in awe. With a little paint and a fresh idea, this studio could really work. She didn't have to try to build something better than her competition.

Without breaking down the old, Anu could create something new.

"Whoever did this did a good job," Neil said, clicking away on the back end of the website.

"My friend," Anu said quietly, thinking again of Imogen. "Imogen. She did do a great job."

"The only suggestion I have is"—he pointed to a text box—"that we integrate the payments systems with the online-booking tool. What do you think?"

She leaned forward. Half the screen was black, covered in green HTML code like in *The Matrix*.

"It sounds great, but you have so much on your plate already. . . ."

"It's easy. Don't worry. It'll only take me a minute." He leaned back suddenly, and his shoulder briefly rested against her forearm. She recoiled. When had the kitchen gotten so hot?

"Do you want dinner?" she asked, rushing to the fridge. Suddenly, she was starving and aware of how many whiskey and Cokes she'd drunk. "It's the least I could do after all this."

"I didn't do much, Anush. It was all you."

"It was a team effort. . . ." She trailed off, saddened. She and Neil had never been a team.

"See, done already." He smiled, standing up.

"Thank you." Her hand gripped the handle on the fridge door for balance. "Now what can I make you? Is *saag paneer* still your favorite?" Of course it remained his favorite. It was both their favorites.

"With rice or *roti*?"

"You may have just saved my business, so you can have it with whichever you like."

"Mom always serves it with *roti*." He walked over to her. "She taught you how to make it, didn't she?"

"That she did."

"Well, instead of cooking for me, would you teach me?" He shrugged. "I think it's about time I learned how to make it, too."

They'd never used to cook together. The rare day she was away in the evening, and neither of their mothers had dropped by, Neil had made do with frozen pizzas or a preroasted chicken from the local supermarket.

Now he was chopping coriander like a pro and taking notes on his phone, jotting down the ratio of cumin to spinach and broccoli, and the exact point at which to add the tomatoes. When her hands were sticky from the soft cheese, he held up the whiskey to her mouth—straight whiskey now; they'd run out of Coke—so she could take a sip, teasing her. Laughing with her.

Had it ever really been like this between them? Surely, it must have been. In university, those first sweet weeks of summer when exams were over and before they started their summer jobs, and there was nothing better to do than fan themselves out on an itchy polyester blanket in Stanley Park and drink warm beer from brown paper bags. Make out behind the girth of the red oak trees, in case any Indian bystanders were looking. Stare into each other's eyes and know, without a shadow of a doubt, that both of them wouldn't rather be anywhere else than right there.

The sudden intimacy of the situation startled her, and she went to the sink and washed her hands. When she turned around, Neil was stirring the *saag* as it simmered on the stove.

What would Paula think if she knew he was cooking with his ex? That he was acting this way with his ex?

Her cheeks were flushed, and the whiskey had made the whole room warm. Her hands shook as she reached for a tea towel to dry her hands.

The moment waxed and waned, and when he looked over at her, she knew it needed to stop. Why was she doing this to herself? And how could he do this to Paula?

She cleared her throat, gesturing him to step aside as she opened the oven so she could take out the *roti*.

"Everything all right?" he asked, as if sensing her shift in mood, her desperate attempt to neutralize the situation.

"Yep." She turned off the stove. "Plates?"

He grabbed two plates, and they served up the food. Her heart was beating fast. She wished they hadn't drunk so much.

"Where are you off to after this?" she asked as they took their plates to the table.

"Nowhere. Just home. I'm not in a rush, though. Auntie Jayani is home with Mom tonight."

"You don't have plans with . . ." She trailed off, incapable of saying her name. She hadn't had to say her name out loud before.

"No." Gently, expertly, he tore off a piece of *roti* with one hand. "Paula and I broke up."

They broke up?

Her heart dropped into her stomach as she tried her best to keep her face calm, her nerves calm. "Oh?" Where was her drink? Why had she finished her stupid drink?

"Yeah," he continued, "a few days ago."

"I'm sorry to hear that."

"Yeah, well . . ."

She could tell he was staring at her now, and she wished she was sitting another chair length away from him.

"I wasn't ready to . . . commit . . . I suppose. Not in the way she wanted."

Anu stood up because at that moment she needed to move, pump the oxygen through her body. She fetched a jar of mango pickle from the fridge, even though neither of them particularly liked *achar* with this meal, and then she sat back down. "I guess," she said, finally, twisting off its lid, "that's a very mature thing to do."

"I know." He laughed. "Who would have thought that word was in my vocabulary?"

"Neil, I didn't mean—"

"But you know it's true." He shrugged, dipping the torn piece of *roti* into the *saag*. He brought the first bite to his lips. "Wow. Anush, it tastes just like Mom's."

"Well, it is her recipe—" She stopped short. Was he crying? His empty fork poised midair, she couldn't read his face the way he was bent away from her. She reached for his hand, and without looking up, he grabbed hers.

"Mom's doing just fine. She's getting through this." Anu squeezed his fingers. "I've never met someone so tough."

Neil nodded, wiped his face. "You have no idea."

Anu glanced out the window. It was darker now, and with the fog like that, she could only see the faint glow of the streetlight in the alley opposite.

He laughed. "Sorry. I must have had one drink too many."

"Don't be sorry."

"I don't know what I'd do without her. It's been . . ." He trailed off, because there was no need to finish. Of course, she of all people understood how close Priya and Neil were, how before Anu they'd had no one but each other.

Wasn't that the reason he never traveled for longer than a few weeks at a time, why he had turned down a life in Silicon Valley when the job offers used to pour in? Why they'd bought a house a ten-minute drive away from her and done everything she'd ever asked of them?

Only now did she understand more than ever.

"I know, Neil." She could feel him watching her face as she lowered her eyes. "I know about your dad."

"What do you know?"

"She told me the truth." Anu flicked her eyes back up. "She told me your dad left."

He stood up in a rush and marched into the guest room, closed the door behind him. Her hands were shaking, but she didn't follow him. Instead, she tried to steady them with her breath, tearing a piece of *roti* with her fingers.

Was he coming back? She watched the clock, and five minutes later, she couldn't wait any longer. Opening the door, she found Neil sitting on the foot of the bed, his head in his hands.

"Can I come in?"

He nodded, drying his face with his sleeves. She didn't bother flicking on the light before going to sit next to him.

"She asked me not to," he said finally. His hands were on his lap, rigid, fingers clasped tightly. "When I was just a kid, she told me what really happened, and I promised her. We promised each other."

She loved their bond, and then she resented it. Was it because she and Lakshmi weren't as close, or was she jealous of Priya because Neil was never completely hers? That Anu would always have to share?

"The worst thing is, my grandparents made her feel ashamed. It's been almost thirty years, and she still thinks it's her fault. That it's something she needs to hide."

She reached for him, and he pressed her hand between his palms.

"She could have remarried. For years Auntie Jayani tried to convince her. But she was punishing herself. She couldn't let it go."

"Neil . . ."

"We never talk about it. It's become so real to me. It's like . . . It's what really happened." A silence, stark and sour, hung in the room. "I hope that bastard *is* dead."

"Neil, I don't know what to say." She squeezed his hands. "I'm so sorry."

"Not as sorry as I am."

She looked over at him, and with the hall light shining on him, she could just make out the profile of his face. "What do you mean?"

"I never let you in." He moved his hand away. "About my dad. About"—he tapped his chest hard—"about anything going on."

"Neil, you were fine."

"I lost you, Anush." Then he turned to meet her gaze. "I'm not fine."

She didn't remember the exact order of what happened next. Who looked or blinked first, who pressed and who pulled. But quickly, and not fast enough, their arms were around each other, their lips and bodies pressed so tight, it was hard to imagine they had ever been apart to begin with.

chapter thirty

✿

They'd waited five years.

Five freaking years to explore each other's bodies, realize firsthand why Rose's and Jack's hearts beat so fast when they panted in sync with each other in that old-fashioned car on the *Titanic*'s bottom deck. Five years in which they remained unsatisfied, frustrated, technically virgins, and therefore technically good kids.

But it was their wedding night, and that was all about to change. Up there on the *mandap* as the priest chanted in Sanskrit, neither of them was thinking about the 486 guests staring right at them or what the mantras they repeated actually meant. They didn't care, unlike Lakshmi, that the flower bouquets they ordered weren't quite the same tones of cream and red as Anu's bridal sari. Unlike Priya, they couldn't care less that the caterer's industrial deep fryer exploded and they'd be serving *kofta* as the appetizer, not samosa as she'd been planning for months.

Nope. While Anu and Neil exchanged rings and garlands,

posed for their thousandth picture, were showered with rose petals and blessings, all they were thinking about was the king-size bed that awaited them twenty-six floors above. Because after five long years, *excruciating* years, they were finally going to have sex.

The ceremony passed in the blur, then the lunch—although both forgot to eat. The afternoon disappeared as Anu, Neil, and their families posed for photos, then changed into their evening wear.

How was it that they couldn't manage a moment alone together? Not even to sneak their first kiss as a married couple? The reception started and the champagne flowed. They skipped dinner in favor of cocktails, and during the speeches—up there at the head table, bored stiff as the umpteenth uncle made a toast—they played a drinking game.

Every time someone whose name they didn't know congratulated them, they drank.

Every time Lakshmi cried, they drank.

Every time an auntie asked them when they planned to have children, they drank.

They were both piss drunk during their first dance, and they clasped each other's hands to keep stable, to refrain from wobbling. Their family and friends joined them, and the whole dance floor became a haze of laughter, sparkles, and sequins.

"Hey!" Neil shimmied toward her. His underarms were drenched, but she barely noticed as he grabbed her—rather chastely—around the waist. "Hey, let's go *fuck*."

"Neil! Shh!"

"We're married," he said, twirling her around. "We're *allowed*."

She went first, and he joined her at the elevators a minute later. He was already unbuttoning the blouse of her *lengha* as they sped upward toward the room, chased each other down the long, carpeted hall. Someone—she didn't know whom—had taken all the flowers from the ceremony and stuffed them in all the corners of the room, and when he pushed her down on the bed, she had the distinct feeling she was in the home gardening center near her parents' house.

"This is so heavy." He pawed at the skirt of her *lengha*, as if he could lift it off her rather than untie it.

"You're not the one who had to wear it all day."

"Do you want me to wear it?" He grinned down at her, his cheeks flushed. "Would that turn you on?"

"Would your fat ass fit?"

"Hey!"

She laughed as they move farther up their bed, shuffled around so their feet weren't hanging off. She'd managed a few buttons, but she couldn't concentrate—there was too much going on at once. Too much to remember. Moving her mouth and tongue—kissing, that she had gotten the hang of. But her head was spinning, and she couldn't see straight, couldn't feel where his clothes started and hers ended.

With a burst of energy she sat up, pushed him over. Eyes half closed, she grinned, slid her hand down his boxers.

"Anu?" He pushed her hand away. "What are you doing?"

"*Cosmo* says sixty-three percent of men like it."

"Sixty-three percent of men are lying."

"*Cosmo*—"

"Shut up about *Cosmo* and kiss me, Anush."

He was kissing her again, and it was bringing her back to the moment. Those lips, she'd known *those* for five years. The lips that made her tremble, even quake; what else could they do?

"Oh, shit." He pushed her back. There was a green tinge to his skin now. "I think I'm going to be sick."

He ran to the bathroom, and when a wave of dizziness passed

over her, she sat up and followed him. The way he was bent over heaving into the white porcelain toilet, it almost looked like he was praying.

"You OK?" She squatted down to rub his back, and suddenly the smell of vomit hit her. "Neil. Move over—"

"I'm not done—"

"Neil!" She just made it to the sink when it all came out. The champagne. The cocktails. It was like acid on her tongue, and she tried to remember what she'd eaten that day.

"I love you, Anush."

She spit and rotated her head to the side. "I love you more." She stood up straight, but when the room started spinning, she leaned heavily back on the sink. "What the hell did we drink?"

"Love potion?"

She laughed. "That's so lame, I'm going to throw up again."

He was smiling at her, his elbow on the toilet seat. Even though there was quite possibly vomit in her hair, she knew that when she thought back to her wedding day, tried to pinpoint that moment of pure happiness, it was going to be this one.

"What is happening here?"

She turned toward Priya's voice. She was standing next to Lakshmi in the bathroom doorway.

"Are you feeling OK, my honeys?" Lakshmi asked, smiling.

Anu swayed her head around and looked at Neil. "They had a *key*?"

"Lakshmi, look how *drunk* they are—"

"Mom, get *out*," Neil yelled, and Anu laughed. Her stomach felt sick again, and she turned back to the sink. Someone was laughing behind her. She couldn't be quite sure because another spasm caught her stomach and she was back over the sink. A hand was pressing at the small of her back, another one cold against her forehead.

"How much did you drink, *beti*?" A sigh. "Priya-*ji*, did we really need open bar?"

"It was your husband who insisted."

"Leave us alone, OK?" she heard Neil say.

"Yeah," Anu said, spitting into the sink, "we're *married*. Mom, please leave us alone. We're grown-ups!"

chapter thirty-one

✾

ANUSHA: Hey, Imogen, it's me again. I'm worried about you. Am I allowed to say that? Please text me back, even if it's just to say "Screw you." I mean, I'd prefer if it didn't but at this point I'll take anything. . . . Anyway, there will be an open house next Sunday for the redesign. It's going to be just the way we imagined. I hope to see you there. xox

"Yoo-hoooo."

Anu turned toward the voice and found the pair of them back-to-back, posed like some sort of girl band. Jenny and Monica were wearing matching T-shirts that read, "WEST BROADWAY YOGA SQUAD," the same ocean blue as the color in the paint cans Anu held.

"You didn't," Anu gasped.

Monica tossed her a T-shirt. "We did."

"Every new business needs merch." Jenny shrugged the canvas bag on her shoulder. "We bought two dozen in adult sizes and a miniature one for Kanika."

Shrieking in delight, Anu hugged them in the foyer, squeezing them tight until they grew annoyed and pushed her off.

She couldn't imagine better friends. For the past three weeks, both Jenny and Monica had been helping her on trips to Home

Depot to pick up paint and primer, accepting deliveries for the brand-new mats, blocks, and other equipment Anu had bought from a distributor down in Seattle. The week before, Monica had even helped her interview the new teachers Anu had found to teach family and prenatal yoga, as well as meditation courses.

They were taking a Friday off work to help her fix up the place. Now that the contractor Anu hired had torn down the wall, and the practice room was double its original size, everything else was up to them.

Anu pulled her new T-shirt over her tank top and then grabbed her clipboard from the front desk. "Who's up for assignments?"

"I already know mine," Jenny said, flipping back her hair in an exaggerated fashion. "Where are my paints, minion?"

Anu gestured behind her. "Yes, we get it. You minored in art and get to paint the feature wall. But please make the mural look ocean-y. Zen and all that."

"She told me she's going to hide a penis somewhere—"

"Mon! Way to tattle."

"No penis," Anu said, laughing. "OK. Well, not a *big* one."

She put Monica in charge of setting up the studio proper: organizing the equipment, varnishing the hardwood floors, and arranging the minimalist decorations. Meanwhile, Anu tackled everything else. She installed the new faucets and fixtures, deep-cleaned the change room and bathrooms, painted all the walls but Jenny's feature wall either a "Swiss coffee" off-white or a "dove" gray. Anu also managed to install a new audio system for the music-inspired classes without tearing her hair out and, later, hung art and other decorations she'd found anywhere from vintage stores on East Hastings to furniture outlets in Richmond.

"You're next," Monica said to Jenny when she caught her taking long breaks from painting to text Damien. "You are *so* going to marry him."

Jenny slipped her phone into her back pocket, ignoring her.

"And you'd better have bridesmaids—none of this 'we're keeping it simple' nonsense."

Jenny rolled her eyes. "Who says you'd be a bridesmaid?"

"Yeah," Monica spit out, *"right."*

"And who says I even want to get married? We don't need a piece of paper, a *party*, to build a life together—"

"You've been dating Damien for three weeks"—Monica smirked—"and already you're 'building a life together'?"

"Oh, my *God*, Monica, you brought it up!" Fuming, Jenny spun around from the feature wall. "You are being so annoying!"

"This is so fun." Monica winked at Anu. "Isn't this fun?"

Anu winked back. "Women in love are so *sensitive*, don't you think?"

"I am *not* sensitive," Jenny said.

"So you admit you're in love?"

"No. Not *yet*." Jenny's face relaxed. "I'm merely . . . sexually sated."

Laughing, Anu turned back to her current task, sanding off the cracking paint on the front windowsill.

"Speaking of being sexually sated," Jenny said nonchalantly behind Anu, "when are you going to go out with Tyler?"

Anu didn't turn around.

"They've been texting," Monica said. "She already told us that."

"According to Damien," Jenny said, "Tyler has asked her out three times, and she keeps making up excuses and postponing it."

Anu gestured at the chipping paint. "Uh, I think *this* is a pretty good excuse!"

"So you're saying that in all this time, you haven't been able to spare an hour for coffee?"

"Jenny," Monica said, "don't pressure her. If she's not ready, then she's not ready."

They were silent for a while, and just when Anu thought it had blown over, she felt someone standing next to her.

"What's going on with you?" Jenny said loudly into her ear.

"Who, me?"

"No, Justin Bieber."

Anu stood up, taking a deep breath. When she was ready, she turned around.

She hadn't let it slip in three weeks. Throwing herself into the studio, she'd pressed it down, flattened it out, pretended *it* had never happened.

Jenny was squinting at her, her face drawing closer. *No.* She couldn't tell them. She *wouldn't* tell them.

"Anusha Manjula Rohini Desai, *what* is—"

"Neil and I had sex."

She'd predicted these reactions; that was why she didn't want to see them: Jenny's shit-eating grin. Monica's gaping mouth, her face instantly a paler, almost translucent hue.

Eventually they calmed down, and when Anu started to explain how the night had unfolded, Jenny interrupted her.

"OK, I don't care about *any* of that," she said. "Was it good? Were you *sated*?"

Anu blushed, and Jenny threw her hands up in the air.

"Hallelujah!"

"It *was*?" Monica screamed.

"It was incredible. It was . . . better, *way* better than it ever was with us." She shrugged. "It was like . . . that passion we used to have—when we were young, when we really, *really* loved each other—was back."

"That's so romantic, Anu."

Jenny rolled her eyes at Monica. "Did you orgasm?"

Anu giggled a shy-schoolgirl giggle, prompting Jenny and Monica to egg her on.

The sex had been incredible. Even the few hours afterward had been perfect as they lay in bed eating *saag paneer*, laughing into the early hours of the morning, limbs in gridlock. But what came after didn't feel so incredible. It was Neil picking up his clothes piece by piece from the floor, telling her he'd better get back home even though she didn't want him to leave.

It was Neil, for once, being the mature one and telling her that their slipup didn't have to mean anything they didn't want it to. It could just be what it was: what was leftover between two people who had loved each other, but were on a path moving forward.

When she eventually said all this to her friends, Monica was near tears. Even Jenny looked morose.

"He's such a good guy," Jenny said after a while. "Sounds like he's really changed."

Anu let her head fall back against the wall. She had painted it only the day before, and the chemical smell was still strong.

"Is there a part of you that wants to give your marriage a second chance?" Monica said softly, turning to Jenny. "I wouldn't be against it. Jen, would you?"

Jenny shook her head. "Not at all."

Anu narrowed her eyes at them. "How long have you felt this way?" Neither one answered, and Anu stood up, shaking her head. "So you guys think I should get back together with Neil? Just because . . . he's learned how to load a dishwasher?"

"Anu—"

"You remember what it used to be like between us, right?"

"You've both changed, Anu," Jenny said. "That's all we're trying to say."

Monica stood up suddenly and disappeared into the back room. A moment later she returned, a piece of hot pink paper fluttering in her hands.

"What's . . . ?" Anu trailed off as it dawned on her.

"You forgot this in my car," Monica said. Turning to Jenny, she added, "This is Anu's—"

"List on how to be a grown-up. I know. I was there when she wrote it."

Monica turned back to Anu. "As I was saying, I found your list in my car . . . and I think it's time you take it back."

Anu took the paper from her. "Why do I need this?"

"Why do you think?" Monica shrugged, turned back to her work. "You haven't finished it yet."

Have you uploaded the new pictures on the website?" Monica asked, the evening before the open house.

Anu nodded. "Yep, and I've updated the class schedule to include Greta's mindfulness seminar."

"And the ads are live?"

Again Anu nodded. She'd paid an arm and a leg for Facebook advertising to hit a huge cross section of her potential demographic starting that very day. The week before, she'd also papered the neighborhood with flyers and e-mailed out a press release about the open house to several hundred, maybe close to a thousand, media contacts that Monica had discreetly borrowed from her publicist friend. Anu had so far received about a dozen calls, a few promises that she'd have local press coverage and that a radio broadcaster would drop by for the open house.

As they lay there in the practice room, ocean blue and calm and lit up by fairy lights, Anu wished Imogen were here to see this. Anu wondered if she'd turn up at the open house. She'd sent several messages inviting her.

"I think you need more lights," Monica said, "in the far corner."

"Yeah?"

"Yeah. Jen, what do you think?" Monica rolled to the side, shook Jenny on the shoulder. "Are you asleep?"

Anu sat up. Jenny was rolled over on her side, texting on her phone. "Nope, she's *texting*."

"Who?"

"I bet it's the man she's building a life with—"

"Oh," Jenny said, sitting up, "you both can fuck right off."

Anu and Monica burst out laughing as Jenny picked herself up off the floor, but there was a smile on her face as she flipped them the bird and left the studio.

"Have *fun*!" Any yelled out provocatively.

Laughing, Monica called out, "We'd better be bridesmaids!"

Anu and Monica put away the new mats they'd been lounging on and shut off the practice room lights. When Anu reached into her purse, her heart dropped when she looked at her phone. She had a missed call from Imogen.

She showed the screen to Monica, and then setting her bag down on the desk, Anu clicked the callback button. It went straight to voice mail.

"Try again?" Monica said.

Anu tried calling four more times, but each time the call wouldn't connect. The room suddenly felt hot, and she took off her hoodie.

Except that one conversation in London, Anu had never known Imogen to use her phone to actually receive a phone call. Why today?

"Something's not right."

"Maybe she wanted to accept your apology, get her job back. . . ."

Anu just shook her head as a dull dread washed over her body. She'd told Imogen to call her anytime, day or night. A call she needed to make, one Anu wasn't around to answer.

Her heart pounded into her chest. Something was wrong.

Out loud with Monica, she went over everything she knew about Imogen, and Anu pored over her social media for information while Monica kept calling. But there was nothing, not a clue, and Anu racked her brain for how to get in touch with Imogen.

Should she call the police? But what would they do? What *could* they do? Imogen mentioned once that she lived near that hip-hop club they'd gone to once; but what could Anu do? Knock on random doors? That neighborhood was huge!

Scrambling, Anu tore through the office, the desk drawers, scavenging for some clue Imogen might have left behind. She got to the bottom drawer, and a lightbulb went on when she spotted Mags' old record book.

"Haruto!"

"Huh?"

Anu pulled out the brown binder and started flipping through the pages. "The guy Imogen is seeing. He took her class." Anu flipped past another page, dragging her hand along the names. "Mags did everything by hand." She flipped another page. "He's got to be in here—*there!*"

She pointed at the sign-in sheet, dated nearly a year before: *Haruto Doi. Age 24. 604-501-9988.*

He didn't answer at first, but Anu kept calling until he did. He sounded surprised to hear from her, and rather stoned, but he had an address. A basement suite, ten minutes away from the hip-hop club.

"When was the last time you saw her?" Anu asked, before hanging up.

"It's been weeks," he said. "She ghosted me."

Weeks?

They took Monica's car; Anu was too rattled to drive. Anu urged her to drive faster, get there *faster*, and so Monica squeezed Anu's hand from the driver's seat and stepped on the gas pedal.

The house was at the end of a tree-lined block and in complete disrepair. There were no lights on. Monica banged hard on the front door, but there was no answer.

"Haruto said it was a basement suite," Anu said, climbing back down the steps. "Maybe there's a separate entrance?"

They both eyed the "BEWARE OF DOG" sign on the back gate. Anu took a deep breath and stepped through, anyway. Luckily, there was no dog, just an old path covered in leaves winding its way back around the house.

She found a staircase leading to a back door. Anu knocked hard, pounding the door with all her might. There was no answer, and so she knocked on the window.

"Maybe she's out . . . ," Monica said, her arms wrapped tight around her body. It was freezing outside, and in the rush, both of them had forgotten their coats.

"She doesn't have a job. I don't think she has any money." Taking a deep breath, she shrugged off her hoodie and wrapped it tightly around her fist. "Mon, I know she's home."

"Anu, no!"

She didn't listen. As hard as she could, she punched a hole through the glass of the door. It was easier than she thought, and carefully, she unlocked the door through the hole, avoiding the shards of glass.

"Imogen?" she called, opening the door. "You here?"

The place was bare. Imogen's faux-fur coat was on a hook down the hall, a few pairs of boots scattered just beneath. There was nothing in the living room but two patio chairs, and on the counter in the galley kitchen were a few empty liquor bottles, an orange, a rogue pizza crust. There, the hallway curved, and she came face-to-face with a closed door.

"Imogen?"

Anu didn't wait for an answer. She pushed through the door, and her chest burst when she saw Imogen, her head lolled back over the edge of the bed, her eyes half open and slits of white.

Anu heard Monica gasp behind her.

"Call nine-one-one," Anu said, trying to stay calm. She bent down by the bed and started shaking Imogen's lifeless body.

"Hello? Hello . . . ?" Monica said in the background.

"Imogen, wake up," Anu pleaded, her face wet. She leaned down, her ear to Imogen's mouth. She heard something. "She's breathing, Mon. Tell them she's breathing."

With Monica on the phone in the background, Anu cleared the mess of hair away from Imogen's face. Her face was so white, it was almost blue, and instinctively Anu glanced at the nightstand, her stomach churning when she saw what was on it.

Shaking, Anu pulled Imogen up and let her torso keel forward over the side of the bed. Without hesitating, Anu stuck her pointer finger and middle finger down Imogen's throat.

Nothing happened, and Anu's heart wrenched; she was terrified of hurting Imogen. Despite her height, her weight, Imogen felt so frail in Anu's arms.

How could Anu have been so blind as not to see? Tears streaming from her face, Anu shifted Imogen's weight more fully on her and tried again.

Come on, Imogen. You can do this.

Anu pushed down and back once more and then felt the reflex and pulled her hand out.

A beat later, Imogen convulsed, vomiting onto the floor.

Monica crouched next to them then, holding Imogen's head with one hand and the phone with the other.

Imogen vomited again and then one more time after that.

With her hand, Anu wiped the rest of the vomit from Imogen's mouth and face, and then Monica helped her push Imogen back on the bed. They laid her on her side, supporting her weight behind her with a pillow.

Monica ran to the bathroom to fetch a hot towel, but Anu refused to leave Imogen's side, brushing stray hair away from her face. She watched the shallow rise and fall of Imogen's chest and swallowed hard as she remembered their fight. What Imogen had yelled: "You take everything for granted. *Everything.*"

The words burned into Anu as she squeezed Imogen's hand, pressed them into her chest.

Imogen was right. Anu had it all, and she took it for granted. She had family and friends who loved and supported her. A career and a safety net and her health.

She had it all and appreciated none of it as much as she should.

Monica returned with a wet cloth. She pressed it to Imogen's forehead, and just then, they heard the sirens.

chapter thirty-two

You are still here?"

Anu looked up. It was one of the nurses from before, the middle-aged South Asian one who reminded Anu of Lakshmi. She was only a few feet away, and Anu wondered if she had fallen asleep; she hadn't heard the nurse approach. Anu squinted. Her nametag read "Avneet," and she had a clipboard tucked beneath her left armpit. Her scrubs were flowery, a cheerful pink standing out against the drabness of the waiting room. Years ago, Anu had worked in this very ward as a nursing student. She wondered if she'd met Avneet before.

"Can I see her?"

Avneet smiled at her, shifting her clipboard to her other armpit. The doctors had gone over this: Anu was not family and therefore not allowed in. Anu glanced at the clock above the nurses' station. It had been five hours since they arrived and two since Anu had forced Monica to go home.

"It is late. Come back tomorrow."

"I can wait."

"You will be waiting a while."

"But her parents aren't here yet."

Avneet pressed her lips together and then glanced back at the nurses' station, empty now. Anu stood up, tucked her hair behind her ears.

"Please? She's all alone in there."

A minute later, Avneet led her to the room and, in a stern tone, warned Anu that she'd be back in five minutes. The rooms running the length of the corridor all had their lights switched off, but she could just make out the vague outlines of all the hospital beds, all occupied.

At the end of the hall, she spotted Imogen's shape on the bed from the doorway and the shadow of a hand moving. The motion of a wave.

"Hey," Anu said quietly.

Avneet left them, and Anu sat in the chair by the head of the bed. Imogen was sitting up, the top half of the hospital bed at a relaxed incline. Her makeup had been wiped clean from her face, and there was crust around her lips and eyes. An IV drip was plugged into her left arm. Anu reached for her right hand and squeezed it tight.

"How are you feeling?"

Imogen grinned, limply. "Like death."

Anu frowned, studying Imogen's face. Anu wasn't family, so the doctors and nurses hadn't told her a thing other than the fact that Imogen was stable. They hadn't told her what had happened, or confirmed that she'd drunk from the bottle of vodka sitting on her nightstand, and that's what it was they'd had to pump from her stomach.

And what about the pills?

Anu had seen the parademics take note of Imogen's antidepressants laying about the nightstand, counting them. It could have been an accident. But it could have not been an accident. The thought of either possibility made Anu's body quake with fear.

"I'm sorry," Imogen said. Shadows danced across Imogen's face as her head leaned farther back on the pillow. "That was a bad joke."

"Don't be sorry. I'm the one who should be sorry." Anu paused, wiping a tear from her face. "I should have been there for you."

"I didn't exactly let you, Anusha." She adjusted her neck on the pillow. "Blaming yourself for this would be so *typical* of you." Imogen smiled weakly. "Only children. You guys always need to be the center of attention, don't you?"

Anu laughed. "Aren't *you* an only child?"

Imogen shrugged, smiling sleepily, as if she might disappear at any moment into a dream. She let go of Anu's hand and reached for a glass of water beside the bed. Anu helped her, Imogen's hand shaking as she brought the plastic cup to her lips.

"Thank you," Imogen said. Such a mild exertion, yet she sounded exhausted. "For finding me."

"Thank you for calling me back."

Imogen laughed. "Took my time, didn't I?"

There were tears in Anu's eyes, and she wiped them away. There was a million things Anu wanted to say, questions she wanted to ask, but there would be time for all that later. Right now, all she could do was be Imogen's friend. Be there for her in whatever ways she was allowed.

"Better late than never."

. . .

Kunal had left Anu a note on the kitchen table.

I made quiche. It is in the fridge. I will be insulted if you do not try it.

Anu smiled and then quietly heated up the quiche in the microwave. Kunal must have gone to bed early that night and not seen Anu's panicked texts from the hospital.

Anu pressed CANCEL on the microwave before the noisy timer went off, and then she took her plate to the kitchen table. While eating, she flicked open her laptop, and her Facebook home page appeared; she must have left it open that morning.

Had it been only that morning that she, Jenny, and Monica had been fixing up the studio? She glanced at the microwave clock. It was four twenty-three a.m. She supposed it had been yesterday morning, and *this* morning—in just over five hours—would be her open house.

When she moved her finger on the mouse pad, Facebook automatically refreshed, and a meme with several baby pandas appeared, posted by Lakshmi only five minutes earlier.

Anu smiled and liked the photo. Why had Anu always been so hard on her for posting enthusiastically on Facebook? For mixing metaphors? For throwing herself so completely into her life?

She remembered Imogen's mother, rushing into the hospital room, in hysterics, trailed by her father, sobbing as he clutched onto his daughter and wife. Just thinking about it, Anu could feel herself breaking down, breaking open.

Lakshmi was there for her. Even in London, she was there for her. Why had Anu pushed her away? Why had Anu been so fuck-ing *petty?*

"*Beti?*" Lakshmi answered her video call on the first ring. She was in bed, the lamp casting a spooky glow over half her face. "Why are you awake at this hour?"

"I saw your meme," Anu said, "on Facebook."

Lakshmi shifted on the bed, an uncomfortable look on her face. Did she, too, realize this was the first time they'd spoken alone in months, maybe nearly a year?

"I never thanked you for the garland you sent," Anu said, wip-ing her wet nose with a tissue. "It's been hanging in the studio doorway this whole time."

Lakshmi gave her a small smile.

"It'll be hanging there today."

"I am sorry I cannot be at your big open house," Lakshmi said, "although your father has promised to let me attend by FaceTime."

"It's OK. I'll show you around when you're home for Kanu's birthday."

"*Hah.*" Lakshmi nodded her head from side to side, a manner-ism that meant both yes and no yet neither. "That will be nice."

The distance between them was palpable, their relationship stiff. Yes, Anu had taken her mother—taken *everything*—for granted, but what about Lakshmi?

Lakshmi had wanted to protect Anu from the world so badly, but she never realized that she couldn't, that she shouldn't, because how else was Anu to grow up? How else was Anu to learn to pick herself up when she fell?

But there was no falling for Indian girls, not *good* Indian girls. Girls like Anu let themselves be guided, graciously, from moment to moment, milestone to milestone. They stayed indoors, and their boots were never muddy. Their hands were always clean.

Good girls listened to their mothers.

But Anu hadn't wanted to listen to anyone. She got tired of *listening*. Yet, still Anu wanted Lakshmi's approval, and so she pretended. She pretended to be her mother's good Indian girl, the lies piling higher and higher, small ones and large alike, until this wall emerged between them.

A wall Anu needed to knock down.

"Mom, I'm sorry." She noted the feebleness in her own voice and cleared her throat. "I'm sorry about our fight in London."

"I'm sorry, too, Anu."

She studied Lakshmi's face on the screen, was tempted to reach out and touch it. "I should never have lied to you." Anu took a deep breath, sucking on the air. "I want us to be honest with each other from now on, OK? Even . . . even if it means I disappoint you."

"*Beti* . . . ," Lakshmi chided. She wrinkled her nose, a smile breaking open on her face. "My daughter is successful nurse. She is . . . *entrepreneur*. She is a wonderful mother and friend and daughter—" Lakshmi stopped. Paused. "She is many things, *unlimited* things, and I am very, *very* proud of her."

Maybe times had changed. They could keep changing. Maybe, from now on, she and Lakshmi could change together.

Anu brought another forkful of quiche to her lips. "I'm proud of you, too, Mom."

"*Hah?*"

Anu smiled, swallowed her food. "I said I'm proud of you, too. I really, *really* am."

"Did your father make dinner? Is it good?" Lakshmi threw Anu a suspicious glance. "He has been bragging about this quiche all day."

"Yeah, it's all right."

"Your father spends few months running the household in England, and suddenly he thinks he is next Anthony Bourdain."

"Wasn't he American?"

"Uh-*ho*," Lakshmi snapped, her eyes smiling. "You know my point!"

Anu took another bite. Chewing it, she caught sight of a textbook open on the bed next to Lakshmi. The words were blurred, but she could just make out lines of neon yellow and orange highlighted here and there.

Anu couldn't think of a single time that she'd video-chatted with Lakshmi and a textbook hadn't been in the frame, that Lakshmi hadn't ended the call by saying, "Back to the books!" or to Kunal, "Now off to study, my lovey-dovey!" Feeling ashamed, she realized that not once had she asked her mother about her master's program. Not once had she taken an interest in Lakshmi's life outside Anu.

"What are you studying today?" Anu pointed at the screen. "What's that textbook?"

Lakshmi squirmed in excitement, sitting up in the bed. "It is heaping mouthful. Are you prepared?"

Anu nodded.

"Gender, *sex*-uality, and women studies." Lakshmi lowered her voice slightly. "And do you know, next term I am taking module that studies the *Kama Sutra*? I will be top of the class, *nah*?"

"Mom, that's disgusting. . . ."

"Because I am a Hindu. Uh-*ho*."

"Oh, is *that* what you meant?"

"You young people. You think we are so old. What can *we* possibly know about the art of making the love? I have been enjoying sex much longer than you, *beti*!"

Anu choked on her food. "*Mom!*"

"Maybe Vātsyāyana did not write *Kama Sutra*. I think *women* truly know these things much better naturally, *nah*? None of this quick-quick testosterone business. You know, I had to teach your father everything, Anu. *Everything.* After our wedding, the first time he saw me undress, it was like he was trying to roll *chapati* with m—"

"I think I'm going to be sick."

"*Kya?* You asked me about my studies, *nah*? You said we should be honest!"

Anu swallowed the bile in her throat. "That I did." She laughed. "So, I suppose, thank you for *that.*"

"Can you imagine this honesty business with *my* ma, Anu? If she was alive, what would she have to say about such filth?"

"Maybe Nani would have surprised you," Anu said. "Maybe she would have told you all about *her* sex life."

Lakshmi made a face, and Anu burst out laughing again, and when the tears started streaming down her face, they refused to stop. It was hard to breathe, because of how much she missed Lakshmi in that moment.

"*Beti.*" Lakshmi tutted at her, soothing her. "No crying. I will see you in less than one week. We are OK, *nah*? Mothers and daughters *should* fight." Laughing, she said, "And now we have made up for lost time."

"It's not just that." Anu shook her head, overwhelmed, as she pictured Imogen's mother hurrying to her side. The images rushed in, bending and blurring. Marianne's moist palm, pressing that pill into Anu's hand. Theo's mouth. The hole in the studio wall.

Paula.

She looked up from the laptop, to Kanika's empty seat, and tried to imagine Kanika in her place, Anu at Lakshmi's age. No matter what Kanika did, no matter how disappointing it might feel, wouldn't Anu want to know? Even if she were far away, even if she couldn't really help with any of it, wouldn't Anu want to hear about it?

She would, and so for the first time, starting from the beginning, she told Lakshmi everything.

chapter thirty-three

NEIL: Hey, Anush . . . I ran into your dad at Costco this morning and he told me about what happened to your friend. I'm sorry to hear that. . . . You'll let me know if there's anything I can do? Otherwise I'll see you at 1 for the family class. Kanu is DEFCON 5 excited. . . .

She managed three hours of sleep after her long talk with Lakshmi, and later Kunal, who overheard their conversation from the basement and came upstairs to join them. Yet that morning, she woke up feeling rested and calm, calmer still after Imogen texted her to say that she'd been released from the hospital and that her parents were taking her home.

Anu hopped in the shower, threw on a bit of makeup, and arrived at the studio a full hour before she needed to be there. Everything was already in place, and so she wandered from room to room soaking it all in.

This was hers. With a lot of help, she had made something new and was about to put it on offer to the world. Would anyone show up? Would people care?

Or would they laugh at her, marvel at the ridiculousness of a single mother kicking off a new business on a lark?

The luxury of the moment startled her: that she had the ability, even the audacity, to worry about something that so few had the privilege to think about. Imogen had been right before: Anu had nothing to lose but her ego. If the business floundered, she'd find herself in debt that eventually she'd be able to work her way out of.

She'd still have her family, her friends. A livelihood of her own. Anu palmed each piece of new equipment as she passed it, let her fingers glide against the surface of the mural Jenny had painted in the foyer—as if they were pieces of a life, and each touch was a recognition of what she had.

And a vow that she would never fail to appreciate it again.

Jenny and Monica arrived early, Monica groggy but pretending not to be. Anu hugged them each in turn, and she decided right then to treat the three of them to a group trip to Seattle as a thank-you for all their help that year. Before Kanika was born, the three of them used to go to Seattle annually for a weekend away. They would wine and dine and get drunk by the water—having the time of their lives talking to no one but themselves.

Why had she stopped going? Why had she insisted they go without her, even though Neil said he could manage things without her? Anu shook her head, now unable to comprehend the decision. This year would be different. She would save and find a way. She would set the time and money aside, and she would make time to be there for her friends.

When the open house started, they kept the front door open, a cool early-spring breeze freshening up the crowded foyer. Jenny, Monica, and Tom manned the coffee machine outside, designed to lure in the foot traffic, while the new teacher Radhika taught a beginner *vinyasa* class in the practice room. Kunal was there, entertaining the back row with his overzealous positions, along with walk-ins, colleagues from the clinic, friends and acquaintances from school she didn't think would come.

Anu let out a sigh of relief when the first class ended. So far, so good. It was all going according to plan. More and more visitors were arriving every few minutes, and even a local reporter turned up to attend Greta's mindfulness session. Just as Anu returned from the back office with another stack of brochures, she saw Neil, Kanika, and Priya through the window. Jenny said something to make Priya—who seemed much stronger than only a few weeks earlier—laugh and just then Kanika looked over and saw Anu. She squealed, and Anu raced through the door toward them.

"There you are!"

She picked up Kanika and smelled the bouquet of wildflowers in her daughter's precious hands, squeezing Priya with her free arm. She could see Neil watching her from the corner of her eye.

"What's that?" Kanika asked, pointing at the mural, as they followed her inside.

"Auntie Jenny did that. She's a good artist, huh?"

"Really, Auntie *Jenny*?" Kanika gasped. "But her makeup is always so funny!"

They burst out laughing, and Anu caught Neil's eye as she set Kanika down on the floor. His gaze made her body burn from head to toe.

"It's wonderful, Anush. It really is."

"Thank you for coming. The flowers . . . For everything, Neil."

"We wouldn't have missed it," Neil said, patting Kanika on the head. "Kanu is *very* excited to see me try to touch my toes."

Anu laughed, but her breath stopped as a pale hand appeared, a small, dainty one on the bulk of Neil's shoulder.

"I'm not late, am I?"

Everyone turned to look, and as Neil moved to the side, Anu saw her. The familiar face, rose cheeks, and lips, Sara's young face shining right at Neil.

"Ms. Finch!" Kanika squealed, running to her. It was like a punch straight to Anu's gut.

"Neil, did you remember the name tags?"

"Yep, got them right here, Sara. . . ."

In a dreamlike state, she watched the majority of Kanika's kindergarten class turn up for the one p.m. family class; many of the children had even brought their siblings. It was a surprise for Anu: Neil and Sara had worked together. They'd rallied the class in her support. Anu had always done so much for the school; wasn't it time, they all said, they returned the favor?

Finally, Anu's new teacher, Mari, called everyone in for the class. The practice room was crowded, but everyone managed to find a space. Why was Anu not surprised to see that Sara snagged a spot right next to Neil?

Anu had planned on taking the class with Kanika, but suddenly she couldn't. She breathed through the jealousy and closed the practice room door behind her, overcome by the urge to be alone.

The foyer was empty now, and Monica, Tom, Jenny, and a few of the teachers were outside by the coffee stand, joking around. Anu didn't join them. Instead, she went downstairs into the empty women's change room and sat on the bench that ran the length of it. She'd bought it used and sanded it down and varnished it herself. Having never had to do anything practical or hands-on before, in that moment she'd been prouder of herself than she had in a while. Then, it had made her feel like she could do anything.

Now?

Now she wasn't sure.

Ten minutes passed down there, and alone with her thoughts, she became angrier with herself. If Neil was with Sara now, she shouldn't *care* that he was moving on, or what he thought about her. She, too, was trying to move forward; how could she expect him to stay there for her in the past?

There was creaking close from above, and she held her breath. It was coming from the staircase.

"Hello?" she whispered, and a beat later, there was a gentle knock on the change room door.

Anu gripped the bench. Maybe it was Sara. Clearly, she wanted to steal Anu's family. Maybe she wanted to slit her throat, too.

"Anush, are you in there?"

She exhaled, and without standing up, she wedged the door open with her toes. Neil poked his head through, and then came the rest of his body.

"Wow, this change room is huge." Scratching at the scruff on his chin, he leaned against the back of the closed door. "I didn't realize you had this much space down here."

"The men's room is just as large," she said flatly. "And there's a big space at the back that's completely empty."

"You could fit another practice room down here."

"I suppose so," she said, even though she had already thought as much. Even though she and Imogen, before their fight, had drawn up fantasy plans for one.

"Are you OK? How's your friend doing?"

"Her name is Imogen, and she's going to be OK. Thanks." Her voice sounded harsher than she'd intended, and she felt a tinge of remorse. Neil had never met Imogen, yet she had become so important to Anu. Anu knew it wasn't Neil's fault that he'd missed out on this part of her life, yet she was still angry at him for it. Albeit unreasonably so.

Anu cleared her throat. "She'll be OK. Thanks for asking." A pause. "She's back home now, with her parents."

Another pause. "Do you want to talk about it?"

Anu shook her head. "Don't you want to take the family class? Why are you down here?"

Neil shoved his hands in his pockets and sat down next to her on the bench. He hadn't turned on the light, either, so the room was dark, only a crack of light streaming in from the slit of a window that looked into the alley.

"I didn't get a chance to tell you," he said. "Sara and I have been talking—"

Anu winced, preparing herself.

"—and the school principal is really into yoga herself, apparently. She's going to call you this week. She wants to schedule an introductory class for every single kid at Kanu's school. Amazing, right?"

Anu turned to face him, not quite believing him—still hanging on to the way he'd said "Sara."

"They're going to take it to the school board." His eyes were shining. "Can you imagine, Anush? If it gets into the school curriculum? Every afternoon, you could have this place *packed*."

"I . . ." Anu grew speechless as her heart pounded in her chest, her stomach. She was touched, yet terrified and overcome with the urge to hug him and run away at the same time. "I don't know what to say."

Why had Neil gone out of his way to help with the studio? Why had he taken the time, the care, to surprise her, to champion Anu's success as her own?

"Sara said that . . ."

She wasn't imagining it; the last few years of their marriage hadn't been a marriage. It had been cohabitation, an *existence*. Neil had taken her for granted.

Had Anu also not failed to appreciate *him* and their life together? Could she not be unreliable, unreasonable? Didn't her mood swing depending on the time of day, what and whether she ate—meaning anything or nothing could be the trigger? Hadn't she wanted from *him*, even demanded something more from life—even before she knew what any of it meant?

What if present-day Neil had existed back then, and he had been the supportive, reliable, loving partner she'd always wanted him to be—would it have been enough for her? Or would she have nonetheless pushed it all away?

"Anush, what's wrong? Isn't this what you wanted?"

This, as in the studio? Or *this* as in us?

"What are you thinking?"

I love you. Her lips were still, but in her head, her heart, it came rushing out.

She loved him, and she had always loved him.

Why had she made him leave without a second thought? Why had she thrown him away on a whim? Why had she convinced herself that staying in their marriage, working through their issues, would inevitably turn her into their mothers?

An Indian woman whose most memorable characteristic was her husband.

"I'm thinking about a lot of things right now."

"Like?"

"Like . . ." She sighed, kicked at a loose pebble on the floor.

"Like?"

The pebble scattered to the far end of the room, knocking up against the wall before settling beneath the coat rack.

"I'm sick of this, Anush."

Startled, she looked over and found Neil violently rubbing his face with his palms.

"You're sitting here, sulking, acting like some jealous, wounded *pup*—"

"So there *is* something going on with you two."

Neil sighed. "Ms. Finch and I—"

"Ms. *Finch*." Anu laughed. "Is that what you role-play in bed?"

"Would you cut it out? She has a crush on me, but there's nothing going on, I swear. She's nearly a decade younger than us—what do you take me for?"

"I—"

"And either way, you have *no* right to be jealous. You left me, Anush. *You* were the first person to date someone else. And don't think I don't know about *Jude Law* or that guy from Tinder—"

"Who told you that?"

"Who do you think?"

Tom. Of course Monica would have told her husband, who would in turn tell his close friend. The information flowed the other way; why had she not thought it to be reciprocal?

"So you think I'm sleeping around?" Anu's voice got small. "Is that what you think of me?"

He stood up and walked three paces. When he was in the middle of the room, he turned around.

Did he really think that poorly of her? That she had changed that much?

Sure, she had gone too far; she had taken risks and had to pay the price. She didn't realize the price would be Neil's respect.

"I didn't . . ." She trailed off. Why did she need to explain herself to him? She didn't, and suddenly, she was enraged. "You know what? Never mind. You should probably join Tinder yourself. Get off your pedestal, Neil, and join me down here with the rest of us." She glared at him. "It's a lot more fun than being *married*."

He stared at her, incredulous.

"Join Tinder." She stood up. "Go be the single guy you never got to be, Neil. Go fuck Sara and twenty-two-year-old interns named Caley and Tiffany who think you're just so damn wonderful."

He crossed his arms. "Maybe I will."

"Good."

"*Good*—" He hesitated, and their eyes met. "But then you can't . . . Anush, you *can't*—"

Her breath caught.

"—keep looking at me like that . . ."

A spark.

It heated up, flashed, and a beat later, he was across the room pulling her up by the waist, pushing her hard against the wall. One leg on the bench, the other around his hips, she fumbled with his jeans as he slipped her leggings down her thighs. His hands winding through her hair, he kissed her, then dragged his lips down to her collarbone.

Their eyes locked. She was in a trance, and she could feel her heart beating hard against his chest as they moved up and down, back and forth, rhythmically, eye to eye and gasping for more.

She pressed her mouth into his neck to keep from screaming as he moved her down onto the bench, and then down to the floor.

Wasn't this the way it was supposed to be? The two of them together: Anush and Neil. Together *forever*.

He rolled off her, pulling her around as she shifted on top of him, and just then, a floorboard creaked.

They both froze.

"Mommy?"

Another floorboard, crackling just outside the door. Anu held her breath, and she looked into Neil's eyes in fear.

"Daddy?"

Silently, Anu rolled toward the door and blocked it with her left leg just as she felt the pressure. There was a soft grunt as Kanika tried to push the door again, but Anu held strong. A moment later, she heard the pattering of feet as their daughter ran up the stairs.

The room spun as Anu sighed in relief. It had been such a close call. What the hell had she been thinking? Decidedly, she rolled over to face Neil. He was lying flat on the ground, his arms bent like he was about to do a sit-up.

There was a lazy grin on his face, like it was a Sunday morning right before Kanika was born. When they could sleep in late and stay in bed even later—goofing around, reading, kissing—until one of them caved and went downstairs to make the coffee. Back then they hadn't had a care in the world, the burden of adult responsibilities made lighter by privilege, by their parents. And then Kanika arrived: the light of their lives. Their new reason for being.

Anu lived as if she had nothing to lose, when in fact she had *everything* to lose. How careless she was. How thoughtless her choices were.

Neil extended his left arm, reaching for her. The tips of his fingers met her waist, but she pulled away and reached for her leggings.

"Come here." His voice was gruff, full of desire.

Leggings in hand, she sidled toward him. He wrapped an arm around her as she tried to put them on. He kissed her forehead. Again, she pulled away.

"Wait five minutes before coming up." She stood. "I'll go outside. You can head back into the class."

"Why?"

She threw him a look, and he sat up straighter.

"Kanu can handle this."

"We can't get her hopes up."

"Her hopes," he said softly, "or mine?"

Anu balked. "Right. As if you want to get back together with your slutty ex-wife."

"I don't think that . . . at *all*."

She glared at him. "Of course you do."

"Anush," he said. Why did it hurt so much when he called her that? "I don't care what you've been doing. . . . It's in the past, and none of us is perfect. Do you think I've been some sort of monk since we broke up?"

She swallowed hard, and suddenly it occured to her that she was hurting them both—all over again. But didn't he realize how easily, again, everything could all slip away?

"Give us a chance, Anush." He drew closer to her, setting his hands on her forearms. "You couldn't before. I get that now. But why not now? Why—"

"And what happens when we start taking each other for granted again, huh? What happens when our daughter is old enough to see on our faces how unhappy we are together? When we split up again—"

"We won't."

"How do you know?"

"How are you sure we will?"

She didn't have an answer for him. She pulled away and sat down on the bench, and she watched him as he roughly pulled up his track pants, straightened out his shirt. After, he sat down next to her. She let her head fall lightly against his shoulder.

They had both changed. They weren't the people who had split up more than a year before, with broken hearts, fake smiles, and vague ideas about what life could be like alone.

"I don't regret marrying you," she said finally. "Not once. Not ever."

He nodded. He was crying, too.

"So many times I've wondered . . . where would we be if we hadn't gotten married so young. If we'd met each other as grown-ups . . ."

"Please," he whispered. His voice was breaking. "Anush, I *love* you."

"I love you, too."

"Then—"

"But I love Kanika more," she said, shifting away from him. "So do you, Neil. And we . . . and *I* . . . can't do this to her again."

chapter thirty-four

✤

Six years earlier

Her back was on the brink of a spasm, and she stuffed another couch cushion beneath her hips, rolling slightly on top of it. Where was the remote? She found it and hit the mute button, silencing the grating voices on TV, some talk show discussing the Kardashians.

She and Neil hadn't exactly tried, nor had they *not* tried, and it had left Anu sitting here feeling fat with her bloated feet up on the table. She was about to pop. Explode. Whatever you wanted to call it. And girl, boy, alien, or demon—whatever it was that was making her pee forty times a day—she wanted it *out*.

"Mom?" A waft of something spicy hit her just as Lakshmi's head peered around the doorway. "Mom, are you cooking?"

"*Hah*. Your favorite."

"Neil said he'd cook today. He's off early—"

"Leave that boy alone, Anu. I am perfectly capable." She dried her hands on the tea towel tucked into her trousers, perching next to the sofa. "Shall I make you some lassi?"

"No, I'm good."

"Just half glass, *nah*? And take off these pajamas. I will start the washing."

"Mom, they're clean, and I don't want lassi—"

"Quarter glass—it will—"

"Mom, can you stop fussing and come sit with me?"

Lakshmi tutted at her as she left the room. Anu heard her turn off the stove.

"Water? Juice? Peppermint tea?"

Anu rolled her head into a couch cushion, suffocating a groan, then pulled away. Why had she told Lakshmi that she had started her maternity leave early? Anu should have pretended she was still at work.

"Water. Thanks."

Back in the sitting room, at first Lakshmi tried to sit next to Anu and massage her, but Anu managed to convince her that she was much too overheated for human contact. Eventually, after Lakshmi nestled into the nearby armchair, Anu started to relax. Oddly, when Lakshmi was around, Anu was unable to relax unless her mother was.

"Any day now . . ."

Anu looked up and found Lakshmi just staring at her. "Yep. Any day now."

"Have you thought of boy names, just in case?"

"We don't need to. I know it's a girl."

"How?"

Anu shrugged, unable to pinpoint how exactly she felt certain, even though she and Neil had declined to find out the baby's gender. "I just know. Didn't you?"

"I suppose. In our family, baby girls have been harder to carry." Lakshmi leaned in, stroked Anu's left ankle. "Our line of women is very strong. The more difficult the pregnancy, the stronger the girl."

"Well, this one had better shoot out of here an Olympic medalist, then."

Lakshmi laughed. "You know, women in our family had to be strong. There was never a choice. But the strength always appeared in different ways. Maybe for this little one, it will be muscles."

"What do you mean?"

"You know my story, Anu. You know it was very hard to leave my mother behind. And back then there was none of this FaceTime."

Anu nodded. She'd never really known her grandparents, had met them only a few times as a young child before they passed away back in India. Phone calls were rare, and once a month they'd receive letters written in Punjabi that her parents read out loud— and usually had to translate.

"And then there was my ma. She had so much—" Lakshmi pressed against her chest, tapped it lightly, and then closed her eyes. "She ran household of twenty-nine people."

"Twenty-*nine*?"

"It was joint family. A big house. All the cousins, brothers, uncles, and aunties, everyone living all together." Lakshmi shook her head. "I remember so well. Can you imagine cooking for them three meals a day? All the washing, the cleaning, the children running around, screaming? From morning to night, my mother worked. I never saw her off her feet."

"Wasn't there help?"

"*Hah*, but never enough. There were a few servants, and the other

women all helped as we could, but she was in charge. If something—
if anything—happened, where do you think they went? If there
weren't enough *chapatis* on the table, who do you think received
blame? The first day she didn't have to work? Her funeral, Anu."

Anu couldn't remember, but had she known that about her
nani? Surely, at some point she'd been told. Maybe as a child. Her
cheeks reddened. She wondered if maybe she hadn't cared enough
to listen.

"And then there was *my* nani," Lakshmi said with a sigh. "Boy,
was *she* pill."

Anu giggled. "What, like you?"

"Uh-ho." Lakshmi laughed, turning to face Anu. "I often think
if she lived in our time, she would have made great military of-
ficer."

"Actually?"

"Or perhaps CEO? No one *ever* crossed my nani."

Anu smiled, watching Lakshmi's face. She couldn't recall if
she'd ever seen a picture of her great-grandmother or even if she
knew her maiden name. Even her first name.

"What was she like?"

"Brutal," Lakshmi said, her face like she had just tasted something sour. "So severe. If I played in sun even one moment, she
would notice my dark skin. If I had a few extra *malai* after school,
she would pull at my *salwar* and say to me in Punjabi, 'Lucky, no
man will want to marry a fatso.'"

"No, she didn't!"

Lakshmi laughed. "She did!"

"She sounds like a . . ." Anu trailed off, catching her mother's
eye. "Sorry."

"A bitch?" Lakshmi held her gaze. "Isn't that the English word?"

Anu shrugged.

"She *was* bitch, Anu. Life made her hard around edges." Lakshmi sat forward in the chair, elbows on knees. "In India, we have a saying. Loosely translated, it means . . . when you put gold in the fire, it shines. It's hot, and it *burns*, but that is life's experiences. . . . They will make you shine. They make us better. But for many reasons, my nani never shined. Too much burning."

"How, Mom?"

"My nani had four children by the age of twenty-three, and then a husband shot dead while fighting for the British. Yet she lived with her in-laws' family her whole life, surviving on *their* generosity. Since she was an *eleven*-year-old girl."

"She was a child bride?"

"Those terms did not exist then," Lakshmi said, completely matter-of-fact.

Anu glanced around the room and wondered if Lakshmi was thinking the same thing she was: Everything around them, every comfort, luxury, every tribulation—none of it had existed back then.

Here Anu was sitting on a nine-hundred-dollar sofa, watching a flat-screen television playing a show that had no societal purpose, having been annoyed her mother was doting on her too much. And what had Anu been upset about that morning? That Neil had shrunk her favorite cardigan in the dryer?

Suddenly, the remote control, her cupboard full of overpriced bourgeois peppermint tea, the sixty-dollar throw rug from Pier 1 were way too much. She kicked off the blanket. Lakshmi's eyes had drifted toward the TV, still on mute. Some tween pop star was being interviewed now, their earlier discussion of the latest Kardashian scandal now in the past. The corners of Lakshmi's mouth curled upward as the tween hopped up to her feet, miming something—making some joke.

"Do you want the sound on?"

Lakshmi shook her head, eyes locked on the pop star. Fleetingly, Anu wondered if Lakshmi had told her all of this to make her feel guilty.

But the thought passed as Anu realized the guilt was already there. That unlike anyone before her, Anu hadn't had to make a single sacrifice.

What had Anu ever sacrificed for anyone? Sure, maybe if she had a do-over, she would have ignored her parents' career advice and trained to be a yoga teacher. Maybe if she and Neil had really stuck up for themselves, they would have bought a condo downtown by the water, instead of a starter house in the same suburb as their families.

But was that sacrifice? Or just not being *selfish*?

Clutching her warm belly, she closed her eyes. Any day now, there'd be a baby in this world who hadn't there before. A girl. Anu can picture her already. Almond brown skin, pitch-black hair. Eyes just like Neil's.

A little girl in their line. A girl she would give up anything for.

chapter thirty-five

IMOGEN: Hey, Anusha. The pictures of the open house looked great. I'm glad you finally understand how Instagram filters work. :P

ANUSHA: Ha, thanks. Take care of yourself and have some nice R&R with your family. I'm looking forward to seeing you back in Vancouver when you're ready! Again, please let me know if there's anything I can do. . . . My guest room has your name on it if you need it.

IMOGEN: Thanks! I may need a job, too. . . .

ANUSHA: I'm pretty sure that can be arranged ;)

Oh, *wow*." Kunal beamed at Anu from the kitchen table as she reached the bottom of the stairs. She was wearing some of her London clothes: a pair of jeans, a black top, and a blazer.

She twirled in slow motion. "Oh, this old thing?"

"You look just like your mother when she was your age."

Lakshmi swooped in from around the corner, cocking her hip to the side. "When I *was* her age? Dear husband, are you saying I am no longer looking young?"

Anu laughed as Kunal's cheeks reddened.

"*Nah*, you are still very beautiful. I am merely saying—"

"You are saying I am showing age. That I am merely a beautiful *old* woman." Lakshmi winked at Anu. "I'll show your father. Do you know, Anu, last month at the Starbucks, a boy *your* age approached me?"

"Really," Kunal deadpanned. "Was he taking your coffee order?"

Shrieking, Lakshmi lunged at Kunal with an oven mitt, playfully smacking him as he cowered and covered his face with his hands.

Anu's heart broke wide open as she watched them. Why had she been embarrassed of their affectionate demeanor growing up? Later, why had she resented it? She was lucky to have parents who loved each other, who—at nearly sixty—could be as silly as a couple of teenagers.

Lakshmi had been home for two days, brightening Anu's home with smiles like sunshine. She'd been cooking, too, despite Kunal's insistence that *he* wanted to plan the meals, despite Anu's warnings that she didn't want to take advantage of her.

Now it was hard to imagine a time when Lakshmi hadn't been there. No, it wasn't perfect, and Anu had already nearly torn her hair out when Lakshmi rearranged her spice cupboard—but Anu was so glad she was home.

Anu had also convinced Kunal to fly back to London with Lakshmi after her spring break, after Kanika's sixth birthday party that Saturday. While his help was invaluable and brought Anu to tears, she knew that he needed to be with his wife. Moreover, Priya was nearly back to normal and Neil was back to work, so as of the following week Kanika would be with them half the time.

The house would feel lonely after they'd gone, when Anu had all the time and space to herself. The open house a success, in the past few days, her roster of enthusiastic teachers had basically run the place without her. The classes were full, the website perfected, the online advertisements and social media posts making the impact she had intended. The day before, a local celebrity had even attended one of Radhika's class and tweeted about it to her fifty thousand followers. Imogen had answered her phone when Anu called to tell her about it, and they ended up talking for two hours. About the future of the studio, how and when each of them had developed a passion for yoga to begin with. Imogen told her that she'd first tried yoga and meditation after a teacher had recommended it to her, mentioned that it sometimes helped people with mental health. Had it helped Imogen, or could it still? Anu hoped so. She hoped that maybe, one day, they would talk about it.

"Your father is correct, Anu," she heard Lakshmi say. Anu looked up to catch her mother brush a kiss on the top of Kunal's head.

"You look very *wow*."

"Thanks, Mom." Anu grinned. "I'm going on a date."

"A date," Kunal said flatly, picking up his newspaper. "With the skiing chap?"

"His name is Tyler. And yes, he's the skier slash schoolteacher."

"Is he taking you skiing?" Lakshmi furrowed her brow. "Your coat is in fashion, *beti*, but not appropriate for skiing."

Anu laughed. She crossed through the kitchen and put her arm around Lakshmi. "No, Mom. It's April. Can you see any snow?"

Over the past few days, Anu had tried not to dwell on what happened with Neil, and whenever she questioned her decision to let Neil fade into the past, she looked at Kanika. Brushed her hair or kissed her head. Squeezed her until Kanu, restless, giggled and pushed her away.

And so the night after the open house, when Tyler had called her out of the blue and insisted they firm up a date, she agreed. She wanted to move forward. Over and over, Anu had said this to herself and to her friends. She wanted it be true, so what else could she do but say *yes*?

"Should I come to the door?" Kunal said gruffly.

"Sure, Dad. Come to the door."

"Kunal Narayan Kapoor, don't you *dare* go to that door!"

"Mom, he can come to the door."

"Do not encourage this business, Anu. Your father can keep those ample buttocks of his in his seat and mind his business!"

"Ample," Kunal repeated, turning a page of his newspaper. *"Ample?"*

Lakshmi and Anu joined him at the table. They had already finished their tea, and they helped themselves to sips of Kunal's until, pretending to be exasperated, he got up and went to the stove to make another pot. When Tyler arrived, Anu didn't let her parents scurry off into the back room and insisted they stay right there at the table. Tyler waved at them from the front door, and tentatively, they came into the foyer to meet him, made obligatory small talk as Anu pulled on her boots and coat.

The date with Tyler was easy, friendly. He took her back to Granville Island, and they toured one art gallery and then another, both exquisite exhibits by indigenous artists local to the area. Tyler bought a print, and then they moved on to the food market and shared poutine and a pork belly bahn mi, traded stories on growing up, growing older.

As it got dark, they walked across the bridge into downtown and shared a carafe of white wine at an unpretentious bar on Hamilton. It seemed very natural, being there with him, and Anu felt the rush of what moving forward could feel like. His eyes sparkled in the low light, and on the walk back to the car, he gently, respectfully intertwined his fingers with hers.

Back home, on the porch step, he kissed her. It was short and sweet, like something Anu had watched in an Eva Mendes movie.

Still, she couldn't help but think of her first kiss with Neil, and she squeezed her eyes shut as she pushed away the thought.

"I've been wanting to do that since the first time I saw you."

She smiled sheepishly.

"Sorry." He brushed a stray hair from her face and then slid his hand gently down to her shoulder. "Actually, I'm not sorry." He drew her closer, resting his hands on either shoulder. "I'd like to ask you out again," he said quietly. "But before I do that, I need to ask you something else."

"Yeah?"

His face grew more serious. "You're separated. . . ."

She nodded, pressing her lips together. "I am."

"Is it . . . permanent? Because I wouldn't want to interfere."

"I understand." She nodded, and the queasiness rose in her stomach. "I get it. And I need to . . ." She trailed off, letting him— letting herself—assume what words came next.

"So you'll let me know, then?"

"Yes." She smiled. "I'll let you know."

I t was her first run in more than a week, since before the open house. Anu slipped out before Kanika and her parents were awake and jogged the half mile to Burnaby Lake. Thank goodness it was warm enough to have the party outside; in addition to more than a dozen family friends, Anu and Neil had asked Kanika's entire kindergarten class to the party, and most had accepted the invite. As Anu ran around the lake, taking short breaks to stretch her calves or catch her breath, she kept her mind occupied as she mentally prepared for the party.

It would be *Moana* themed, of course, and the kitchen and back porch would be covered in tasteful Disney decorations and fresh flowers. Lakshmi baked a cake, and as a surprise, Kunal had rented a mechanical surfboard for the back lawn. Neil, knowing how busy a week Anu had had, insisted on bringing over all the food and beverages.

She kicked a piece of driftwood, and it scattered off the curved path. All week, she and Neil had been planning the party together—being civil, exchanging ideas, and dividing up tasks by text message. He was an involved and loving father to Kanika and a considerate ex, and she forced herself to dismiss all other thoughts about him that kept bubbling up.

After showering, she brought Kanika upstairs to get ready for the party. She'd braided her daughter's wet hair the night before, and unwinding it, Kanika beamed at her reflection in the mirror.

"I look like Moana!"

Anu laughed, spritzing her hair with a bit of hair spray. "That's kind of the point, huh?" She helped Kanika into her dress, red and tan with similar patterns to Moana's dress in the movie, and then—as a treat—let her put on a bit of lip gloss; she always ended up licking it off, anyway.

As the final touch, Anu pinned a fresh flower into Kanika's hair and then smudged a touch of black eyeliner behind her ear. "There. You're ready."

Kanika turned to her. "Why do you and Nani always do that?"

Anu hesitated. It was only the second time Kanika had asked her about the ritual. What had she told her the last time?

It's makeup.

Wasn't that what Lakshmi had told Anu as a child? To stave off the difficult conversation about what their superstions meant until she was older?

Kanika wrapped her arms around Anu's waist and let her head drop back as she stared up at her. "What's it for?"

"It's for protection," Anu said eventually. "Well, Nani and I think so, anyway." Slowly, carefully, Anu explained what a superstition was, and how it was passed on from one generation to the next. And that while sometimes the meaning became lost, the purpose didn't.

"Does that make sense?" Anu asked after a while.

Kanika had a far-off look in her eye as she stared out the front window. Neil and Priya had arrived, and she could see Kunal helping them to bring the food inside. "Sure, Mom."

Anu was tempted to laugh by the confidence and charisma in Kanika's voice, the way she could sound like a child one moment—and expertly mimic an adult the next.

She was growing up, slow and fast at the same time, and pretty soon she would be a grown woman herself. Her sixth-birthday party—her whole childhood—would be a hazy, hopefully, happy memory.

Anu tucked Kanika's hair behind her ear, studying her. What did she remember? Even if she didn't show it, what did she understand?

More than anything, she wanted to protect her daughter; of course she did. But she wanted to be an honest mother, too.

"Kanu," Anu said, sitting next to her on the bed, "do you remember what happened right before Christmas?"

Still staring out the window, Kanika said, "Dadima got sick. But she's all better now."

Anu nodded, scooted closer to Kanika. "Do you remember what happened before that?"

Slowly, Kanika turned her head and looked up at Anu, her eyes shining clear and wide.

"I went away for a whole week—do you remember that?"

Without blinking, Kanika nodded.

Taking a deep breath, Anu looked her daughter straight in the eye. "I'm sorry I missed your Christmas concert, Kanu. And I left in kind of a hurry, didn't I?"

Kanu shrugged, her expression unreadable.

"I was very sad, and I needed to be away for a little while, sweetie."

"Why were you sad?"

Anu smiled at her, thinking of a way to explain it. "Kanu, you love acting in plays, right? In drama class?"

She nodded her little head.

"And dancing and singing? And you love coloring and playing outside—"

"And *Moana*?"

Anu laughed. "Especially *Moana*." She paused, gathering her thoughts. "And I guess, Kanu, I didn't know what I loved to do. And I needed to leave to figure it out. Do you understand what I mean?"

"Did you figure it out?" Kanika said "figure it out" with the exact same intonation as Anu, as if it was the first time she had ever used that phrase and was trying it on for size.

She was growing up. Anu could feel the weight of it all, as Kanika climbed onto her lap.

"*You*, Kanu." Anu squeezed her. "I love you!"

"Just me?" Kanika rolled her eyes expertly, just like her auntie Jenny. "Mommy, you're allowed to love more than just *me*."

Anu was taken aback, and she shifted away to look her daughter in the eye. She was just a little girl squirming away on her lap, yet just then she had sounded decades wiser than her years.

The moment froze around her, and her breath was short as

she came to understand. Could it really be that easy? Could Kanika, her sweet little girl, really have the answer?

Anu could be a good mother and be herself, too. She could be there for Kanika and love and live how she wanted, too?

The world came back to life when she felt Kanika pulling on her hand. Anu sat up, startled, and kissed her daughter hard on the head.

"You're right, Kanu." Anu set her on the bed and then ran toward the door. "You're absolutely right!"

The hot pink piece of paper was still in her desk drawer where she had left it. Anu grabbed it and then raced down the stairs. The kitchen was empty, and after she moved to the patio window, her eyes skirted across the lawn. Her parents were out there with Priya, chatting near the mechanical surfboard. Next, she checked the living room and the basement. What about the front yard? Opening the door, she spotted Neil on the driveway, a tray of baked goods balanced on his left hand.

"Where should we store these?" He smiled as he looked up at her. "Garage?"

"Good idea." She keyed in the punch code, and the garage door opened. She suddenly felt nervous. Neil set down the tray on a nearby shelf. The sun was behind her, and as he walked back onto the driveway, he shielded his eyes with his hands.

"Do you need a hand with something?"

Anu pressed her lips together and walked down the steps to meet him. Her hands were shaking.

"What is it?"

She pressed the paper into his hands and watched Neil's face as he unfolded it, as his eyes moved across each of the items.

"What is this?"

"I wrote this," she said, "when Ryan and I were together. When I thought I had it all figured it out."

He handed the paper back to her, his eyes down on the pavement. "And did you?"

"Do you remember our first kiss?"

She could tell her words caught him off guard. Slowly, a slight grin stretched across his face.

"How could I not? I nearly broke your front tooth."

"And I think I actually chewed your lip."

"Your tongue," he said, "felt like a dead mouse in my mouth."

Anu laughed, remembering the way he'd held her awkwardly in Priya's car. "I got pimples on my chin from all the drool."

"It was the worst first kiss in the history of first kisses."

"No, Neil. It was perfect." Her hands trembled as she stepped closer toward him. "It was perfect for *us*."

He blinked, his eyes glistening. "We got it right eventually, didn't we?"

"I reckon we got pretty good at it."

"Anush." He breathed hard, stepped away from her. "Don't toy with me—"

"I'm not." The wind had picked up, and she brushed away the hair that had flown into her face. "I'm right here, Neil. And I want—" She hesitated. "I want *you*."

She reached for his hand, and when he didn't pull away, she squeezed it. "I was so hell-bent on being a role model for Kanika . . . I never realized the best thing I could do for her was be . . . *me*."

His voice caught. "And who are you?"

"I'm Anush." She shrugged. "I'm just . . . *me*. And I want to be with you." She pressed their hands to his chest, looked him deeply in the eyes. "I've realized that our marriage, our separation, Ryan, *punching* Ryan—none of it was a mistake. Because otherwise I wouldn't have realized how much I love you. How much I want our family back."

She could feel him shaking, and he was gazing at her the same way he had when they were eighteen years old and sneaking desserts off Auntie Jayani's dining room table. The way he looked at her when he had first told her he loved her, when they were puking their guts out on their wedding night. When they drank their coffee by the crib every morning, after their daughter was born. Or Anu accomplished something as insignificant as beating another level of Fruit Ninja.

"It's always been you, Neil. I'm sorry it took me so long to realize it."

She wrapped her arms around him, holding him close. A moment passed, and she felt the weight of his arms around her, too.

"You have to promise me something, though."

"What's that?"

"You have to shovel the driveway."

She pulled back, smiling. "*Excuse* me?"

"You heard me. I hate it. I'll do any chore—hell, I'll do all the chores—but for the love of God, woman, I *hate* shoveling snow."

"Deal. Any other requests?"

"Well"—he pulled away—"if we get back together, I have one more condition for you."

"And what's that?"

"Even though we're still married, if you want me back, you're going to have to propose to me." He shrugged. "*Formally.*"

"Oh, yeah?"

"Yeah. It's nerve-racking. Women need to go through that, too. . . ."

"Really, you were nervous? But you knew I'd say yes."

"Still," he said, "it was the scariest day of my life."

A garbage truck rumbled past, and as he turned to look, she sank to the ground.

"Do you think—" He stopped short, taking in the sight of her down on one knee.

"Neil."

He toed toward her. "Anush."

"I'm going to make you a proposal."

"What's that?"

"I propose that if you move back in, if we give our marriage another chance, you'll never have to shovel the driveway again."

He laughed, set his hands on his hips.

"As long as *you* clean the bathrooms."

"Deal."

"And I promise to love you—" She choked up as Neil dropped to his knees in front of her, took her hands in his. "I promise to never give up on us again."

He was smiling at her, and she felt exactly the way she had on the day they first met.

"I promise to always be a woman our daughter will be proud of."

He kissed her then, slow and soft. She wound her hands through his hair, pulling him close as he clutched her waist. After what felt like an eternity, they pulled away.

A rush of color flashed to the side, and they turned to look. Kanika was standing there, beaming at them. She ran to them, and Anu and Neil pulled her in, wrapping her tight in their arms.

Anu wasn't grown-up—not yet. Not even close. But maybe, just maybe, she wouldn't have to do it alone.

acknowledgments

Thank you to Mom, Dad, and my whole family for your love and support, and for our afternoon "writers' room" sessions that have been a wealth of inspiration to me. Thank you for giving me the freedom to be truthful and encouraging me to follow my dreams, regardless of whether they were what a "good Indian girl" would do.

Thank you to my brilliant agents, Federica Leonardis and Martha Webb, for believing in me, and to all my creative writing teachers—formal and informal—over the years.

I am immensely grateful to everyone at Berkley for throwing your heart and soul into this book, in particular my insightful editor, Kerry Donovan; Fareeda Bullert; my publicists, Brittanie Black and Dache Rogers; and Sarah Blumenstock. And a huge thank-you to Penguin Random House Canada for your incredible support in my home country, especially Claire Pokorchak, Kara Savoy, and Kyrsten Lowell.

Thank you to my work family at House of Anansi Press and Groundwood Books for your daily doses of encouragement, and to my wonderful friends—my personal hype squad—who are there for me every day regardless of time zones.

And to Simon, for everything and every day.

Grown-Up Pose

SONYA LALLI

questions for discussion

1. As much as Anu loves Neil, she chooses to separate from him rather than try to keep working on their marriage. What reasons led her to make this decision? Do you think she resented him, or resented the traditional roles each of them had taken on in the marriage?

2. Anu often uses labels such as "good Indian girl" or "good wife and mother"—and she feels the weight of the expectations that go along with those characterizations. Do you think such labels are ever black and white? How much did you think the burden Anu was feeling came from expectations she placed on herself?

3. Anu and Jenny lament over the fact that their alumni magazine, and society in general, tends to celebrate milestones such as marriage and children, and fails to give recognition to personal accomplishments. Do you agree with their viewpoint? In what ways does Anu's viewpoint influence her decisions?

4. Initially, Anu believes she is more grown up than her best friends because she is, among other things, a mother and wife, although she ultimately comes to realize she's wrong. What do you think it means to be "a grown-up" in today's society? Is there a difference between acting like a grown-up and truly being grown up?

5. Comparing her own family to Monica's and Priya's friend Auntie Jayani, Anu talks about how there is a spectrum of Indian families in terms of how traditional they are. Do you see this kind of spectrum in your own community? How do you think social mores change over time?

6. Do you think Anu's decision to take over Mags's studio was impulsive? Irresponsible? Are there ways in which following her dream to run a yoga studio helped Anu grow as a person?

7. Anu partially justifies her decision to leave for London by telling Monica that if she doesn't go, she doesn't think her daughter will ever be able to think of her as a role model. What does Anu mean by that, and did you agree with her reasoning?

8. Anu has a close relationship with both her parents, but at the same time, she's felt that she has needed to hide a lot about who she is and what she wants in order to meet their expectations. How has her relationship with both Lakshmi and Kunal evolved? And why do you think Anu was never able to be honest with them until their confrontation in London?

9. Is Anu's jealousy of Neil's love interests reasonable, considering that she was the one who asked for the separation and first started dating other people?

10. Anu feels responsible for Imogen's hospitalization, and thinks she should have done more, even though she tried to respect Imogen's decision to deal with her depression on her own terms. Do you think Anu did enough as a friend? What further action could or should Anu have taken?

11. Toward the end of the novel, when Anu and Neil are discussing their marriage, Neil says, "We started a family so young and had to grow up so quickly, sometimes I think we didn't have time to grow up at all." Did you agree or disagree with his statement?

12. In Anu's own words, she "goes off the rails" for a while in a bid to find her own sense of self and independence, much like an adolescent. By the end of the novel, do you think Anu was ultimately able to "grow up"? What do you think she struggled with the most in her bid to become a grown-up?

Photo by Ming Joanis at A Nero's World

SONYA LALLI is a Canadian writer of Indian heritage. She studied law in her hometown of Saskatoon and at Columbia University in New York, and later completed an MA in Creative Writing and Publishing at City, University of London. Sonya loves to cook, travel, and practice yoga. She lives in Toronto with her husband.